PRAISE

*"If you are looking for a story that wraps around you like
a warm blanket and reminds you that there is good in the world,
then grab a copy of the* The Healers, *make yourself a cup of tea,
and hang out for a bit with this engaging group of friends."*

—Allison Shadday, LCSW, author, *Handling the Ups and
Downs of Multiple Sclerosis*

*"A beautifully written reminder to embrace your true self.
This book stays with you long after you've finished reading it."*

—Lauren Fike, Owner, Pure Barre West Portal

"Reading The Healers *made me ask, 'Why do I worry?
Why am I creating this negative energy?' When you let go of the
past, you accept the now. That is when true happiness happens.
Thank you for this gift."*

—Cam Karr

*"From the very beginning, I was hooked. The characters
are so well developed that it's as though I know them personally.
I saw a bit of myself in Marlee, Maggie, Juliette,
Sophia, and Annie."*

—Joan Ulibarri

The Healers

MICHELLE DAVIS

DEDICATION

To all the Healers who shine their light.

PART ONE

Chapter 1

MARLEE

March 23rd – 24th

What am I to know?

Why are you so hard on yourself? Do you expect Tom, Patrick, or your friends to meet the standards you strive to achieve? Of course not. For them, you allow grace.

While you've come light-years these past fifteen months, there is still much to learn. Remember, your time on earth is a journey filled with valuable lessons designed to propel you toward your higher self. But you want perfection. Continuing to self-criticize will only impede your progress.

Prior to incarnating, you—like all humans—agreed to master specific truths during this lifetime. However, to do so, you must take risks. You are still afraid to explore new ways of thinking and being, trust what you cannot see, let go of the familiar, and venture into the unknown. Instead, you prefer the reliable path, forgetting you are meant to make mistakes so you may learn from them. That is how true growth occurs.

Of course, the choice is always yours. If you continue to play it safe and slip into old patterns of fear, all will be fine. Yet, know that remaining rooted in your comfort zone only blocks new and exciting experiences from appearing.

These unforeseen opportunities and challenges are all part of the Universe's plan. We each play a critical role in this Divine design. There is no chance, coincidence, or happenstance. Everything has meaning. And, while there is always free will, an underlying purpose exists. Consider it a blueprint in our DNA to support access to our highest calling. Sadly, too many humans ignore their greatness. They opt to stay small, never becoming the magnificent creatures they are created to be, because they are afraid.

My fingers stop moving. The session is over. I reread the words that came *through me*, not *from me*. I'm still baffled by what occurs each morning, but I've come to accept this unusual ritual. Will the messages I receive and type serve a specific purpose at some point? Are they for my personal evolution? Or is there more to it?

These transmissions have been happening for almost a year now, since my private healing session with Daniel, the channeler from the retreat in Costa Rica. Daniel explained that, like him, I can convey messages. His guides *speak* to him. He hears their words then repeats them aloud. Mine mainly communicate to me through writing.

At first, I doubted every word my fingers typed out … as well as the mysterious voice I began to hear in my head. I thought I was just making things up. Sometimes I still do. However, from what I've read, it appears that what comes through are not *my* actual thoughts. Whose thoughts are they? I have no idea. I'm just trying to trust and be at peace with the process.

The sound of the garage door opening jolts me back to reality. It can't be Tom. He has a 3 p.m. surgery on his schedule. Patrick must be home.

"Hey, Mom." My son sounds unusually cheery as he walks into the kitchen in his oversized, mud-covered sweatshirt. Grinning ear to ear, Patrick drops his lacrosse bag onto the floor.

"I heard from Colgate," he says with a toothy smile.

"You got in!" I blurt. When he nods, I rush toward him for a hug, inhaling his oh so familiar musky scent.

"Does your father know?"

"No, just you," he says. Tom is a legacy, a fact that might have held huge benefits in the past, until this recent string of higher ed abuses. I was actually worried that Tom's alumni status would hurt Patrick's chances.

"So, is Colgate *it*?" I ask. "Because I'm sure your dad would understand if you want to go to another school."

"It's Colgate," Patrick beams. His eyes dart to the ceiling for a moment. "I'm gonna commit right now," he says, then runs upstairs.

The muscles around my neck tighten, causing my shoulders to crimp closer to my ears. I should be happy, shouldn't I? Isn't this what a mother wants? If so, then why do I feel sad? It's been a given that Patrick would go to college. Still, this feels like a huge leap closer to him leaving.

Three weeks ago, unbeknownst to Patrick, I made a dinner reservation at his favorite restaurant. Had "Acceptance Day" turned out differently, I would have cancelled. However, somehow I knew he'd receive an offer.

I carry his lacrosse bag to the laundry room, then toss his maroon jersey, with the number seventeen on its back, into the washer. It's clear that this is one more opportunity for me to practice letting go, something I find very difficult. I release a sigh, then return to the kitchen to make a cup of Tulsi tea. One of its benefits is to calm the mind.

Focus on something besides Patrick.

The voice that speaks is not Margaret, the critical inner voice that sabotaged my self-esteem for years. Instead, this voice guides and inspires. Could it be my intuition? I suppose it's somehow connected to the voice that writes through me. It's all so confusing. I'm just not sure.

Despite my best efforts, all I can think of is Patrick leaving in August. I sit down and rest my elbows on the countertop. As Tom has reminded me again and again, Colgate isn't *that* far away … *only* a four-hour drive. I'd secretly hoped Patrick would pick Villanova, Drexel, or St. Joe's, all of them being closer. I let out another sigh. At least he didn't choose Tulane.

I take a bite of an oatmeal raisin cookie and allow it to dissolve in my mouth while I consider what's ahead. Kids are receiving acceptances now, but early May is when the real chaos begins, especially for parents. First, there's the lacrosse team's senior night. I take another bite of cookie. I'll have to keep my shit together as Tom and I walk with Patrick across the field while the announcer shares his career milestones. He'll be so embarrassed if I become emotional. Next comes senior dinner. Then graduation parties begin. Before I know it, it will be time for the academic awards, baccalaureate, and actual graduation.

That punched-in-the-gut feeling returns as the kettle whistles. While the tea steeps, I think back to last May. Impressed by Colgate's campus and course offerings, perhaps it was how the tour ended, with a Chipwich for each prospective student and their parents, that sealed the deal for Patrick. After all, who doesn't love an ice cream sandwich?

We visited eight other schools. Patrick applied to six. Looking back, the process wasn't too bad, probably due to how mature and self-sufficient he's becoming. I wish I would listen to the words I'm using to describe our son. It's hard. I want to believe he's ready, but I'm worried. What if he doesn't get along with his roommate, has trouble keeping up with classes, or can't manage the new freedoms in his schedule? Then there's the thing that concerns me most, the fraternity scene.

"Well, I guess that's done," Patrick announces as he bounces down the steps, reminding me of Tigger from *Winnie the Pooh* stories, the character he dressed as for Halloween in kindergarten. His upbeat voice interrupts my imaginary doomsday scenario session. Not wanting my fears to dampen one of his biggest days, I suggest a diversion.

"How about we get some ice cream?"

His huge smile answers my question.

I toss him the car keys as we head to the garage. These outings will become fewer and fewer. A constriction forms across my chest right above my heart when I think about it. Colgate's freshmen move-in date is five months away, but incoming freshmen can attend a wilderness adventure in July. These five-day trips are supposed to foster the bonding process before the semester starts. When Patrick applied, he shared that, if accepted, his first choice would be the canoe excursion. Ever since he and Tom spent a few days paddling during a father-son trip to Michigan, Patrick has been wanting to canoe again. Of course he chose the only offering labeled *spicy*. Knowing him, he'd be bored with something easier.

As we pull out of the garage, my phone rings. It's Maggie. I let it go to voicemail. As much as I love chatting with my sweet young friend, it can wait. Patrick and I are headed to Scoops. Maybe they have Chipwiches.

***

Later that night, after our celebration dinner at Pietro's, Tom and I crawl into bed. Emotionally exhausted, I forgo the book on my nightstand for mindless TV. Reaching for the remote, I remember Maggie called earlier. I grab my phone and scan the transcription of her message …

Hey Marlee. How are you? I can't wait till June when you all come to Bend. It's going to be amazing to be together… I need to talk to you … don't worry … but when you have a chance … can you give me a call?

It's a little after ten o'clock my time, seven out in Oregon. I wiggle my feet into my slippers, put on my robe, and do my best to be quiet as I slip out of our bedroom. When I come to Patrick's room, I pause. No doubt he's awake, headphones on, listening to music or playing X-box Live with friends. His homework has already gone by the wayside, but I wish he'd start studying for his AP tests.

Once downstairs, I call Maggie. She claimed she was OK, but something tells me she's not. There were too many pauses in her message. Besides, she usually leaves upbeat voicemails, peppered with flowery language and inflected tones. This one seemed sad.

She answers after three rings.

"Marlee … "

"What's going on?" I ask, skipping the pleasantries I usually evoke at the beginning of our conversations. "I'm sorry I didn't answer earlier. Patrick and I were heading out to get ice cream … to celebrate. He was accepted to Colgate."

"That's wonderful." Her voice reflects her natural sweetness. Then she cushions her statement by adding, "How are you doing? I know the idea of Patrick leaving for college is a difficult subject." Only Maggie would put the focus on me when she, apparently, is dealing with something.

"I'm fine," I say. "It's you I'm concerned about. Did something happen?"

"I … well … I found out something … that I wasn't expecting." The phone goes silent. Several seconds and a few audible gulps later, she whispers, "I'm pregnant."

Maggie's pregnant? I assume Bobby's the father. When I met him in February, he seemed self-assured, kind, and smart, the perfect guy for Maggie. There was no denying the fire between them, the exact opposite of how Maggie described her previous relationship with Pete from Pittsburgh.

Hoping the right words flow through my mouth, I do my best. "I'm happy for you. You and Bobby will make incredible parents."

Silence. I check the phone to make sure we're still connected.

"He doesn't know," she says.

"You didn't tell him?" The words blurt out before I'm able to consider their impact.

"No," her voice lowers. "I'm not so sure I want to have the baby."

I'm stunned, not because Maggie grew up in a strict Irish Catholic family, but because she'd be an amazing mother—loving, nurturing, giving. And Bobby's crazy about her.

"I'm sorry," she says. "I shouldn't have sprung this on you."

"You have every right to be upset," I say. "An unexpected pregnancy can be shocking, even when you're in a loving and committed relationship." If only I were in Oregon, sitting next to her, I could give her a reassuring hug and tell her it's going to work out. "Why haven't you told Bobby?"

More silence. Then I hear crying.

"Oh, honey," I say. "Everything is going to be fine."

"It's just …" she sniffs several times. "I'm repeating the cycle. This is exactly what happened to my mother."

Why didn't I think of that? Now it all makes sense. Knowing Maggie, she probably doesn't want Bobby to feel obliged to marry her, or to take care of the baby. I suppose her mother felt the same way when she became pregnant with Maggie and never told her boyfriend.

"But Maggie, *this* is different. Your mom was only seventeen. You're twenty-nine. You have an established career and a mature partner who adores you." I let out a deep exhale before continuing.

"Don't you think you owe it to Bobby to tell him? After all, think how much your dad missed not being there for you." I keep myself from saying the second part—how angry he must have been with Maggie's mom for never telling him she was pregnant.

"My mom did it on her own, and I ..." but she cannot finish the sentence.

"How far along are you?"

"Not sure, somewhere around nine or ten weeks, I think. With all the running I do, my period has been irregular. I didn't think much about it when I was late the first month. But then ..." she clears her throat. "At first, I thought it was all a mistake. But I've taken four tests over the past three days. They all say I'm pregnant."

Knowing she most likely is pregnant, I avoid suggesting she may not be. Instead, I ask for guidance. *Please, give me words to help my friend. I have no idea what to say.*

"You always have a choice, and that choice is yours," I share. "If you keep this from Bobby, though, it might jeopardize your relationship. It will probably weigh heavily on you for a long time ... maybe the rest of your life. You've been together for eight months now, right?"

"Almost seven," Maggie says.

"Bobby's crazy about you. If you don't tell him, and he finds out later, he might never get over it. It will linger ... like a deception ... even if you have the purest intent."

Maggie is silent. I wait, then go on.

"I think you should share what's happening. Let him digest the news. Give him space to respond ... listen to what he says and how *he* feels. You can trust Bobby." I take a breath and wait before asking, "Why do you assume he'll feel obliged to marry you?"

"I don't know," she says, her voice sounding childlike.

"What if he wants to? Give him some credit. You owe him that, right?"

I sit up straighter and shake my head, unsure if this is coming from me or the voice that speaks when I write. However, I think the last few sentences were mine.

"You feel that certain?" Maggie asks, now sounding more like the Maggie who is thriving in Bend, not the frightened girl I first met in Costa Rica, afraid to make decisions.

"Yes, I do," I say.

"I don't want him to do anything out of duty," she says with conviction. "*If* I choose to keep the baby, *I* can care for the child. I do not need a man to support me." Her words, bold and strong, could be her mother's. No doubt Carr women are resilient, reliable, and responsible.

"I don't know Bobby that well," I begin, "but I get the impression he wouldn't do something if he doesn't want to."

"I know," she says, then sighs. "Bobby's amazing … caring, independent, and always encouraging me to be the same."

"Hasn't he noticed you're preoccupied?"

"Bobby's been away the past week and a half, at a conference in Boise. Then he tacked on a few days to spend time with his parents in Bozeman."

"When will he be back?"

"Tonight," she says. "He left Bozeman this morning. He's stopping at his place in Tumalo first, then heading here."

Maggie gets quiet. Perhaps it's best to shift the conversation and talk about something else. "Are you still OK with Juliette, Sophia, Annie, and me coming this June?"

"Are you kidding? I can't wait to see everyone. I've especially missed Juliette. Have you spoken to her?"

"No. There's no internet where she's staying. But she sent several letters."

"Same here." Maggie pauses before asking, "How's Michael?"

"He seems nervous … unsure what will happen when she's back."

Tom and I are also concerned about Michael. This hotshot orthopedic surgeon has gone inward since Juliette left in October. They called off their wedding last April, after she admitted to her affair with René, the chef from our resort in Costa Rica. Though they didn't break up, Juliette and Michael decided to put their relationship on pause until she came back from Peru.

"I can't imagine how tough their separation has been for him," Maggie says.

"Michael has definitely not been himself," I add. While I've always pictured them together, Juliette is anything but predictable. And, after studying with a shaman, I can't imagine what she will be like when she returns.

"Oh, before I forget, I booked an Airbnb," Maggie says, shifting the conversation slightly.

"Why? We're all comfortable sharing space in your apartment."

"That's silly," she laughs. "We're too old for that." Now I'm laughing, since I'm almost twenty years older than Maggie. "My place is too small for the five of us," she continues. "I thought it would be fun to stay somewhere closer to restaurants and shops. Plus, this place has a hot tub, and a sauna … like a mini getaway."

"Well, it all sounds wonderful, but I'm worried about you," I say. "Let's get back to Bobby. Don't you think you should tell him?" She goes silent. I ask, "What if you reached out to your father?"

"I couldn't share this with him." Her tone drops. "He would be so disappointed in me."

"Would he? Did he ever express regret that your mom kept you?"

***

The next morning, I hit snooze three times. Maggie and I talked well past midnight. She finally committed to telling Bobby. Maybe my question about her dad hit home.

Although miles apart, Maggie and I grow closer with each conversation. In some ways, she's like the daughter I'd always hoped for. Something inside me wants to protect her. She's so vulnerable. Though almost thirty, she still possesses the innocence of a young girl.

Growing up without knowing her dad seriously impacted her. Her mother refused to tell her who he was, what he was like, or whether he was even still alive. Then it became too late for her to find out anything. Two months before we met at the retreat, Maggie discovered her mom dead on their kitchen floor.

"Morning," I say to Tom, and gently kiss his cheek. "How did you sleep?"

"Like a rock," Tom yawns before turning on his side to face me.

"I was up till almost one, talking with Maggie. She called earlier."

"Is she OK?"

"I think so. I'm glad I didn't wait too long to call her back." I give Tom a quick recap, starting with the pregnancy. After hearing it, he agrees she's in a tough spot.

"What do you think she'll do?" he asks.

"My gut says she'll have the baby," I say, then add, "I just wish I could understand why she's adamant about not getting married. I get that she doesn't want Bobby to feel like he *has to* marry her … but what if he *wants* to?"

I crawl out of bed, arch my back, then roll my neck side to side. As much as I crave more sleep, I have a busy day ahead. "Oh, before I forget, tonight is yoga night," I remind Tom.

"That's right, it's Wednesday." He raises his eyebrows. "No husbands?"

Since Juliette left for Peru, our former Wednesday night yoga at Bliss, Juliette's studio in Rittenhouse Square, turned into evening yoga at a new place in Wayne. Afterwards, Annie, Sophia, and I go out for dinner, sometimes with our husbands.

A small smile etches across my face. I shake my head. "Girls' night," I say. "I'll defrost lasagna for you and Patrick. Lacrosse practice won't be over till after seven. He'll need to shower afterwards," I say, hoping to manage Tom's expectations about dinner. It would be easier to eat separately, of course, but I insist on family dinners. It's one of those traditions I work hard to keep.

"Maybe I'll see if there's a court available at the Y during your yoga time," he says. "Jonathon owes me a rematch. Sounds like there'll be plenty of time to get in a few games of racquetball before Patrick gets home."

Two months ago, Annie and Jonathan Thompson, Jefferson Hospital's Head of Orthopedics, left their downtown high-rise to move to Bryn Mawr. Their new house, zoned for a sole proprietorship, also has a separate apartment above the garage, perfect for their nanny, Mary. Now, Annie, who's a therapist, can meet clients in her home office, while Mary cares for five-month-old Ella. Annie schedules breaks between appointments to spend time with the little one, which was impossible when she worked downtown. Mary, who's a little older, loves living with them. It's a beautiful arrangement, and everyone has become quite close. In fact, Mary is almost like a grandmother to Ella.

Sophia and Jared Robbins, Tom's co-worker and good friend, have lived in Wayne for more than twenty-five years, longer than we've been in Radnor. Now that the Thompsons moved to the Main Line, we've discovered there's a triangle between our houses, making it easier to get together.

It's hard to believe Sophia, Annie, Juliette, and I only met a year and a half ago at a Jefferson Hospital holiday party. We quickly became close friends. Maybe it was our weekend in the Poconos that bonded us. I can't imagine not having them in my life.

Before yoga and dinner, I'm meeting with our local bookstore's events coordinator. In May, I'm releasing my book, *The Best Is Yet to Come*. At first, I thought it would be exciting to publish a book. Now I'm absolutely terrified. Whether conscious or not, there's a lot of me, my history, and my baggage in those pages. What will people think?

***

I take a big swig of what's now cold coffee. What possessed me to commit to an opening event *on* May 19th? Patrick graduates eight days later. It's all too much!

While part of me looks forward to time alone with Tom, there's an ache in my heart when I think of Patrick being gone. I know how to do *the mom* thing. What will life be like once he's away at college?

It's just after eight in the morning here, too early to call Maggie in Oregon. I decide to shift my attention to today's meeting. Instead of contemplating questions for the bookstore's event coordinator, I think about what made me write the book in the first place.

It started during the retreat. Francisco, the shaman, told me I'd be writing a book. I didn't believe him. Then, when I returned from Costa Rica, I met with Brad, my editor at the *Inquirer*, and gave my resignation. I felt ready to focus all my efforts on a different kind of writing. Leaving the paper created time and space to begin my journey as an author. Besides, I was no longer excited about writing "lifestyle" articles for the newspaper. I craved something deeper.

Beginning the book was easy. Francisco gave me enough hints as to the theme. Still, writing a manuscript is a monumental task. Approximately midway through the process, I stumbled, facing writer's block head-on. Despite wanting to quit, I kept at it. Eventually, I finished a very long, *very rough* draft. Multiple revisions later, the story seemed presentable. With Tom's encouragement, I sent a copy to a former college friend who is now an editor. Four months later, she and I were both very proud of the final product. She connected me with a woman who helped me self-publish.

Now that the book is printed and ready, I'm beginning to second-guess myself. What will others think? Will anyone buy it? Then I'm reminded of the upcoming book launch. What if no one shows up?

A ray of sunlight shines through the dark clouds, bouncing off my laptop's screen. I lift my head, straighten my spine, and place my fingers on the keyboard. Pausing in reverent silence, I begin the now familiar ritual by asking, "What am I to know?"

Chapter 2

MAGGIE

March 24th

Turning the corner by the Unitarian church, I make a right onto Skyliners Road. My stride lengthens as gravity pulls me toward the roundabout. From there it's all uphill. I don't mind. I want to push myself. Shit, I'm going to have to stop running at some point, won't I? Instinctively, I pat my belly and say good morning to the tiny human growing inside me.

What was it Bobby said last night? "I will *totally* support you no matter what." His words run through my mind as my feet pick up pace. My breathing deepens. "I've always wanted to be a father," was the next thing he said. How vulnerable, the way his face softened. He wasn't trying to convince me to keep the baby. Both of us believe in the right to choose.

I relaxed after that. We both cried. I dropped my armor and admitted the truth: part of me wants this baby. When I said the words, Bobby took my hands and asked if I would marry him, which wasn't what I wanted—not then, not like that. If I get married, I want an unconditional ask. I want it to be for me, because of me, not because of an unexpected infant. But now that I've decided to have the baby, I trust Bobby will be there … for me *and* our child.

***

At my apartment, I toss my sweaty clothes atop the washer, then head to the shower. I'm meeting a new client this morning, and I have a boatload of prep beforehand. Plus, I have to call the doctor. I told Bobby I would.

Washed, rinsed, and dried off, I step into my favorite taupe corduroys. Are they getting snug around the waistline already, or am I imagining things? I try on three sweaters until one works, then glance in the mirror. Eh, professional enough. I grab a banana and a protein bar, then remember I'm eating for two now. I toss some cashews, almonds, and dried apricots into a reusable snack bag, add it all to my tote, then head out.

Driving to work, I think about all the people with whom to share the news. Right now, only three people know: Marlee, Bobby, and my father. I was nervous about admitting it to my dad. Our relationship is still new—he didn't even realize he had a daughter a year ago. When he came to meet me this past winter, we formed a pretty strong bond in our little time together. Then Bobby and I visited him in Florida and met his family. I trust my dad. Maybe that's why I needed to let him know. As I'd hoped, he supported me and our decision.

I half expect it to be my dad calling when my cell rings. However, it 's Bobby. He asks how I'm feeling.

"Good," I say, crossing my fingers. "Actually, never better." Yes, it's a white lie, but I'm really not myself right now.

"How was your run?" he asks, a tone of concern in his voice. "You were careful, right?"

"What do you mean?"

"You're carrying precious cargo," he says, his voice deepening. "I've seen those gashes on your shins and hands from the trails."

"I'm gonna need bigger running shorts," I say with a sigh.

"That means the baby's growing." His encouragement relaxes me a little. "Did you have a chance to schedule the doctor's appointment?"

"I'm guessing their office opens at nine," I say. "I'll do it this morning, promise."

This is a good thing. I'm going to love being a mom. I'll learn how to properly care for the baby. And Bobby will be by my side the entire time. Juliette believes in affirmations. Maybe they'll work for me.

"So, I'll see you tonight?" His voice returns to that of the seductive cowboy I fell in love with. Bobby's coming over later and making dinner. He insisted, claiming I need to get off my feet and start taking better care of myself. Truthfully, I know nothing about being pregnant, or babies for that matter. I'm an only child. All sorts of questions have been ping-ponging in my head. I plan to bring a list to the doctor's appointment, even if I'm not sure I want to know all the answers.

"Can't wait," I answer Bobby, meaning it with my entire heart.

Despite this unexpected twist in our relationship, I'm more in love with Bobby than ever. Maybe that's what scares me the most. Will everything change when the baby arrives? What if our relationship stalls because we're focusing on being parents? If this new life becomes too overwhelming, will he leave?

The truth is, I always expected to have a husband first, then a child. But we don't always get what we want.

***

Rain starts falling as soon as I get off the phone with the obstetrician's office. Spring in Bend is strange. In Pittsburgh, the daffodils start popping up in late February. By the beginning of April, the smell of spring is in the air. Not here. It's as bleak and cold outside as it was in November—kind of like how I feel. Locals say this is normal. They warn not to plant too early. There can be frost till mid-June. Even in July and August, when daytime temperatures might reach the nineties, you need a jacket in the morning and evening. That's life in Oregon's High Desert.

I text Bobby the appointment date and time: Friday, April 1ˢᵗ, 2:30 p.m. How ironic … April Fools' Day. In a minute, he replies with *got it!* I'm so grateful for his care and support. Considering everything, I'm pretty lucky. What if this had happened when I was dating Pete? I can only imagine how clingy he'd be. Bobby anticipates my needs, and he supports me in what I want to do. Pete probably would have smothered me. Sure, he was super sweet and had the biggest heart, but my relationship with him felt more platonic, nothing close to how I feel about Bobby. Thank God I ended that when I did.

***

A year ago, I didn't even know Bobby. I still lived in Pittsburgh. I shake my head when I think about how we met. It was late August, and I was in the parking lot next to Riverbend Park—embarrassingly in a bikini—struggling to strap my paddleboard on top of the Subaru. From the corner of my eye, I see this incredibly hot guy with shoulder-length brown hair, hoisting his board into the back of his pick-up truck. A yellow lab stood by his side. Then, without a word, this guy, dressed in flops, navy shorts, and a pair of Wayfarer sunglasses, walked toward me, his lab following. He nodded his head as he reached for my paddleboard. With ease, he lifted the board on top of my car, securing it with two quick tugs on the strap.

"You looked like you could use a hand," he said. "I'm Bobby." His jaw-dropping, chiseled abs caught me off guard. Then, he reached his hand toward mine. I remember being surprised by his firm, yet gentle grip. But it was the length of the shake—as well as the intensity of his dark brown eyes—that I most recall. He then introduced me to Harry, his lab, who wagged his tail upon hearing his name. Bobby and I must have talked for close to an hour that afternoon. By the time I left the parking lot, he had my phone number ... and my attention.

I rest my forehead on my fist. Since finding out about the pregnancy, I've only thought of how everything's affecting *my* life. Not once have I considered how this will impact Bobby.

Sitting up, I close my laptop and try to consider having a baby from Bobby's perspective. How will this child change his life? What responsibilities will he feel compelled to take on? What will he have to give up? I pause with this last question.

Freedom. Bobby's losing his freedom. But don't most new dads? I wonder how others deal with this loss.

Bobby loves long mountain bike rides and fishing on the weekends. And God knows his workouts are sacred, especially after a stressful day on job sites. But there's more, like what Bobby does late at night when we're not together. He spends time in his woodshop in the back corner of his barn, behind the horse stalls.

As a kid, whenever Bobby visited his grandparents, he'd help out in the woodshop. Bobby told me he'd hand his grandad tools, or hold the wood steady, so his grandfather could make exact cuts. Afterwards, Bobby cleaned up the debris, tidying the place. Even as a boy, he understood how special this space was. Now it's Bobby's. Maybe just being there provides solace.

Recently, he began building things ... a step stool, shelves for the kitchen, a bench. Last week, he told me about a swing he wanted to make for the front porch of the guest house. I need to tell Bobby that I don't want him to give up any of this for the baby, or for me.

***

The alarm on my phone rings. Toph will be here in fifteen minutes. I think I'm ready, but I take one final glance at my PowerPoint, just in case. I use my compact mirror to make sure there's nothing in my teeth, then dab a bit of lip gloss on my lips.

Toph Harris and his family are relocating to Bend from the Bay Area. They're building a home in the outskirts of town. Their move is scheduled for mid-June. He worked as an investment banker in Manhattan for ten years before moving to Mill Valley, where he runs a start-up venture capital firm. Viv, his wife, teaches yoga and has a reiki practice. She doesn't know this, but the reason we're meeting today is because Toph wants me to design a space on their property where she can teach yoga and see her reiki clients.

Sandy, my boss, gave me this client. Toph and her college roommate were old family friends. Sandy knows nothing about yoga or reiki. In fact, she doesn't subscribe to anything that might be even remotely *woo-woo*. I suppose that's why she referred him to me. Of course, the project immediately intrigued me. I had plenty of ideas to incorporate into the design, many of which I modeled after the beautiful yoga studio at Nueva Vida.

Toph wants to surprise Viv by giving her these plans on her birthday, which is less than two months away. To create a blueprint, I need more information to ensure the design will meet her needs and inspire her work. I have a long list of questions for Toph.

Once in the conference room, I open PowerPoint on my laptop, projecting it onto the wall screen. Unsure of Viv's tastes, I took several approaches—Zen, mountain rustic, modern organic, and farmhouse. Once Toph identifies a style, the fun begins.

A bell chimes. I say a quick affirmation to myself. *Today's meeting will be productive and positive.* Juliette shared this practice—she says something similar before she teaches a yoga class. Now I use it before all client meetings.

I walk out into the lobby just as this tall blonde gentleman, probably in his early forties, collapses an umbrella and rests it against the wall.

"Toph?" I ask.

"Hi," he says, offering his hand. He's dressed in crisply ironed khakis, a burgundy and gray plaid Oxford button-down shirt, and white Converse sneakers. I sense something different about Toph. Perhaps it's the black tourmaline bracelet on his right wrist, or the fact that his unkept wavy hair and earring do not go with his clothing. He doesn't project a New York or a Bay Area vibe.

"Welcome to Bend," I say. "How long are you in town?"

"Until tomorrow. Flew in last night so I could meet with the contractor about a few final details. Viv stayed home with our son, Ben. She didn't want him to miss school." He pauses then adds, "It seems ridiculous, since the kid's only in second grade." Then he shrugs and offers a boyish grin.

I laugh, as if I can relate, even though I can't. I know nothing about second graders, or babies for that matter. Instantly, my right hand goes to my stomach, and I remember what's percolating inside.

"But since this studio is a surprise, I guess it's good Viv's not here." His eyebrows raise, as if we're co-conspirators on a top-secret project.

When seated in the conference room, I start right into the presentation, explaining each slide and sharing my thought process along the way. I pause to glance at Toph. So far, he appears on board.

We discuss square footage, materials, and sustainability. Toph's quick to addresses each issue. He envisions a space larger than I anticipated. And he wants to include a bathroom and changing area. As predicted, sustainable practices are important to him. And he expresses a strong interest in incorporating natural elements—stone, wood, metal, fire, even water—into the plans.

"What's your ceiling for the overall cost?" I tentatively ask, curious if my *guesstimate* is close.

A shyness comes over Toph. His eyes fall to the floor, and he shakes his head. "The sky's the limit." He looks up shyly. "I almost lost my wife two years ago. She received a diagnosis that didn't provide much hope. But she beat the odds." He pauses, takes a breath, then continues. "Luckily, I'm in a position to do this for her." He becomes quiet.

I nod. There's an undertone of love and adoration in his words, nothing flamboyant or entitled. His wife, I think, is very fortunate.

Next, I project a layout of his current property on screen. The home he's building is situated in the front of a five-acre rectangular lot. We discuss possible locations for the studio, conscious of parking and privacy issues. When I ask about a permit for business zoning, he says that's already taken care of.

Thirty minutes later, Toph has answered all my technical questions. Now it's time for the fun part—the style slides. After viewing all options, without a bit of hesitation, Toph says, "Modern organic … but with a touch of Zen."

This man just provided the exact answer I was hoping for. "I can do that," I say. While I've never met Viv, something told me this is the look she'd want.

We spend the next several minutes chatting about ourselves and why we've chosen to make Bend our home. Toph thanks me for meeting with him. Halfway to the door, he pauses.

"Is there something else you've thought of?"

"Actually, there is, but I'm not so sure it's possible." His crystal blue eyes narrow as he clears his throat. "Viv's fascinated with astrology. This goes way beyond reading her daily horoscope. She's been diving deep, talking about conjunctions, trines, sextiles … things I barely comprehend. I think she's trying to make sense of everything she's gone through … and do whatever she can to make sure it doesn't happen again." With this statement, he grimaces before his eyes meet mine. "Is there *any way* you can incorporate some type of astrological aspect into your design? I realize that maybe I'm asking the impossible. I'm not sure I even know what I'm requesting. But *if you could*, I believe it would mean the world to her."

My heart starts pounding, quickly and loudly, like it's about to explode from my chest. He wants me to combine astrology and architecture … exactly what Francisco said I'd be doing. Our conversation from last April replays in my head:

I am meant to understand astrology?

Most certainly … and I suspect once you master this subject, you will use it to help others." He smiles, then says, "I am not suggesting you quit your job as an architect. Not in the least. But perhaps see the connection between the two. Might one benefit the other?"

Speechless, I try to process the synchronicity.

"I'm sorry," Toph says, his face blushing. "You must think I'm crazy."

"No. Not at all." How can I explain this? "You see, last year, I went to a retreat in Costa Rica and worked with a shaman." I swallow several times. Now it's me who's feeling embarrassed. But Toph leans in, waiting for me to continue.

"During a private session, he presented me with a book … on astrology. Francisco, the shaman, told me I would combine astrology and architecture in some way … to help others." The words fly from my mouth.

"And that is what I just asked you to do," Toph smiles. "Well then, it seems as though I've chosen the perfect person to design this studio. I can't wait to see what you come up with." With that, he bows his head, picks up his umbrella, and walks out the door.

What the hell just happened? I flop onto the conference room chair and let my forehead fall to the table. How could Francisco have known? And how will I make Toph's wish come true?

The office door opens. Quickly sitting up, I wonder if Toph forgot something. It's not him. Sandy and Mark are back from their trip to Pittsburgh.

"Hey! How's your dad?" I ask, putting on my best happy face. Sandy's father just sold his house and moved into a retirement community.

Sandy rolls her eyes. "Just as I suspected, he loves it there. Finally, he admitted how miserable he was living alone. Now he has people nearby if he wants company. And if he doesn't, he lives in a beautiful cottage with more than enough space and privacy."

"Of course, he didn't want to admit any of that," Mark adds with a chuckle. "I swear Sandy's dad looked younger than I've seen him in ages. And yesterday, I caught him eyeing up this cute older lady who lives across the street from his new place."

"That's great news," I say.

"Anything happen while we were away?" Mark nonchalantly asks.

"I just met with Toph Harris, from the Bay Area. He wants to build a studio for his wife as a surprise."

"I knew you'd be perfect for him," Sandy says.

"I'm excited. He liked my preliminary ideas. And he's giving me carte blanche with the budget," I add, suspecting this tidbit will make Mark ecstatic.

"Really?" Mark asks. "That's wonderful."

"Anything else we need to be aware of?" Sandy asks.

I wasn't planning to share my baby news with Sandy and Mark today, but now seems as good of time as any.

"Well …" My voice quivers, causing an instant reaction from them both. "Can we sit down?"

Sandy places her hand on my arm. My body trembles. Before I know it, tears begin to form. It's futile to try to stop the inevitable flow. Within moments, salty streaks cover my cheeks.

Squeezing my eyes shut, I do my best not to totally lose it in front of the two of them.

"What's wrong?" Sandy asks.

"I'm pregnant." The words blurt from my mouth despite my intention to be as graceful as possible about things. While it's not unusual for an unmarried woman to have a baby, my Catholic upbringing kicks in. Suddenly, I'm worried they'll judge me.

"A baby," Mark says, sounding delighted. "That's awesome news."

Sandy quickly adds, "You'll be a fabulous mother." With a tender look, she hands me a tissue from the box on the conference table.

"Do you really think so?" I ask, confused yet grateful for their reaction.

"Absolutely," Sandy says. She puts her arm around me. "Every time I see you and Bobby together, it's clear that you're meant for one another. I can't imagine more perfect parents."

Chapter 3

MARLEE

May 16th

The temperature is over eighty, too warm for a Monday in mid-May. But I suppose weather is merely one more thing that's become unpredictable.

I pull into an empty spot in front of LaScala's. Juliette didn't care where we had lunch, but she mentioned craving pizza. It's probably been a while since she's had a slice.

Juliette's usually prompt. Who knows what she's like now. She could have changed. Studying with a shaman in the jungles of Peru tends to do that to people.

Does this make Juliette a shaman? While she just spent eight months learning from one, I'm not so sure it equates to becoming one. I suspect she will explain everything in detail. She usually does.

Juliette's soft top Jeep Wrangler enters the lot. After pulling into a corner space, she gracefully emerges from the driver's side in a short jean skirt and sleeveless embroidered tunic. She excitedly waves and hurries toward me. She looks the same, except her hair is braided, and her skin is several shades darker than it was in October.

"Hey!" she yells. I pull her tightly to me. It feels good to have her home.

"Let me look at you," I say, taking a step back. She's glowing, almost glistening. Sure, she's always had sparkly turquoise eyes and a vibrant complexion. Plus, her yoga teacher body sets her apart from most women. However, today there's something else going on.

"It looks like the past eight months agreed with you," I say.

She nods. "It exceeded all expectations," she shares. Then she gives me her trademark smirk. While I suspect Juliette has shifted in many ways, it's reassuring to know a part of her remains the same.

"Come on, let's go inside." I put my arm around her as we walk. "I can't wait to hear about Peru."

***

The restaurant is empty. Perhaps everyone is outside enjoying the weather. A middle-aged woman seats us by a large bay window.

"Oh my God, Marlee," Juliette begins as soon as the hostess walks away. "The past eight months were utterly amazing. My shaman, Juana, is as knowledgeable as Francisco, maybe even more so." Her eyes widen. "He taught me so much … about life, about how I've been showing up … everything." Then her voice lowers. "The truth is, I'd been fooling others … and myself. Juana helped me realize how dishonest I've been. Sure, I spent my days at Bliss sharing uplifting messages with my yoga students. But I wasn't following my own advice. At first, I attributed this to my fear of abandonment. You know, I did whatever I could to protect myself so no one could hurt me … like my mother did when she left."

I nod, remembering how this was one of Juliette's critical takeaways from our retreat.

"But then I understood there was more, you know … *underneath*. After diving into my shadows, I learned that I lacked faith in myself and my abilities." She swallows, as if still trying to digest this discovery.

"How so?" I ask. Juliette's always come across as extremely confident.

"Well, for the past several years, I created an image of this spiritual yoga teacher and energy worker who had a doctorate in philosophy from Yale, then studied at an ashram in India." She rolls her eyes. "I used all the right terms and phrases. I was a good actress. Fooled everyone, including myself, into believing I was the real deal. I wanted to be *the best*. But working with Juana helped me realize I really wasn't who I pretended to be. Only then could I see how fear, jealousy, and ego ruled my mind and body. Instead of accepting my gift, I wanted to be able to do everything other healers could."

Our server pops over and takes our orders—Juliette's spinach, mushroom, and goat cheese pizza, my margherita, the specialty, plus iced herbal teas for both of us. As the waiter walks toward the kitchen, Juliette takes a sip of water, then continues.

"I said and did what's expected from someone who's *enlightened*," she explains. "Deep inside, though, I was as confused as anyone … but I'd never admit it." She leans across the table, dropping her tone to something close to a whisper. "For years I ignored my fears of not being good enough by stuffing them deep inside."

Right then my heart skips a beat. *Juliette is really no different than me.*

"So, what did you do?" I ask. "How did you *fix* it?"

"Once Juana let me in on the secret, it was super easy. All I had to do was surrender and trust myself," she says with a shrug of her shoulders. "Who knew it would be so *uncomplicated*?" She waves her hand through the air, as if admitting this was the easiest task. "Actually, it was hard at first." She bites her lower lip and looks at the ceiling. "I suppose the biggest challenge was releasing the need to know … and being right."

I can't help but chuckle, having noticed Juliette's need to do both. Her eyes widen with my reaction. Then she scrunches her nose. "You knew that about me?" she asks.

"Yes, but it was kind of cute," I fib.

"Anyway, when I was able to admit I didn't know everything and never would, life became easier. I stopped resisting, controlling

… you know … trying to make things happen *my way*. That's when I began to *understand*. After that, 'aha moments' started to happen all of the time. Information would flash in my head just as I needed it. It was as if the Universe knew I'd waved the white flag. Whatever I required magically appeared."

"So, only when you showed up as yourself, without trying to influence the outcome, did things come together, maybe even better than you expected?"

"Yup," she grins.

"That would be impossible for me to do." My throat tightens as I say it.

"Why?" Juliette's head tilts. She stares at me.

"Because I'm still afraid to let go."

"But what about the premise of your book? I read the draft you sent me. I distinctly remember chapters where you discuss trust, letting go, and believing." Apparently, I, too, proclaim one thing, but deep down believe the opposite.

Juliette leans closer again. "See, no matter who we are, we all deal with the same shit, right? We're afraid to let go because we're terrified we won't be able to handle the outcome. That's why we're all control freaks." She pauses. "But I can help you. Would you trust me?"

Right in front of my eyes, Juliette's face transforms. She appears older than twenty-nine. Her eyes glisten, and her tanned skin sparkles like iridescent crystals. There's something else too … about how *I feel* in her presence. My body calms, as if a wave of unconditional love envelops me, assuring I'll be fine. But just as quickly as the sensation appeared, it vanishes.

"What the hell just happened?" I ask, wide-eyed and trembling.

"Oh, that was the Divine Mother working through me to help you," she says, then leans closer. "Growing up, I never had a maternal figure in my life. Juana showed me how to connect with the

Divine Mother. You can think of her as Mary, or even Gaia, Mother Earth. She's the supreme nurturer. The Mother flows like water and provides comfort. She helps you walk through your fears … eases your pain. I never knew She existed before Juana introduced me to Her." Slowly, Juliette returns to her normal self. "Are you in?"

Unable to respond, I remain silent.

"Please say yes," she goes on. "Besides, I have an assignment to complete before I return to Peru in November. You'd be helping me out."

"You're going back? For good?"

"God no. Don't get me wrong. I *loved* the entire experience. But I am not meant to be a traditional shaman, or to live in Peru. I'm more of an *urban* shaman type. I like life here in the States, if you know what I mean."

I don't. Actually, I'm confused. Maybe that's the point.

"It's like this … for me to *earn* the title of shaman, I have to complete a project this summer. Then, when I'm back in Peru, I'll present what I learned to Juana. If he believes I have the necessary skills to heal others, I will receive my final rites."

"And where do I fit in?" I ask.

"You'd be like a case study. I'll use what I learned from Juana to help you advance to your *next level.*"

My next level? I glance at the floor. Just like that, Juliette's trying to convince me to be her guinea pig. She wants to practice her shamanic ways on me. However, she is right about one thing. How can I release a book about trust, letting go, and believing, when I continue to struggle with these exact topics? Could Juliette's plan actually work?

"OK, I'll do it." I try to force a smile. While I feel many things, *happy* is not one of them. *What is she going to do? Will I have to face my fears?* But then a bigger question surfaces. *What if I'm unable to change?*

Our server arrives with two iced teas. As soon as he leaves, I shift the conversation. "How is Francisco? Dominique told Sophia that her husband spent most of January in Peru with you." Dominique is Francisco's second wife. Together they own and operate Nueva Vida. Sophia and she connected while we were at the retreat and have remained close.

"Oh, Francisco's amazing." A serene expression comes across her face.

"Did you study together or separately?" I'm curious as to how these things work when someone trains with a renown shaman. "Was your day scheduled from dawn to dusk? Did you have free time?"

"We studied separately," she says, answering my first question. "Francisco was there to sharpen his skills. It was wonderful to be in his presence." She adds, "As he was leaving, he asked me to come to Nueva Vida again … as a presenter." Her face lights up.

"Wow. Well, that makes you an *official* shaman to me."

As much as I'd like to hear more about the retreat, I really want to know about Michael.

"Juliette," I pause, cautious not to be too nosey, "how are things with Michael?" My voice softens when I say his name. Michael's always been special to me, almost like a little brother. "Was it strange when he met you at the airport?"

"Well," she begins, "it was *soooo* good to see him." Then she sighs and places both hands over her heart. "I wasn't sure what to expect … or how I'd feel. What worried me most was how he would act. After all, it's been months since we were together." She takes a sip of iced tea then leans closer. "But it was as if we hadn't missed a beat." Her face blushes.

Thank God! Michael's emotional well-being has been a frequent topic between Tom and me. It's been hard watching him turn inward with Juliette away.

Then her eyes narrow and her smile fades. "As we were leaving the airport, he told me he'd booked a room at a resort in the Poconos, at Skytop. It's beautiful. The place has this old-world charm, plus all the trees were starting to bloom." For a moment she appears to drift off.

"So … it was a good weekend?" I ask.

"Well … not at first." Juliette slumps when she says this.

"Did you talk? Were there awkward moments? Are you still together?" I fire one question after another, unable to restrain myself.

"Yes, yes, and yes." She wrinkles her nose before taking in a big breath. "We barely slept Friday night. However, it wasn't as I'd hoped. Instead of, well, *you know*, Michael wanted to talk about our past eight months apart." She rolls her eyes. "He had doubts about our future … *and* a one-night stand with some hospital resident." Her nostrils flair as she admits this.

Unsure how to respond, I remain quiet. Juliette will share what she wants to.

"Of course, I had no grounds to stand on," she continues. "We never said we wouldn't see other people. And besides, after what I did in Costa Rica …" Her glance falls to the floor. She stops mid-sentence.

"What about the rest of the weekend?" I ask, hoping they were able to move on after his confession.

"That's when things got interesting." Once again, she leans closer. "After a late, leisurely breakfast, Michael suggested we go for a drive and explore the area. Did you know Skytop is not that far from your family's home in Hawley Falls? Anyway, we stopped at this darling antique shop, just to browse. That's when we saw your aunt and uncle."

"Sue and Pete were there?" I ask, amazed by the coincidence. Last August, when Juliette, Sophia, Annie, and Maggie visited my family's home—Eagle's Landing, as we call it—everyone met my mom's brother and his wife. Sue and Pete live in the house from May through October, then they go to Florida for the winter.

"It was great to see them. I introduced them to Michael, and the four of us started talking. At one point, they mentioned friends who recently bought a house in North Carolina and were planning to list their home."

I nod, wondering where Juliette's going with her story.

"You see," she goes on, "one of the things Michael and I talked about the night before was what I wanted to do now that I'm back … my overall *game plan*."

She pauses when our pizzas arrive, pulls a slice from the metal pan and takes a huge bite.

"Oh my *God* … I'd forgotten how incredible pizza tastes!" We eat for a bit, then she picks up the story from where she left off.

"Friday night, I told Michael about a dream of creating a retreat center, one that offers mini getaways for women like us … to help people heal. I'd do most of the programming, but I'd also invite other practitioners to run sessions." She stops, eyeing the metal pan. "It would resemble Nueva Vida, but on a much smaller scale."

I try to envision this as she continues. "Michael asked Sue and Pete if we could see the property. Then he turned to me and said, 'It might be the perfect spot.'" Juliette sighs.

"This was Michael's idea? Did you see it? What was it like?" Once again, I can't help but forge ahead with a barrage of questions.

"Sue and Pete insisted on taking us there."

"And?"

"We met the owners. They're nice. The six of us spent the entire afternoon together. By the end of the day, I made an offer." A faint blush comes over her face.

"You bought a property in Hawley Falls?" Never in a million years would I imagine Juliette wanting to have anything, especially a retreat center, in the Poconos. Mexico? Yes. Arizona or Colorado? Maybe. But Hawley Falls, Pennsylvania? No way.

"It sounds crazy, but it feels right," she says, taking another bite of pizza. Then she tilts her head in a knowing way. "Actually, the property is perfect. There's a stone house to live in. It's quaint, with a craftsman flair. They just built it four years ago. Everything is practically new. Three bedrooms, two and a half baths, and the most beautiful patio that looks out onto a charming pond, all on twenty acres." Her eyebrows arch. "The best part is a little creek runs through the back of the property and feeds a pond that's filled with trout." She takes another bite, then washes it down with iced tea.

"Of course, I'll need to build the retreat center," she concludes. Her nose scrunches. "I'm still trying to figure out how much space I'll need … and how I want it to look. But this land will be the perfect backdrop for whatever I build." Then she adds one more huge detail. "Michael said he believes in me … in my future, and in ours."

A ray of sun comes through the window and bounces off Juliette's hand. We both notice the vibrant sparkle.

"Later Saturday, we finally had the passionate reunion I was hoping for," she says. "That's when things got real." Juliette exhales. "It's when I knew. Finally, I was ready to commit. The wedding's back on!" Her trademark smirk appears. "Guess you're going to be my maid of honor after all."

I get up from my chair to hug her. "I couldn't be happier for you both. Tom is going to be so relieved when I tell him. Or maybe Michael already shared the news today at work?"

"Not sure," she says. "Anyway, when I was in Peru, despite my strongest intention, I couldn't stop thinking about Michael. A part of me wanted to release him, let him follow his path as I traveled mine. But I couldn't. If anything, the time apart taught me how much I wanted him." By the tone of her voice, I doubt Juliette will question their relationship again.

"Just to be clear, you and Michael are getting married, you're building a retreat center in Hawley Falls, and you are using me as a guinea pig to see whether you will qualify as a shaman," I say. An unexpected giggle emerges.

In pure Juliette fashion, she shrugs, as if this is an everyday occurrence. "I know. It's a lot. But, if I came back to Pennsylvania and everything remained the same, the entire time away would have been pointless."

"What about Bliss?" I ask. "Are you going to sell the studio?"

She bites her lower lip. "I love that place, but I can't run a yoga studio in downtown Philadelphia and direct a retreat center in the Poconos."

"Why not? Will you live in Hawley Falls full time?"

Juliette shakes her head. "Michael's committed to Jefferson, at least for now. We're planning to stay at his place during the week, then go to Hawley Falls on the weekends. I've decided to sell my apartment in Northern Liberty. That'll give me some cash to secure a construction loan."

She's carefully thought out all angles, but I still don't know why she wants to sell her yoga studio. She's worked so hard to cultivate her clientele. Besides, what will she do when she's in Philadelphia?

"Sabrina has been running Bliss while you're away," I say. "How has that been going?"

"Great. Enrollment hasn't dropped at all. I think it may have even increased over the winter. She sent me the stats. Class numbers are strong."

"Why not ask her to continue to manage the studio? You could keep Bliss and teach a few classes during the week without worrying about day-to-day operations. Besides, your students miss you."

Juliette inherited a large sum of money when her father passed, and I assume she won't have to sell Bliss. However, knowing her, she wants to make sure her yoga studio runs properly.

"You've got a point," she agrees. "And I already miss teaching. Plus, what would I do all week in Philadelphia without the studio? I'll talk with Sabrina this afternoon." She pauses. "Fortunately, Bliss has been very profitable, which helped me pay off the mortgage ahead of schedule." Juliette is comfortable talking to me about these types of things. She knows I won't judge her for having the advantage of inherited money. After all, it came at a huge cost. She'd give it up in a heartbeat if it meant more time with her father.

We switch from iced to hot tea and spend the next two hours catching her up on everyone else's lives.

"Annie and Jonathon left Rittenhouse Square and now live in Bryn Mawr," I say. "Their home is beautiful. Annie moved her office there. And Mary, their Irish nanny, has her own apartment over the garage." I take out my phone to show Juliette pictures of little Ella at their new house.

"She's grown so much," Juliette says. "Annie sent me pictures, but the last one was from February." Her voice deflates a bit, and I note how disconnected she must feel after being away.

"Sophia's doing well too. Her practice began to flourish after she returned from studying with Jack at Nueva Vida."

"Francisco shared how impressed Jack was with Sophia," Juliette says. "Apparently, she's the smartest doctor he's ever trained to incorporate holistic methods into an existing practice." Her eyes widen with this statement.

"I always suspected Sophia was brilliant," I say in awe of my friend.

"How's Maggie?" Juliette asks, her voice softening. "Besides you, I've missed her the most."

"Well …" I pause, wondering how much I should reveal. Then I remember that Maggie is telling people, and from what she mentioned, is beginning to show. "Her life's definitely taken a turn." I smile, not wanting to alarm Juliette.

"What do you mean? Is she OK?"

"Maggie's pregnant. The baby's due the middle of October."

Juliette's mouth drops. "Pregnant? I assume it was a surprise?"

"It was. But she and Bobby are embracing the situation." I let out a long exhale. "At first, she felt overwhelmed. But when I talked with her last week, she sounded more excited about becoming a mom."

Without a word, Juliette seems to digest this information, perhaps considering how she and Michael would handle a similar situation.

"Maggie will be a great mother," she says. "I haven't met Bobby, but I can't imagine Maggie would fall in love with just *any guy*. I'm sure he's fabulous." A curious grin comes across her face. "Maybe I'll throw her a baby shower."

"We'll all be together in less than two months," I say. "The end of June will be here before we know it. First, I have to get through Patrick's graduation."

"I know how much you're dreading that day," she says, lightly touching my arm. "I suppose that's what being a parent is about … preparing kids to be independent, then letting go," she says with a twinge of sadness. Maybe she's thinking about her own mother, who certainly didn't do that for her.

Her demeanor shifts. She gets bubbly again. "You know, the timing for us going to Bend couldn't be better," she says in an upbeat tone. "There's a lot going on in your life. Patrick's going to college … and you're releasing your first book." I note she uses the term *first*. "Some girl-time is just what you'll need."

"Everyone's busy," I say. "Look what's ahead of you!"

"Sure, but we all process change differently. Remember, I just broke off an engagement, went to Peru to study shamanism, and now, I've recommitted to marrying Michael and am creating a healing center in the Poconos. I guess I'm OK with uncertainty."

She laughs dismissively. "But I have a hunch these transitions—becoming an empty nester and an author—are pretty big for you." She stares into my eyes, gauging my reaction. Suddenly, I don't feel apprehensive about what's ahead. A calming sensation courses through my body. Juliette has always had a healing way about her. Now, after studying with Juana, her gifts seem to have magnified.

I'm proud of her for following her soul's calling to the jungles of Peru. She came back knowing she is ready to be with Michael. Her vulnerable, childlike side has transformed into a wise woman—confident, accepting, and real. That last word resonates most. There's a true presence about her. Releasing the need to label this transformation, I decide to trust her. I'm not sure what working with her will lead to, but I know that staying where I'm at isn't an option. It's been more than a year since our retreat. Now I'm ready to take my next steps.

Chapter 4

MAGGIE

May 21ˢᵗ – 22ⁿᵈ

The building design is complete. I finished it several weeks ago. However, the astrological component—Toph's special request … which Francisco prophesied—is still missing. Despite my best efforts, nothing resonates. I cannot figure out how to incorporate astrology into Viv's yoga studio. I tried using the moon as the theme. Then I dabbled with various zodiac signs. I even spent a ton of time studying where the sun rises and sets on the lot, as well as the moon's positioning throughout the year. Still, I'm at a complete loss.

Maybe some sugar will give me inspiration. The unopened bag of Starbursts at the back of the snack drawer reminds me of Sonya, the astrologist I met at the retreat. At the end of her workshop, she handed out her business card, with a Starburst attached. Could Sonya help me?

On a whim, I leaf through the filing cabinet in the back of my closet until I find a folder labeled *Nueva Vida*. It's thick, filled with a week's worth of notes, plus the journal I kept. The last entry captures my attention …

Still mourning the unexpected death of Mom, my mind struggles with three looming decisions. Should I break up with Pete? Despite being with him for three years, he never stokes any fireworks … not even a flickering sparkle of passion. Would it be better to remain in

Pittsburgh and search for a new job,
or take a risk and follow my bosses to
Bend, Oregon, where I don't know a single
soul? And the most difficult question:
should I search for my father? Do I have
the courage to contact a man who
doesn't know I exist? What if he doesn't
want anything to do with me?

It seems like I wrote this in another lifetime, though it was merely thirteen months ago. I return to the contents of the folder. About a third of the way through, I find it—a light pink business card, embossed with silver stars and planets. Sonya's contact information is on the back. Might she provide some answers, or at least help me find them? Is reaching out to her is a dumb idea? Would she even recognize my name? I'm sure Sonya holds multiple workshops and does tons of readings each year. Why would she remember me? *But what if she does?* With a renewed conviction, I open my mail app and start a new message:

Dear Sonya,

We met in Costa Rica—at Nueva Vida—last April. I loved your workshop. You were so helpful during our private session. Your wise insights guided me in making several critical decisions after I returned home.

When I met with Francisco later that week, he told me I'd be combining astrology with my job as an architect. At the time, I had no idea what this might mean. Then, at the end of our session, he gifted me one of his books, Truths of the Night Sky. *I've read it several times. I also enrolled in an online astrology course, hoping it might give me further insight. Still, I can't see a connection between architecture and astrology.*

Strangely enough, a new client recently requested I add astrological elements to a yoga studio I am designing for his wife. She teaches yoga, practices reiki, and follows astrology. As this project is a surprise, I cannot ask her what aspects of astrology she finds most interesting. To say I am at a loss is an understatement. I've tried various angles, but nothing makes sense.

Then I remembered how perceptive you were, and I wondered if you might be able to offer direction. Of course, I understand if you're unable to help right now. Still, if you could share any thoughts on how to design this studio to include astrological elements, I would be incredibly grateful.

Thank you,
Maggie Carr

Before I can change my mind, I hit "send." Then I head to the kitchen, open that bag of Starbursts, and pull out a yellow square. Maybe a vision will *miraculously* appear as the sugar slides down my throat. Sadly, not even the tiniest idea comes through. I may never figure this out. Four more Starbursts later, I'm back at my desk without any solution. Luckily, tomorrow is a new day. Maybe Sonya will respond.

***

"Damn, this chili's awesome," Bobby smiles as he runs his hand down my thigh. His touch feels electric. The further along I am in pregnancy, the more I want to have sex. Of course, Bobby doesn't mind one bit. At first, he was a bit leery. I've read most men are. But once they realize there's no harm to the mom or the baby, well …

Bobby takes a final bite of his second helping, then begins the dishes. Harry leaves the table to curl up on the new dog bed I bought. I want him to feel comfortable every time he's at my place.

"Don't forget the cobbler," I say. I take it out of the oven, scoop two healthy servings into bowls, add some vanilla ice cream to both, and carry them to the table. Bobby's eyes fixate on me as we enjoy dessert.

"What are you thinking?" I ask.

"You're just so beautiful," he smiles. I playfully swat his arm.

"My skin's breaking out like I'm a teenager," I argue, "and I barely fit into my clothes. I had to buy more leggings … and bigger tops."

"You're so wrong," he says. He gazes into my eyes. "It's this glow you have. Like you're part of some grand plan … to create a tiny human." He gently touches my cheek. I blush.

"Hey, it took both of us, mister," I tease. Then Bobby leans over to pull me onto his lap.

"Best thing I've ever done," he whispers and begins to nuzzle my neck. I feel my mood shift, suddenly way less self-conscious about my body. Embracing the strong femininity that moves inside me, I stand, take his hand, and lead him to my bedroom.

My body has shifted, and so have we. There's something much deeper about being with him now. I keep my eyes open as we make love. I don't want to miss one moment with him.

***

The sun streams through the slightly parted curtains. Turning onto my left side, I watch Bobby sleep. Strands of dark, wavy hair fall across his face. His muscular chest, slowly rising then falling, captivates me. Breath, so fragile, is a force we cannot understand. I touch my belly, wondering about the new life inside me. Instead of any panic this morning, there's a sense of ease … as if this is what's meant to be.

Thinking back to last night, there's no longer any doubt concerning Bobby's commitment to our baby or to me. I feel more secure about our relationship as well as my decision to become a mom.

I reach my hand toward his face and lightly graze his lips. He stirs. "Hey, beautiful," he murmurs. "Sleep well?"

"Amazingly," I say. Then I remember that tomorrow, I'll be telling my new favorite client I can't deliver on his astrology request. A wave of nausea comes over me. Ignoring it, I reposition to spoon Bobby, intertwining my legs with his. After a few minutes of snuggling, I slip out of his embrace and head to the bathroom, beginning my morning routine. When I'm done, the bed is empty. It's then I notice an aroma of coffee coming from the kitchen.

After slipping on my furry pink slippers and lavender robe, I make my way to join Bobby. He hands me a mug of coffee as I quickly check the emails on my phone. There's a message from Sonya. I carefully read her reply:

Hi Maggie,

I definitely remember working together. I recall sensing a familiarity about you, as though we'd met before. If my memory is correct, you had just lost your mother. Hopefully, life has become easier since the retreat.

Regarding your question: I know nothing about architecture, but I do have a pretty good grasp on astrology. And I keep notes on all my readings. When I reviewed your file, I found some information that might prove helpful.

You have Mercury in Pisces. You're empathic! You can pick up on the feelings of those around you. You don't know the woman whose studio you're designing, but you've met her husband. What can you feel about her through him? Pause and go within. Ask to sense her personality and desires so you can paint an image of her in your mind. Then, utilize that information to determine what she would want in this space.

Success and achievement are important to you. They've helped you move forward in life. Part of this is because your Mars is in Capricorn. However, these traits are holding you back in this project. There is no winning solution. Instead, follow a heart-felt approach. Tap into your emotions. Your conjunction between Venus and Neptune will help. This will stoke your creative fires.

Also, as an Aquarian, it is important to remain true to yourself. Create what you believe will make her happy. Do not worry about meeting anyone's expectations of you or your abilities.

Finally, one more thing. What is it about astrology that most reso-nates with you? Which aspects do you find most alluring? You were chosen for this project. Trust yourself. The answers lie within.

Sending love and light,
Sonya

I'm grateful for Sonya's email … but I wish it came with spe-cific directions for the blueprints. Still, I know there's wisdom and purpose in her words. It's up to me to decipher the meaning.

"Everything OK?" Bobby asks. He hands me a warmed crois-sant slathered with butter.

"The astrologer I told you about responded," I say. There's a glimmer of hope in my voice, but I'm not sure it's warranted.

"And?" he asks.

"Her email was *kind of* cryptic," I say. I stare into my coffee. "Maybe if I spend some time thinking about it, I'll find clues." I tear off an end of the croissant.

Bobby walks toward me and takes me into his arms. "How about I head out to Phil's trailhead for a ride, while you give yourself some space? Can Harry stay here?"

"Of course," I say. Harry nudges up to my knee.

"Looks like he's already claimed you," Bobby smiles. He kisses my forehead, then goes off to change into his bike gear. A few minutes later, he's dressed and ready for his ride.

"Be careful," I say, kissing him goodbye.

"Of course. Now I have two reasons." He leans down to kiss my belly. Harry gives a playful grumble. "OK Harry, sorry … three reasons."

Once Bobby is gone, I reread Sonya's email several more times. I still have no idea what to do. With a pen and notepad in hand, I start writing …

> Empathic – what can I pick up from Toph's energy?
> What do I know about Viv?
> How does Toph feel about her?
> How does she feel? What might she desire?
> Heart-felt approach … no "right" solution.
> What would make her happy?
> What would make me happy?

The last two questions stick. If I were to design this space for myself, how would I want it to look? Working from that idea, what would Viv desire? *Think … imagine Viv, not Toph. She's the client!* I move to the sofa, stretch out, prop my head on a throw pillow, and shut my eyes. Harry joins me on the other end of the couch. My body begins to melt into the cushions. My mind sets off to another place. I'm in an empty room. There's a woman next to me. I can't make out her features. Is this Viv? She has a small object in her hand that she uses to point to different areas of the room.

My eyes dart around. I sense that this space wants me to dictate its textures, colors, features, angles … everything. The woman and I stand in the middle of the room. In front of us appears to be a babbling creek. Now everything shifts. It's actually a narrow water feature in the floor. The water flows over multi-colored river rocks. Soothing, bubbling sounds fill the space. The woman then points to the floor … long, narrow floorboards set on a diagonal. The color catches my attention … sage green, almost mossy in appearance … like the forest. *I'm getting it!*

I look up at the front wall and scan a row of mirrors, smoky and textured. In the muted reflection I can make out a raised steel gas fireplace behind me. I turn toward the structure that lines the back wall. It creates a serene environment, and its dancing flames will provide heat whenever Viv wants to make the yoga room toasty.

I pivot to the right, toward bay windows with plants at their base. The woman in the room with me points upward to a circular skylight. Oiled bronze pendants hang from the domed ceiling. The off-white walls allow the rich lighting fixtures to pop.

My mind drifts to where there are no rights and wrongs … only possibilities. A thought surfaces. *I can incorporate Viv's birth chart into the ceiling.* A faint circle appears above me. There are twelve sections to the sphere … *the astrological houses.* Gray Roman numerals appear on the ceiling above each house. Hanging pendants depict archetypes of each zodiac sign … a lion for Leo, a crab for Cancer, a scale for Libra …

What about the planets in Viv's chart? Adding them to the ceiling might become confusing. I don't want anything to distract people while they're lying on their yoga mats. I rub my forehead, hoping to open my third eye. Sparkling objects start to populate the floor below me. I walk in a circle around the room and count seventeen unique gemstones, the exact number of planets and coordinates in a birth chart. *Now I understand … embed the planetary placement of her birth chart in the floor.*

I open my eyes, unsure what just happened. Harry pants and stares at me. "Pretty wild," I say to him. "Sure, there are lots of loose ends, but things are beginning to form." I pet him on the head and start pacing.

Will people even never notice this theme? Some might find the water feature interesting … maybe they'll wonder about the stones in the floor. I doubt they'll comprehend the big picture. But Viv will. That's all that matters.

Harry follows me to my desk, then curls into his dog bed. I begin sketching … and quickly crumble paper after paper, tossing them into the can next to me. Harry lifts his head and tracks every toss. But I keep going, and eventually the sketches begin to make sense. I'm ready to launch the design program on my laptop.

When the front door opens, Harry runs to greet Bobby. However, I'm too focused to look up. "I guess you found your inspiration," he says, grinning, sweaty, and covered in dirt.

"I have," I say, then motion for him to come over. Showing him the drawings, I do my best to explain the reasons behind my thought process. At first, Bobby's quiet, absorbing how the details will work together in the physical space. He asks several questions. His years as a contractor give him great insight into interpreting blueprints, but astrology is pretty new to him. Finally, he squeezes my shoulder. "You did it," he says. Three simple words in a straight tone, like he always knew I'd find my answers.

***

Toph is quiet. I wait, biting my lower lip in anticipation. Then his voice comes through my laptop. "You nailed it, Maggie. It's brilliant." There are few things more satisfying than meeting a client's request. "Viv will love this," he adds, his voice cracking a bit.

"Thanks," I say. I can hear the humility in my voice. These ideas came through me, but not from me. "Toph," I say, "I know you want to surprise Viv with these plans for her birthday, and I will have the designs ready before then. I'm wondering ... do you think she'd like to give some input? I can make assumptions about what she might want, but I'd love her guidance in certain areas. For instance, which gemstones would she want to represent various planets? I want to make sure we're meeting her needs ... current ones, and anything for the future."

"You have a good point," he says. "Knowing Viv, I suspect she'll also have opinions about where the studio should sit on the property."

"When will you both be in Bend?"

"Once school is over. I just booked our flights for early June. We're staying downtown at The Oxford until the house is ready."

"Maybe we can schedule a meeting before you move in."

"Perfect. Viv will need something to keep her mind busy while she's waiting for moving trucks."

***

Later in the afternoon, I sip a cup of decaf chai and look ahead to the month of June. The calendar is already filling up. I'm most excited about what I've highlighted in hot pink. My friends—I always think of them as The Healers—are visiting for four days. I wish they could stay longer, but it's hard for everyone to get away.

I pull up the confirmation email for the Airbnb. The house is just off Galveston. At first, I thought we'd stay downtown, but this is better. Five bedrooms, two and a half baths, a hot tub, sauna, fire pit, and twinkle lights outside. Bobby told me not to worry about him that weekend. He's met Marlee before, and I was hoping he could spend time with Annie, Sophia, and Juliette. But he insisted on me having girl time.

Kenny Chesney will be at the amphitheater on Saturday night. I bought our tickets months ago. Friday night we have reservations at Bosa, my favorite local Italian restaurant. We can figure out the rest later.

Sandy and Mark said I can borrow their stand-up paddle boards. They have four, which is perfect because I already own one. But then I realize I haven't been on my board since last October. How will my balance be? Will the extra weight make a difference?

Placing my hands on my stomach, I whisper, "What do *you* think?"

Chapter 5

MARLEE

May 26th – 28th

A text from Tom pings my phone. *Can you meet for lunch?* Can I meet for lunch? Today? Doesn't Tom realize tonight's baccalaureate?

I text back, asking where and when. I don't have time to go downtown. There's too much to do. All I can think about is keeping my shit together. The last thing Patrick needs is an overly emotional mother during his last two days of high school.

I let out a big sigh, then try to release the idea of having some downtime this afternoon. For whatever reason, Tom needs to talk. Seconds later, he replies …

Noon. You pick, close to home. I'm taking the afternoon off. I know we have a tight timeline, but something came up that I need to discuss.

I suggest a place, and he replies with the thumbs up. My mind starts rerouting the day. This is pretty unlike him, but clearly, whatever it is can't wait.

I go back to my to-do list, bouncing from one task to another … unloading the dishwasher … changing beds … wrapping Patrick's graduation present. I water the plants, confirm our dinner reservations, and start vacuuming the downstairs. Next on the list is to make the chocolate cake for the post-baccalaureate party. The funniest part of it all: today's stress level will probably be mild compared to tomorrow's.

At Radnor High, every student gets eight tickets for graduation. A lot of families scurry around for more. Not us. Patrick's grandparents have all passed on, Tom is an only child, and my siblings are essentially estranged. We're bringing the Thompsons, the Robbins, and Juliette and Michael. Patrick looks up to Michael. It was his idea to invite everyone.

***

Tom's already seated when I arrive at Sullivan's. Instead of his usual calm demeanor, his face has an uncomfortable seriousness to it. My pulse quickens.

"Are you OK?" I ask after giving him a quick kiss. I sit down, anxious to know what's going on.

"I'm fine." He sips his water, sits up, then places his hand on top of mine. "I know the timing is horrible, with graduation and all, but a recruiter reached out to me this morning about a *big* position. I need to give him an answer by tomorrow morning."

"A recruiter? You're looking for another job?" My stomach clenches. "Why haven't you mentioned this?"

"I wasn't looking," he says. "They found me. That's why I wanted to talk as soon as possible."

"I thought you loved your job. Wouldn't you miss working with your team?" I'm baffled. Why are we having this conversation right now?

"I do, and I would," he says. "That's what makes this so difficult." The color drains from his face. A pit forms in my stomach. I'm not so sure I want to hear what Tom has to say.

"The job would be the Head of Orthopedics, at Mass General."

"Boston?" I can barely spit the word out. Tom nods.

"Yes," he says, then inhales deeply. "An opening came up. The former department head resigned … health reasons." He pauses and sips his water again. "Before they advertise the position, they have a small list of people they're contacting. Apparently, I'm at the top of it." Tom's tone is humble, but there's a slight redness to his cheeks. "That's why we have to decide kind of quickly."

I pause. What would a move like this mean for his career? Orthopedic surgeons do well. Being an administrator will add to his workload, but also his prestige … and salary. My mind goes to Annie, remembering how much their lives changed when Jonathon took the same position at Jefferson.

"What do you want to do?" I ask, even though I already know the answer. Tom leans closer and squeezes my hand.

"It's more than what *I* want," he reminds. "Would this work for *us*?" He pauses, trying to gauge my reaction. I keep my emotions in check, hoping Tom will continue. He does.

"Patrick will be at Colgate. Us being in Boston will probably be strange for him, but it's not a deal breaker. He can always visit old friends over breaks. What concerns me is *you*. I know you can write from anywhere, but what about everything else? The house? Your friends? Routines?"

Tom knows how much our farmhouse means to me. We put enormous sweat and equity into the place. And we finally have it just as we'd hoped. More importantly, I'd be leaving my friends. Before Annie, Sophia, and Juliette, I struggled connecting with other women. Now these three mean the world to me. Our bond is much deeper than any I could have imagined.

I scan the floor. A sigh escapes my lips. It's a huge honor for Tom. I squeeze my eyes tight, trying to imagine life in Boston, away from home and friends. Just as I'm about to focus on what I might lose, the voice comes through.

What if you said yes?

I feel a divine wisdom in these words. What if I did? What would life in Boston look like? There's no way we could recreate what we have in Radnor. We'd have to start from scratch. Then my mind turns to more practical matters.

"Did they share the salary?" I ask. Tom's eyes widen, surprised I'm not showing my usual hesitation.

"They're offering $825,000, with a $300,000 signing bonus," he says. His tone stays even, and I suspect he doesn't want money to be the deciding factor … but we can't ignore it either. That's almost twice what he currently makes. The signing bonus would cover close to four years of Patrick's tuition.

Dozens of possibilities swirl through my mind. We could create a brand-new home that meets our new lives as empty nesters. Red Sox games. The Freedom Trail. Italian food in the North End. I bet we could even find a place with extra bedrooms for when friends visit … and explore the city together.

"Let's do it," I say. We're both shocked when the words come out of my mouth.

"Seriously?" Tom's jaw falls open. "You'd move to Boston? Leave everything here?"

"We can try it … rent an apartment downtown, near the hospital, and see how it goes. If we hate it, we can move back. Maybe we can hold onto to the house, in case it doesn't work." I wave my hand in a non-committal fashion, completely unlike me. "Plus, with the house, we can come back on weekends whenever we like."

"Are you sure?" he mutters. "I need to tell the recruiter tomorrow morning, before eight. Don't you want more time to think about it?"

Do I? Even though I usually don't perseverate on decisions, this one was unusually quick for me. Should I pause, weigh options, and consider the pros and cons? I've always lived in the Philadelphia area, except for college in Vermont. This will be a *huge* move. Something is pulling me toward taking this leap. Perhaps it's an unconscious desire to explore someplace new. Or maybe there's more to it. Perhaps moving to Boston will help me grow.

My rational side begins kicking on. There's so much involved with packing up and moving. I'll need to find new doctors, a dentist, a yoga studio. Tom used the word *routines* a moment ago. What about my hair stylist? Then there's Patrick. How will this *really* impact him? Boston is six hours from Philadelphia. Most of his high school friends will be in Radnor during the summer and on breaks. Sure, he could visit, but where will he stay? In our house without parents being there? No way.

Tom sees I'm lost in my thoughts. He reaches across the table and touches my face. I rest my cheek in his hand.

"You want this job?" I ask. A smile etches across my face. He nods. "Then let's do it." A spark ignites. My thoughts take off in all directions again, like a pack of kindergarteners at recess. Where's the best area to live? Do we want a new apartment, or a classic townhouse? A brownstone? What will we bring with us? What will we leave? When will we tell Patrick? How will he take this news?

My heart sinks. Leaving Radnor will rock his world. Still, he has surprised us before. Perhaps I shouldn't make any assumptions. Either way, we can't say a word till after graduation.

An hour and a half later, Tom and I walk into our farmhouse. That's when the decision hits me the hardest. My pulse quickens, and I feel an undeniable weight across my chest. I was barely ready to experience the *lasts* of Patrick's high school career … now I have to face the *lasts* of life in Radnor. Tears form in the corners of my eyes. I swallow and hope Tom won't notice. I don't want to spoil our celebratory mood.

I blot my eyes with the back of my sleeve, take Tom's hand, and lead him to our bedroom. I have no idea what life as an empty nester will be like. The best thing Tom and I can do is test things out. Maybe it will take my mind off all that is changing around me.

***

A long line of seniors enters the gymnasium to the sounds of "Pomp and Circumstance" playing over the loudspeaker. My throat tightens. I do my best to fight back the inevitable tears as Patrick's classmates, in their maroon and white caps and gowns, proceed down a makeshift aisle toward rows of folded metal chairs. Tom squeezes my hand.

Sophia, to my left, understands. She's been through this twice. Annie, Jonathon, Michael, and Juliette sit in the row behind us. It's nice to have our closest friends with us during this special, emotional milestone.

Several students address the audience. Their passionate speeches are filled with anticipation for what lies ahead, which gives me hope for their generation. Soon, the principal begins calling names in alphabetical order. Students rise, walk to the stage, and receive their diplomas to applause. With nearly three hundred kids graduating, I wait patiently as the principal begins with "B" names. In ten minutes, he's up to "F's." Another twenty-five minutes go by before he hits the "R's." Soon it will be Patrick's turn. The muscles in my chest tighten. I inhale deeply, followed by long exhales. Still, nothing calms me.

"Here we go," Juliette says right before the name "Patrick Ryan" rings out across the PA system. With a huge grin, Patrick jumps up and practically vaults on stage. One vigorous shake of the principal's hand later, he proceeds toward the superintendent for his diploma. Then … it's over. He's back at his seat, high-fiving the kid sitting next to him.

"Are you OK?" Tom asks. He wraps his arm around me. I nod … I am.

"The hard part is over," I say.

***

The hostess at the White Dog Café seats us at a large round table in a spacious corner. Patrick grabs a seat next to Juliette. He's so excited she and Michael are back together. Much like Tom has been Michael's mentor, Michael has been a big brother to Patrick for some time. And Juliette … well, what eighteen-year-old boy wouldn't want to sit next to this gorgeous woman?

Between courses and conversation, Patrick opens gifts. Annie and Jonathon give him a generous gift certificate to Colgate's bookstore. Next is a set of books from Sophia and Jared, including Sean Covey's *7 Habits of Highly Effective Graduates*, *The Four Agreements* by Don Miguel Ruiz, *The Celestine Prophecy*, by James Redfield, and finally, *Seuss-isms*, by Dr. Seuss. Then a large box from Juliette and Michael makes its way onto Patrick's lap. His eyes go wide as he pulls a round object from the crumpled tissue paper.

"It's a drum from Cusco," Juliette says. "A shaman made it. The top is goat skin."

"It's awesome," Patrick utters. His fingers trace the cording along the drum's edge. "Is it OK to play it, even if I'm not a shaman?"

"Of course," Juliette laughs, then tilts her head toward Michael.

"I was fooling around with it this past week," Michael admits. "But then *she* told me it was for *you*." He gives Patrick a wink.

Tom stands and clinks his wine glass. "Patrick," he starts, "I hope you know how proud we are of you. You've done well in school … but it's the man you're becoming that matters most." I gulp. Tom has always been a stickler for achievement. Hearing him share this makes me realize that he is shifting too.

"We've had some ups and downs," he goes on, "but you've always manned up, been honest, and taken your responsibilities seriously." Patrick grins a bit. "Your mom and I, along with everyone here, can't wait to see where you are in ten years. I'm not talking about your career ... or how much money you make. I mean, will you be happy, and will you feel like you're making a difference? Those are the true measures of a fulfilling life."

With that, he raises his glass, then quickly wipes away a single tear. I look around the table. There's an undeniable connection among us ... an unconditional acceptance, plus a level of trust you can't find with just anyone. These people are special. They've become my family.

When will the nine of us be together like this again? In a few months, Patrick will be at Colgate, and Tom and I will be living in Boston. I feel my mood spiral downward, restoking my fears about everything coming to an end.

Last night, Tom and I decided to keep the move to ourselves until we found a place to live. We definitely didn't want to share the news tonight. It's Patrick's night. Now I'm starting to doubt things. Was I right to say *yes* so quickly? I never do things on a whim. Why didn't I give myself more time to think things through? Would that have been selfish? Tom's ecstatic about the offer. I would never want to keep Tom from his dream job, just because I'm afraid to move and leave my friends.

I dig my fork into a slice of chocolate cake, tonight's dessert, and inhale its sweet, bitter aroma as I lift a bite to my lips. For a moment, I forget about moving, but the feelings of uncertainty are still there ... maybe even stronger now. I do not want to ruminate. I take another bite, then another. My fork scrapes up the last bit of frosting when the voice appears.

Do not worry. Your decision may seem impulsive, yet it is in your and Tom's highest interest. Each of you will discover new opportunities for growth and expansion. If your friendships are what you imagine them to be, you will find a way to stay close. Remember, we each must choose our path. What is yours?

***

When the doorbell chimes in the morning, I know it's Juliette. It's our first session. After I committed to working with her, I blocked out all thoughts of what this might entail. Once, when she offered to do an energy healing with me in the Poconos, I didn't accept or decline. I merely avoided the topic. Eventually, she forgot … or did she?

"Are you ready?" she asks when I open the door, "…because *I'm* excited!" She charges in with her zippered tote. "Where should we do this?" she asks, scrunching her nose as she scans the room.

"Should I be lying down?" I ask.

"It works best that way," she says.

"How about outside on the patio? Our backyard is private. No one can see through the hemlocks."

Juliette walks to the sliding glass door and surveys the space. "Perfect," she says. Outside, she pushes one of the cushioned loungers away from the others, unzips the tote, and pulls out a container of sage and a lighter. She sets them on a small table, then takes a smaller, golden cloth bag from the tote. Carefully, she places its content on the table as well—setting pieces of black obsidian, crystal quartz, amethyst, rose quartz, and lapis lazuli in a circle.

"Make yourself comfortable," she says. I lie down. "To start, take in a long breath, then slowly exhale." Her voice shifts lower, sounding even more reassuring than usual.

My body sinks into the cushioned lounger. Juliette lights the bundle of sage, then moves around the patio in a deliberate manner, waving the sage to cleanse the area. Closer to me, she circles my body with the lighted bundle and chants in a language I can't place. Perhaps she's speaking Quechua, the predominant language in the area where she studied.

She fans the sage with a large feather. The smoke fills my nostrils and helps me settle. I close my eyes as she places gemstones on top of my body.

Trust.

The voice reminds me to let go as Juliette does her thing. Mesmerized by her deep, resonate chant, my mind begins to swirl, unraveling from its tightly coiled state.

"You have so many fears about the future," Juliette says. "You try your best to do what you think is right, almost to the point of perfectionism. You believe that by controlling your actions and words, you will mitigate any negative outcomes from occurring ... but it's futile."

I try to focus on what she's saying, while slow, steady drumbeats stream from her phone's music app.

"Instead of trying to control yourself, and attempting to control others as a way to keep them safe, you must *be* in the present moment. Focusing on the uncertainty of tomorrow makes you worry, which isn't good for your mind or body, or for those around you."

The drums become flutes. The pace quickens. So does my heartbeat.

"Your task for the next two weeks is to catch yourself whenever you reflect on the past, recall the cause-effects of yesterday, and use old information to dictate how you view *the now*. For example, you may think, 'This is what happened that one time ... when someone did this or that ... and now it will happen again.'"

She pauses. The lighter flicks. My nose fills with a fresh onslaught of burning sage. "For years, you've relied on the past to predict the future, hoping to keep yourself and those you love safe. This creates expectations about what will come, which actually limits what's possible."

I close my eyes, trying to synthesize everything she's saying. Have I really done this … projected the past into the future?

Juliette continues. "If what you *assume* will happen isn't something you like, you become fearful. This uncomfortable feeling propels you into *control* mode."

I think about Patrick and my fear of him going to college. Suddenly, what Juliette's saying makes complete sense. I've focused on his mistakes—like the party he went to while we were in Costa Rica—instead of considering the beautiful future that's waiting. Now I'm certain that my thoughts about past actions are causing me to worry about what will happen when he's at school … and the fact that we won't be able to bail him out if he makes a poor choice.

What about being empty nesters? Will my relationship with Tom shift? When I dig into our life together, I can't find a reason why I'm worrying about this. All I can think of is how things were before Patrick. As a new surgeon, Tom's schedule was horrible. We rarely had time alone. But it's different now. Or maybe it won't be with his new job.

Just as that sinking feeling arrives, I realize I'm doing *exactly* what Juliette said … giving into memories from a prior experience and believing they'll *predict* or dictate how the future will go. Ahh, now I get it. This is what makes me afraid … the idea that the past will repeat itself.

"How do I stop this cycle?" I ask, my eyes still shut.

"You must stay in the present moment and trust everything will work out as it's meant to," she says.

"Not exactly the easiest thing," I mutter. "How can I be certain things *will* be OK? And … what if I don't like how it's meant to be?"

"Do you have faith, Marlee?" she asks. "Because, only when we believe in something higher than ourselves can we loosen our grip to trust and surrender. That's what letting go is all about."

As I contemplate Juliette's words, a memory surfaces … Daniel, the channeler from Nueva Vida. I can actually hear his words:

You have a gift, Marlee. It is your ability to shine your light through your writing as your authentic self. You do not have to do anything with this gift, but if you desire to do so, the sky is the limit regarding what you can share with the world. Now is the time to decide. Again, there is no right or wrong answer, though some choices are higher in vibration than others. And if you wish to travel the higher path, it will require you to trust and believe in yourself and your abilities. This includes your intuition … and God. It is critical for you to have faith that something higher has a Divine plan for you. It is there. It always has been. However, you have been choosing in fear, not love. That is why you must trust and believe. Only then will you find your true voice, for you will no longer be afraid of how others will view you. Your true voice knows what you are meant to share.

It's the exact message Juliette's telling me now.

"So, I must choose from love, not fear?"

"Yes," she says.

"And speak my truth?"

"Go on …"

"And trust in God." I gulp as I say the last sentence.

"Exactly," she agrees. Then she becomes silent, turns off the music, and claps three times. I prop myself up on my elbows. One of the gemstones she placed on my chest falls onto the cushion.

"What happened?" I ask.

"You now understand the problem ... what's holding you back," Juliette says. "It's simple. You lack faith. For you to release your fears, you must strengthen your trust in God." Juliette tilts her head and gives me a big smile. "Figuring this out may be the most difficult part of your journey."

I rub my eyes with my peace sign fingers, as if doing so will offer additional clarity. "But how do I strengthen my faith?" I ask. Then I fall back and squeeze my eyes shut.

Juliette lets out a light laugh. "Ahh ... *that* is your work. Instead of trusting in God, you've been making decisions from a state of fear, turning to the past, then assuming you know what will happen in the future. Now you can choose differently ... from a state of love. When you have faith that God, the Universe, or Source ... whatever term you prefer ... will provide what's in your highest interest, then you're able to be OK with what comes your way. This is what *letting go* means. It's about *not* being attached to the outcome."

"Still," I start, then pause and shrug. "I just don't get it. What am I supposed to *do*?"

Juliette exhales, pauses, and closes her mouth for a moment. "Marlee," she says, "this is an entirely new way for you to approach life. Think of it as consciously responding to what happens, instead of reacting out of fear. You have to be in the present moment, not preoccupied with the past, or worried about the future."

A strange sensation stretches across my chest. Juliette's hands hover over me. I assume she's removing some old energy that's not supposed to be there. I hope she's taking out fears that hold me back.

"When we feel afraid, we are not in the *now*," she says. "We're too focused on what's next. We become anxious about the uncertainty of it all. If we can return to *what is* ... meaning *the present* ... we can respond mindfully, instead of reacting *mindlessly*." There's a pull in my chest. It's slightly uncomfortable at first, but then my muscles relax. My body falls deeper into the chair.

"Let me share an example," Juliette says. "Let's say it's October. Patrick sends a text that reads *'Can you talk now?'* What's your first inclination?"

"Something's wrong!" I blurt. Panic runs through my veins just thinking about it. Juliette places her hands over me. I start to relax.

"*That* is choosing from a state of fear," she says. "That choice holds a low vibration to it." Her tone becomes stringent, like a teacher trying to make a point.

"Wouldn't most moms react that way?" I ask.

"Did you hear the word you chose? How would it feel if you *respond* to that text, rather than react?" I feel her hands pulling something from deep within me. A new idea begins to emerge. *What if nothing's wrong?*

"Maybe Patrick just had a few minutes between classes and wanted to share some good news," I say.

"Exactly! How does your body feel when you approach things from that perspective?"

A lightness overtakes my apprehension. "Curious," I say. "Maybe even a bit excited to hear what's happening in his life."

"Yes! This is choosing from love." I feel a swoosh of air as Juliette waves her hands above me, shooing away any lingering negative thoughts.

"It's really that simple?" I ask.

"It sure is. But it will require some rewiring. I can do some of that on my end, but you've got homework. Be aware of when you slip into your old patterns of acting from fear. Make note of what you're taking from the past and projecting onto a new situation."

"So, you want me to monitor my thoughts?" I ask. "Whenever I become anxious and backtrack … I should see if I'm making assumptions based on what's occurred in the past?"

"Precisely," she nods. "Remember, Marlee, yesterday is not today, and today is not tomorrow."

Chapter 6

MAGGIE

June 9th

I write "21 Weeks" on top of today's page, then close the "I'm Expecting" journal that Bobby's mom, Midge, gave me. I'm over halfway there. Apparently, this is the *sweet spot* of my pregnancy. No longer feeling or looking fat, it's now clear the bump is a baby. Women at the grocery store stop and smile before saying something kind or sharing a memory from when they were expecting. At work, Mark constantly asks if he can bring me water or a cup of tea, or if I want a muffin from the bakery. Sandy, the mother of two sons, seems to understand everything I'm going through. I'm not sure what I'd do without her. The knowing glances she sends my way calm me whenever I'm overwhelmed.

Running has become a challenge, but I'm not ready to quit. Instead, I'm adapting, choosing smooth blacktop instead of rocky trails. I've also cut my mileage in half. Still, Bobby's afraid I'll lose my balance and fall. I do my best to reassure him, reminding him how important exercise is for me and the baby.

Bobby and I spend most of our free time together. I've never felt this connected to anyone. He seems to anticipate my thoughts and needs. Somehow, I do the same for him, which strengthens our bond. I suppose both presence and open communication leave little room for assumptions and misunderstandings. It's as though our worlds are merging.

We've retained our individual identities, while our relationship as a couple grows stronger. I've become more aware of his work, for instance—the scope of projects, the names of clients, the peculiarities of some of his subs. Bobby has been more tapped into my interests as well. Last night, he started asking me about yoga. I thought he was just making conversation, but then I realized he *wanted* to know about the physical and spiritual aspects of the practice. Mostly, he was curious about what's *underneath*.

We talked about how the asanas—the poses—are only one of the eight limbs of yoga. I did my best to explain the other seven, emphasizing their equal importance in the grand scheme. Bobby's eyes narrowed whenever I got too technical, but he asked great questions. What surprised me most was when he said he wants to go to a class with me this week. I pulled up the schedule and reserved two spots for an early evening class. Before that, I'm meeting with Toph and Viv Harris.

***

Last week, Toph called to share what a hit the gift had been. But I already knew. Viv sent an email earlier that day thanking me profusely, reiterating how much she *loved* the way I incorporated her birth chart into the design. She also said how excited she was to meet in person. I still can't explain how the ideas germinated, but I'm extremely grateful for Sonya's advice, as well as the mysterious image that led me to visualize the studio's features.

When I spot Viv in the office, my first thought is that she does not match the image I held in my mind. Long straight black hair and darkly penciled eyebrows frame her vibrant green eyes. She's shorter than I imagined, probably five foot three without her heels. Dressed in snug black leather pants and a crisp white blouse, I can't help but wonder if she'll like Bend.

Once she starts talking, my assumptions evaporate. Even if her outward appearance screams Manhattan, there's no denying her warmth and kindness. "I'm Viv," she says with a huge smile. "You must be Maggie."

"That's me." I extend my hand. Viv has a different idea.

"Come here, you," she says, giving me a heartfelt embrace. Then she steps back and looks directly at me, hands on my arms. "You have no idea what you've done for me. The plans are perfect." Tingles course through my body when I hear this. There's nothing better than a happy client.

Toph walks in holding hands with a small boy. The child's hair color resembles his mother's, but his eyes are definitely Toph's.

"This is Ben," Viv says. "He just finished second grade." Toph lets go of his son's hand, then gently pats him on the back. Ben steps forward, extends his right hand toward me, and says, "It's nice to meet you, Miss Maggie."

I lean down to shake his hand. "It's great to meet you, too, Ben. Your dad says you're excited to move to Bend."

"I am!" His blue eyes sparkle. "I can't wait to learn how to ride a mountain bike. Dad told me he'd teach me. He said Bend has lots of dope trails."

Toph clears his throat when Ben falls into slang. Viv just laughs. "Bend is going to be a huge shift for all of us," she says. "Ben was born in New York, but he grew up in California. I'm originally from Long Island. And Toph is from Connecticut."

Now it all makes sense. They are a true mix of both coasts. Often, when people move, they abandon their identity to fit into their new environment. Something tells me the Harris family will not fall into that trap.

At the conference table, Viv pulls out the first *Harry Potter* book from her handbag and slides it to Ben. I can't imagine it's an easy book for a kid his age.

"He's able to read that?" I ask.

"Yes," Viv says. "He's been in a Montessori program since he was two. When he was four, his teachers told me he was ready to start reading. So, we let it happen. He picked it up pretty easily. He'll ask about certain words, but he's always loved complex books. But let's talk about you, Maggie. Was it odd when Toph asked you to integrate astrology into the studio's design?"

"Well, the funny part is, I love astrology and yoga. So, this was the perfect challenge for me."

"Maggie, how did you know … what made you incorporate my natal chart into the plans?" As Viv tilts her head, a quizzical look stretches across her face.

"Actually …" I pause, "last year, at a retreat in Costa Rica, a shaman named Francisco gave me a book on astrology. He told me someday I would combine astrology and architecture." A sigh escapes my lips, then a chuckle. "I thought the idea was crazy. How could the two be connected? But I trusted Francisco, so I read the book at least three times. Then I enrolled in an astrology course, hoping it would provide insight about how my career and this new passion might connect. But I still couldn't understand what Francisco meant. I didn't see the link."

Strangely, sharing this with Viv feels perfectly normal, not uncomfortable at all. "Almost a year later, Sandy asked if I'd take this project. When Toph and I met, my goal was to get a feel for what he thought you might want. He did a great job. As he was leaving, he asked if there was any way I could add an astrological component to the blueprint." An unexpected smile eases across my face. "I realized it was a test … and that Francisco knew something after all."

Viv and Toph just nod, waiting for me to go on.

"Trying to actually incorporate astrology into the design was a whole other thing," I laugh. "Believe me when I say I *struggled*. My mind was a complete blank. Eventually, I reached out to an astrologer I met during the same retreat. She didn't tell me *what* to do, but she challenged me to explore certain areas of my own chart … to imagine what I'd want, as well as what you might. Then the ideas starting coming in."

"That's amazing," Viv says. "You know … there's a great deal more behind this, right?"

"What do you mean?"

"You *read* me. I'm not sure how you did it, but you were able to tap into what I've always wanted. Did Toph tell you I've been obsessing over my birth chart, hoping to understand the reasons behind my illness?"

A slight ache comes into my heart. "Toph told me how important astrology is to you … and that you've been through a great deal. But he never mentioned anything about your birth chart."

Viv leans toward me. "How long have you been doing this?"

"Doing what?"

"Reading people."

"I honestly have no idea of what you're talking about," I say.

"I'm curious," she says, standing up now. "Could it be since you've been expecting?"

My pulse quickens. I remember Marlee mentioning Annie's clairvoyance … how it showed up during her pregnancy.

"You think pregnancy opened something inside of me, like an intuitive knowing of sorts?"

"I do," Viv says. "Would you like to explore it further?" Her eyes peer into mine. "I know this work can be frightening, but you seem to have something special." She shifts her gaze, offering me a knowing glance, as if she's been down this path before.

"Did this happen to you when you were pregnant?" I ask. Viv nods.

***

I stop home to change before meeting Bobby at the studio. He doesn't have a yoga mat, so I grab my old one from the hall closet.

Thalia's teaching today. She's my favorite. I love the way she approaches her flow classes with grace and ease. It will be the perfect style for Bobby, especially if he's interested in the deeper elements of the practice.

I arrive at the studio before Bobby, choosing two empty spaces in the back of the room for our mats and blocks. I'm lying in *supta vata konasana* when Bobby walks in, dressed in gray board shorts and a black Counting Crows t-shirt. He looks a little uncomfortable, but oh so cute. It's strange to see him unsure of himself. He's always confident, but this is new territory. I smile and motion for him to join.

"We're going to begin in a few minutes," I say. "Do whatever feels comfortable, to help you settle in." I sit cross-legged, spine erect, hoping to quiet my mind while fighting the urge to check in on how Bobby's doing. He's scanning the room, watching others, trying to figure out if he should lie on his back, do a twist, or settle into a deeper stretch. When he turns to me, I smile. He mimics my posture, sitting cross-legged on his mat as well. His knees have trouble relaxing toward the ground. I prop up on a block, then motion for him to do the same. After he adjusts, his legs soften, moving closer to his mat.

"Thanks," he whispers. I give him a wink and gently nudge his thigh.

Thalia enters and moves to the front of the room. She's dressed in white tights and a coral tank, her blonde hair casually pulled into a high ponytail. The tip of a tattooed pine tree covers the back of her neck, and I can't help but notice her bright blue toenail polish.

"Let's begin class lying down, legs bent, your feet about a mat's distance apart," Thalia says. "Let your knees fall inwards, so they touch one another. Then feel the small of your back widen and anchor onto your mat. Now breathe slowly, to the count of four." She pauses then counts aloud. "Good … hold it there … sip in a bit more air. Hold for one … two … three … four. Now, slowly release … one … two … three … four. Wait before inhaling again."

We repeat this pattern of box breathing five times. My pulse slows as my diaphragm expands with each inhale, then deflates with every exhale. Bobby's staring at the ceiling, fully focused on his breath.

"Pull your knees to your chest, then rock back and forth several times, up and down your spine. Eventually, you'll end up in a standing forward fold at the top of your mat."

Everyone moves at their own pace. Some have no trouble transitioning from rolling to standing. Others stop and prop themselves up with their hands. I can still do this with ease, but I suspect not for much longer. My belly is already impeding some movements in class. Soon I'll need to make more adaptations for the baby's well-being.

Thalia instructs us to slowly rise, one vertebra at a time, with our head coming up last. Standing in *tadasana*—mountain pose— with arms by our sides and palms facing the mirror, Thalia asks us to set an intention for today's practice. I choose, "I am here now," hoping to remain present throughout class. I realize this may be a pipe dream with my boyfriend right next to me, taking his first yoga class ever. I'm more concerned about Bobby having a good experience than about myself staying present. But perhaps that's my work.

Thalia guides us through lunges, twists, sun salutations, warrior one and two, side angles, and triangles. Bobby's amazing for a beginner. Sure, he mixes up his lefts and rights, looks at me when Thalia uses Sanskrit words, and takes a tumble when he gets too brave during crow pose … but none of it matters. He's here, trying something new. By the end of class, the proud look on his face makes me think he'll be back.

As people begin to roll up their mats, I ask Bobby how it went. Sweat falling down his face, he grins. "It was hard as fuck … took a ton of focus to follow what she was saying."

"The more you do it, the easier it becomes," I reassure, resting my hand on his shoulder. "Just learning the names of poses takes time. Eventually, you'll figure out how to align your body and transition from one position to the next."

Thalia approaches and thanks us for being here. "Was this your first time?" she asks Bobby.

"Was it obvious?" he laughs. "Maggie's been saying yoga would be good for my tight muscles. I'm kind of curious about the other stuff too."

"Did you get a glimpse of what's underneath?" Thalia asks. Her voice softens, as if she's the keeper of some magic secret.

"I know something's there," Bobby says. "For today, I was more focused on trying to keep up."

"That's why it's important you return," she goes on. "Maggie knows … it takes time. Once you catch a glimmer of the bliss that happens when you surrender, you'll become a regular." She turns toward me. "How are you? Would you like me to show you some adaptations?"

"That would be awesome."

Thalia motions for me to follow to the front left corner of the room. "The balancing poses may become tricky soon," she says. "I don't want you to fall."

Bobby nods his head, agreeing.

"If we're doing tree or eagle, instead of balancing unsupported on one leg, use the wall." Thalia demonstrates both poses. "Now you try."

A part of me feels like I'm *cheating*, but I do it anyway and feel myself relax deeper into both poses. Maybe I was unconsciously afraid of tumbling.

***

Midway through dinner, Bobby pauses and sets his fork down. "There's something I've been meaning to ask." His face grows serious. "The guest house has been fine for *me* to live in. But," he stops then smiles, "it's not *just me* … and Harry … anymore." He clears his throat, then takes a sip of water. Where is he going with this? "What I am trying to say is, I really want you and the baby … all three of us … to live together."

Live together? The three of us? My pulse races as apprehension and joy swirl throughout my body. It's impossible to respond. Seeing this, Bobby takes my hand. "It's time to renovate the main house," he says. "I can do the barn later." His stare locks on my eyes. "Some of the subs owe me favors," he continues. "If I start now, work in the evenings and on weekends, I can finish by the time the baby's born." He stops and waits. I still can't speak. "But I need blueprints," he goes on. "Nothing intricate. The guys and I know how to build. We just need direction."

He leans toward me. "There are several architects I've worked with in the past. Before we met, I always figured I'd use one of them. But that doesn't make sense now. I want *you* to draw up the plans." He pauses before asking, "Would you?"

This may be the most Bobby has ever said at one time. I'm still speechless. Did I hear him correctly? He wants all of us to live together, and he just asked me to design the space?

Does he really want us to be together? Or is he just saying this? Then another part of me wonders, *What if this could work? Is this something I can do?*

"You, me, and our baby, together at the farm … like a real family?" I'm honored he asked me to be the architect, but what matters more is that he wants us all to live together.

He gently pulls my hand to his lips and kisses my fingertips. "I can't imagine it any other way. I mean, your apartment's great, but it will be too small for us and the baby. I know the farm is twenty minutes from your job, but it seems like the better option, especially after we renovate. The baby gets a room, plus we'd have two guest rooms, for Marlee, my parents, your dad … whomever. You could even use one as a yoga room … or a home office."

"And you want *me* to design your renovation?" I ask again.

"*Our* renovation, babe," he reassures. "If it were up to me, we would also be getting married, which would make this all so much more real." His eyes narrow, his face softens. "I understand you need time before you say *yes*. Well, I need you and the baby with me. Can you understand that?"

"I want to pay my share," I say. "I won't have rent anymore. Let me do my part." I sit up straighter, hoping he knows I'm not kidding. He just shakes his head.

"I get it," he says. "We'll figure it out."

"You promise?" My eyes widen for emphasis.

"Yes," he says. "But you should consider your architectural fees. Designs are expensive." His lips form a straight line as he leans closer toward me. Even with his serious look on his face, all I see is an incredibly hot man with the most mesmerizing eyes … and he just asked me to move in with him.

I shake my head. "As if I'd charge you for creating blueprints for the renovation," I laugh. "I'd do that for you regardless."

"Then you are beginning to understand how I feel about supporting you and our baby."

I try to put myself into Bobby's shoes. This entire time I've resisted everything he proposes. I won't discuss marriage, even if it's something I might want. Now, here I am insisting on paying my fair share of our living expenses. We've been brought up differently.

I was raised to take care of myself. He wants something a little more traditional and old-school. I need time before things sink in.

"OK," I say, placing my hand on his. I'm ready to turn the subject back to the remodel. "Tell me about this project. What would you want an architect to consider when designing this space? Pretend we're not a couple." I no longer think *girlfriend* is the appropriate word, and I've never been a fan of *partner*.

Bobby's face goes distant for a moment. He's doing his best to pretend this is a business interaction, instead of us planning our future. "Well, materials are important," he says. "So is open space … and light. High ceilings, large windows. Clean lines. We'll have to remove walls and add support beams, maybe eliminate part of the second floor, but I want to keep enough space for two guest rooms and a full bath. There will be a main room, plus kitchen, dining, and living space." He pauses. His look is content now. "I'd like an entry with a distinct presence," he continues. "And the master should be on the first floor, along with the baby's room. Plus, it would make sense to design the main house and the barn at the same time. We can section off part of the barn for a gym and an office. Of course, I want to keep the woodshop."

I nod and make mental notes, staying in my professional mode.

"What about outside?" I ask. I'm curious how much detail he's thought through. It's no surprise when he easily describes the exterior.

"We'll keep the stone, but replace the wood," he says. "We'll need to repoint the stone in spots, which isn't a big deal. How about a wraparound porch? We could watch the sun rise and set." His eyes gaze toward me. Then he refocuses. "In the back, I'd like a flagstone patio with a fire pit."

"And a place for the Traeger," I grin.

"Of course," he laughs. "I'm not too worried about landscaping. Let's figure that out later. Maybe we can incorporate a large willow, or some fruit trees."

"What about a garden?" I ask. "I've always wanted to grow my own vegetables."

"Yes, but we have to protect it from deer. What do you think about a small greenhouse? Remember, growing season is short here."

I walk to my desk and retrieve a sketch pad and pencil. I begin drawing, blocking Bobby's view with my shoulders. Twenty-five minutes later, I hand my ideas to Bobby. He studies them as I clear dishes. Once the dishwasher is running, I brew tea for both of us.

At the table with mugs and cookies, I ask him what he thinks, hopeful I captured his vision.

He leans forward and gently touches my face, his watery eyes locked on mine. Sometimes, words are unnecessary.

Chapter 7

MARLEE

June 22nd

Thinking back to the beginning of the month, telling Patrick about the move was brutal, but he took it like such a trooper. First, he was stoic and congratulated his father. Then he sat down at the kitchen counter and quietly worked through his thoughts about how the move would impact him. He asked a few clarifying questions, then excused himself and went upstairs to shower. Before he headed out with friends, we asked him to keep a lid on things.

"Don't worry," he said. "I won't tell anyone about it right now. We're all in such a good mood, there's no reason to bring anyone down." He forced a smile, but the glassiness in his eyes told the real truth.

Right now, Tom is down to his final two months at Jefferson. Jonathon is the only person who knows about Tom's new job, and he agreed to keep the news quiet. We're still not telling everyone until we sign a lease.

As our moving date approaches, I keep racking my brain, trying to think of any unfinished business here in Radnor. Thankfully, my book release has come and gone. I can't imagine trying to fit that in now.

The event went well. I was nervous to read a passage from the book, but I made it through without any blunders. The bookstore sold forty-two copies that afternoon. In the end, it was about owning up to finally publishing my story, even if the title "author" still sounds strange to me.

However, there is still one commitment I'm concerned about … my promise to Juliette. How can we continue our sessions if I'm in Boston? She needs me here to complete our work. I have to tell her about the move. I gulp, knowing we're meeting this morning at 11 o'clock.

"Does June 30th through July 4th still work to go to Boston?" I ask Tom in the kitchen.

"Yes," he says. "I cleared the dates with our scheduler. I have a ton of vacation days to use or lose."

"Can we talk about the move?" I ask him. Maybe now is a good time to broach the subject of telling our friends.

"Of course," he says.

"I understand why we've waited to share our news," I begin, "but I'm feeling the need to let people know, especially Juliette. She's using me as her case study, so she can become a shaman. We have at least two more months of sessions. I'm worried I'll mess things up when we leave." I sigh. "I think it's time. I don't want to walk on eggshells about it. I've actually been avoiding certain people, afraid I'll slip up."

Tom takes a long swig of coffee, stands, and walks toward me with a grin. He pulls me into his arms. "You're right," he says. "It's time. I can only imagine how difficult this is for you. I've been dodging conversations too." Then he kisses my forehead.

"I feel horrible not telling our friends," I say. "It's like I'm lying to them. I can't commit to any plans after August." Suddenly I'm choking back tears, resting my head on Tom's chest, burying my face in his warm embrace.

"Then we agree," he says. "Let's make it public knowledge." He squeezes me tighter.

"I'll tell Juliette this morning, then I'll call Sophia after that. Do you think Jonathon has mentioned it to Annie?"

"I asked him to keep it between us … but who knows? You and I tend to share everything." He looks into my eyes. "Are you sure you want to do this?" he asks gently. "It's not too late. I can tell them I've changed my mind."

I swallow and nod. "It's going to be exciting," I say, trying to believe myself. "A new chapter for both of us."

He leans down and kisses me like nothing else matters. "Yes, it will be," he says. When I pull back, I see a sparkle in his eyes that I haven't noticed in some time. He's been craving a challenge, ready for something new. I always thought my *meat-and-potatoes* husband preferred life the way it is. In the past, he's been resistant to change. We're both shifting.

I try to hold onto the excitement, but then I realize that I'd done the very thing Juliette and I talked about last time … my pattern of projecting fear into the future. I'd assumed Tom would be opposed to telling people. I was wrong. He's actually energized by the uncertainty of it all. I wish I was as well.

***

I'm agonizing about telling Juliette. As she walks in, dressed in purple flowered yoga pants and an indigo racer-back tank, all the eloquent explanations I worked over in my head fall by the wayside. I simply blurt out the bombshell.

"We're moving to Boston!" Her jaw drops when she hears it. "But we're keeping our home, so we can come back whenever we want." Of course, I say this more for my assurance than hers.

"This is amazing!" She takes my hands in hers. "I am so excited for you both." She pulls me to the couch and plops down next to me.

This is not the reaction I expected. I know I'd be sad if she told me she was leaving. It's suddenly clear how much I fear losing my friends.

After I tell Juliette about Tom's new position, she slumps deeper into the couch. "Wow," she says. "To be sought after as Head of Orthopedics for Mass General ... what an honor for Tom! You must be so proud of him."

Her last sentence catches me off guard. I get this is a big deal, but I've been focused on how the move will affect me ... and Patrick. I haven't fully considered the opportunity that has come Tom's way.

"Yes ... it is," I say, embarrassed by how self-centered I've been. As the words come out, I'm unable to control tears that form in the corners of my eyes. "I'm going to miss you," I say.

"Oh, Marlee," Juliette smiles. She straightens up and wipes my cheeks. "We'll still see each other. And remember, I won't be in Philly too much either. I've decided to spend at least three days a week in Hawley Falls. God knows I need to keep an eye on this project." Her eyebrows raise as if she's had an ingenious thought. "Maybe you can spend some time at Eagle's Landing, especially during the winter when Sue and Pete are in Florida. I mean, we'll be *almost* neighbors." Her upbeat tone comforts me. She'll be pretty close to our family home.

"But what about your case study?" I ask. "Won't my move mess things up?"

"Don't worry about that," she says and waves her hand. "We'll make it work." Juliette shrugs, as if everything will be simple.

She stands up from the sofa and pulls her cell from her tote. "When do you leave?"

"Tom's first day is the Tuesday after Labor Day," I say. "We're driving to Boston when I get back from Bend, to look for an apartment. Ideally, we'll be able to lease a place starting September 1st ... my gosh, that's only ten weeks away!"

"Oh, we'll have plenty of time," Juliette smirks. She tosses her phone back into the tote. "I'll make sure we get most of our sessions in before that. If not, we'll Zoom ... or I'll drive to Boston. Wouldn't that be fun?" She scrunches her nose. "You know, moving to Boston will make you confront one of your biggest fears."

"Which is?"

"Uncertainty!" I'm a little shocked to hear her say it, but I can't deny she's onto something. "Let's use this to our advantage. We'll incorporate your move and any apprehensions into our work. OK?" I nod. "Great. Then let's get going."

Juliette walks out onto our patio. It appears our session has started.

***

The homework from our last session was to leave my comfort zone and try something I've never done before. I suppose deciding to move to Boston fulfilled the assignment.

"Today, we'll focus on your fears," Juliette announces. She motions for me to lie on the lounge chair. "You are already aware of how they appear, often tied to your past. Our next step is to learn how to release what frightens you. There are many ways to do this. What may work best for you is mental imagery."

I shut my eyes as a gentle breeze moves through the birch trees to my right. With the slight rustling sound, and the smell of burning sage, I fall into a light, soothing trance. There are no drums on today's playlist. Instead, this music is lighter, fluid, somewhat melodic. My solar plexus, the third chakra where we hold our power, begins to pulsate. When the music shifts, so do the sensations. I feel movement in my sacrum, one chakra lower.

"Singing bowls?" I murmur. I remember these magical crystal healing instruments from Nueva Vida. I begin to relax, surrendering to the sound as vibrations move through me, clearing away stagnant, negative energy.

"Imagine you are in a beautiful garden," Juliette says, her voice deep and comforting. "There's a small pond with fish … and lily pads. Butterflies flit about. Honeybees savor pollen from an abundance of flowers."

I see myself in an English garden, where bright pink hollyhocks line a flagstone path. There's lupine in one corner. Two hummingbirds hover over delicate purple flowers. Pale yellow roses, carefully planted against a wrought-iron fence, catch my attention. Then I'm drawn to foxglove, sweet pea, and peonies. It's almost too much to take in at once. I'm about to lose myself completely when Juliette speaks.

"There is a wooden bench directly in front of the pond," she says. "Take a seat." I follow her directions in my mind. "Now, the bench you're sitting on is slatted, and there are open spaces beneath you. This is important. Through these openings you will release your fears into Mother Earth. She will repurpose them for the good of humanity."

I envision the bench's slight openings between strips of wood. The music shifts to something deeper. The singing bowls begin activating my root chakra.

"I want you to quiet your mind, Marlee. Once you feel settled, allow whatever scares you to appear. You are safe in the garden. And you're safe here, with me. Feel the emotions that attach to your fears. Let them flow through you … so they can leave your body, falling between the bench's slats, far away from you."

It takes a moment, but when the fears appear, they come on strong. My arms twitch, my stomach rumbles. I'm fighting to release what I hold so tightly.

"Feel the fears," Juliette emphasizes. "Surrender. Let them go!"

Vivid visions flash in my mind. There's Patrick leaving our car, carrying suitcases. He fades into the distance, out of sight. There's Tom going to work. But his cell phone is still on the counter.

How will I reach him if there's an emergency? There's me, going into the operating room. Tom holds my hand. What is this? He kisses my forehead as they wheel me away. My body shakes. I know this scene, from my mastectomy.

Juliette touches my arm. "You're safe," she reminds. "Let the fears go."

Terrifying thoughts run down my spine, then start to release. My body contracts. I squirm on the lounge chair. Then things begin to calm. After several minutes, a sense of peace overcomes me. The images evaporate into nothingness.

But then more fears surface, and the intense physical sensations return. My mother takes her last breath … my father consoles himself with Johnnie Walker. I gulp and the pain flows from my root chakra through the slats, then into the ground. My siblings refuse to come to family reunions … they cut off all contact. I'm at a party, surrounded by women who pretend to be my friends. Deep down, I know they're not … I just don't want to admit it. I fight to embody these sensations … to acknowledge them … and to surrender.

Several minutes pass. My body quivers as more visions come and go. Finally, the music softens, and the images begin to slow. My muscles relax again.

"Wonderful work, Marlee," Juliette says. "You've released quite a bit. This practice is available to you all the time. All you need to do is recreate this exercise and allow your fears to surface. As they come, feel them, then let them pass through you." Her voice resonates with the singing bowls, almost sounding like one.

Lying on the table, I feel a sharp yank in my chest, similar to what I felt during our first session. Juliette's hands move across my body, and she begins to pull any remaining negative energy up and out.

"I'm just tidying things," she confirms. "You had a lot of fears pop up. There's definitely more down there, but we've accomplished a lot today." When the tugging sensation stops, I know Juliette is done.

"Now that you've let go of so much, there's *empty space*. It's important to fill it with things you find uplifting. That will help keep new fears from settling there."

I try to digest her message, wondering what she's going to use to fill in the emptiness. In no time, she continues. "Imagine sunlight is penetrating your crown chakra, straight into the top of your head. The light travels to your feet. Then your calves, thighs, and core begin to fill with it from the bottom up. It flows all the way to your chest, then overflows down your arms, into your hands and fingertips. Your shoulders and neck fill next. Finally, this light fills your entire head."

I follow Juliette's directions, and an unexpected warmth comes over my body, releasing any remaining tightness. My fingers tingle. I gaze at my hands. Never has my skin looked this shimmery.

"What's happening?" I ask.

"Letting go of your fears, then adding light, is like rewiring your brain. When you release negative thoughts, your mind gets a break from the looping ... those repetitive, troublesome thought-cycles we all have."

"Worrying about things that haven't happened," I say.

"And that may never occur," she adds.

"Like being afraid of something bad happening to Patrick at college," I go on. "Or losing my friends when we move to Boston."

"Yep," she agrees. "Let's focus on both of those for your homework. Any time you have a negative thought about either, imagine you're on that slatted bench. Let your fears flow from you ... straight into the earth. Can you do that?"

"I think so," I say, unsure if I'll be able to catch myself.

"Afterwards, remember to add the light to take up the empty space." She smiles and brushes her hands together. The session is over. She's discharging any lingering energies she may have absorbed.

"Remember, Marlee, you are not your thoughts," she adds. "You are the observer of your thoughts. You choose what to hold onto … and what to release."

"It's really that simple?"

"Hell yeah! Life is supposed to be easy. We just like to complicate things."

***

When I finally text Annie to see if she has time to talk, and mention that I have something important to tell her, she calls immediately.

"Jonathon swore me to secrecy," she says. "He told me I needed to wait until you reached out to me." She sounds relieved that we're finally able to talk about it. "I'm really going to miss you," she adds, "but I understand keeping your house here, so you can come back and visit." Her voice lifts.

"Yes," I say. "I'm sorry it took so long to tell you. Tom and I wanted to wait until we found a place to live. But I realized I couldn't hold out till then."

"I understand," she says. "But damn … I'm going to miss you."

"We'll still be here … sort of," I say.

"You will … but still … anyway, let's talk about Bend!" She wants to review what she plans to bring to Oregon, to make sure she's not overlooking something essential.

"Sounds like you're ready," I say. "I'll see you bright and early tomorrow morning!"

"You bet."

***

My next call is with Sophia. As soon as I start to speak, my voice cracks.

"Is everything all right?" she asks.

"I'm good," I say, biting my lip. "I have some news to share. It's something kinda big."

"Is this about our trip?" she asks, some worry in her voice.

I let out a slight sigh. "No. We're all set." As I say this, unexpected emotions rise. My throat constricts, as if warning me to keep my news to myself. Maybe if I don't say it, it won't be real.

I take a deep inhale and share the twist in my life, the one I'm still trying to process. "Last month, Tom accepted a job offer … at Mass General."

"In Boston?" Sophia asks.

"Yes," I say. The phone goes silent. I'm worried about catching her off-guard like this, so I try to explain. "He wasn't looking," I add. "They approached him." I swallow before continuing. "It's a big salary bump. And now that Patrick's going to college, we have more options." I sound like I'm trying to convince myself, not Sophia, that this is what's best. Then, for good measure, I add the fact that Patrick is onboard, even though it's not entirely true.

Despite my best attempt to explain why we're leaving, Sophia says nothing.

"We have only committed for a year," I continue. "And we've decided to keep our house, so we can come back as much as we like. We're going to look at apartments after Bend. Tom and I decided to focus on the Back Bay area. It's beautiful … and historic. Plus, the location's not far from his work."

That's when I hear muffled cries over the phone.

"Sophia?" Shit! This isn't going well. "I'm sorry. I should have told you before now. It's just that … well, I've been having trouble accepting it all. And we wanted to wait until everything was finalized before we told everyone." My throat constricts again. "It's happening so fast … and at the worst time. Tom told me about the offer the day before Patrick's graduation."

Still no response. I sit on the sofa and wrap my arms around my knees. Tears stream down my cheeks. After another moment of silence, Sophia finally speaks. "I understand this is a wonderful opportunity for Tom, one he could not pass up." Through intermittent sniffles she continues. "But why did you wait to tell me? I thought I was your closest friend? You are mine." Her voice sounds riddled with pain.

Everything becomes crystal clear now. I focused on myself and my emotions, oblivious to how our move would impact others. Maybe Sophia feels like I didn't trust her, or as if she's irrelevant. Damn. I should have considered how hard this would be for her. Annie has Ella. Juliette is back with Michael, planning their wedding, and immersed in creating her retreat center. And Maggie's expecting a baby. Plus, where I live doesn't really impact her.

My relationship with Sophia is in a totally different place. These past few months, we've spent more time together than anyone else, often without Annie, since she's occupied with work and motherhood. How could I have been so insensitive to Sophia's emotions?

"I guess I've been in my own world," I admit. "I've been thinking about how this impacts Tom, Patrick, and me … well, mostly me." I clear my throat. "You are my *dear* friend, Sophia. My dearest, in fact. Our lives run in parallel lines. We understand what the other is going through, especially since we're at similar stages." Tears stream down my face now. "I made a mistake. I didn't consider how this would impact you. Nor did I think about how you could help me through this. Instead of trusting you, I took it on all by myself."

"Marlee, true friends let one another in," she says. "You supported me as I worked though transitioning my practice to include holistic methods. Did you not know I would be there for you as well? Why did you shut me out?"

"I didn't mean to. I just felt like I had to process this move alone." It was true. I had been so wrapped up in my own emotions that I forgot what true friendships are about. Real friends are there to celebrate the good times … and to help shine their light when things get dark.

In the silence that follows, I hear the voice.

Remember, others' reactions frequently have nothing to do with you. Often, we trigger another's wound, one we do not realize exists.

"Is there something else?" I ask. "Something you're not telling me?" My question comes from nowhere. Sophia exhales deeply before speaking. "Jared started to talk about retiring."

"That would be a huge change for both of you," I say.

"Yes. He turns sixty-four this October. I have just started the next phase of my career." She pauses and takes another big breath. "He wants to travel, but I am focused on helping patients with these new methods I have been learning. The timing could not be worse."

"Oh, Sophia." Like me, her husband's career is impacting her life. "Jared has worked hard for so long. Similar to Tom, he's endured long hours operating, juggling schedules … everything. It's natural for him to want to enjoy life."

"Of course," she says. I say nothing in reply. It's difficult for me to be quiet, but I want to give Sophia as much space as she needs to share what's on her mind. However, she stops talking as well.

Finally I ask, "Does he know how you feel?"

"Yes and no," she says, then sighs. "I have mentioned how much I love my work, and how I hope to offer my services to more people. However, he does not grasp how serious I am about the holistic practice. Instead, he wants to know if I would move to Manhattan, so we can be closer to our children."

"If my career was tied to a certain geographic area, I would have had way more reservations about Tom taking this job," I say. "Luckily, I can write anywhere."

"That is true. And yes, I could open a practice in Manhattan, but I do not want to leave my patients. They trust me. And I care deeply about them and their health. I wish Jared understood this."

"So here we are … two women who want to support our husbands in their transitions, yet also want to preserve our own identities." I feel my body deflate as I speaks these words. "So, what are you going to do?"

"I am not sure," she says. "Fortunately, there is time to decide."

Neither of us speak, yet one thing's clear. There's a deeper understanding that no matter what lies ahead, Sophia and I can trust that the other will be there, willing to listen and support.

"Marlee," she says, "I am sorry I overreacted. I had broken my rule … I *assumed* you did not trust me."

"I'm the one who was being insensitive," I counter. "I shouldn't have tried to handle this alone. I guess I wasn't ready to accept it. I figured that if I didn't talk about it, maybe it wouldn't happen."

"Just know that no matter where you are living, you and I will always be connected."

At that moment, something within my fourth chakra stirs, creating new space in my chest. Yes … my heart's expanding, allowing for more love.

Chapter 8

MAGGIE

June 22nd

"Maggie, there's something I need to ask," Juliette says as soon as I answer the phone. Leaning back into my office chair, I subconsciously place one hand on my belly. I find myself doing this from time to time, as if assuring the baby I'm here.

"Is everything OK?" I ask. Juliette clears her throat.

"Sorry," she says. "I guess that wasn't the best way for me to start a conversation." Immediately, I'm relieved by the lightness in her voice. She continues. "As I mentioned when we last spoke, I'm building the retreat center, on the property in the Poconos. Well, last week, I finished interviewing four contractors. It's clear which one I'm going to hire," she pauses, "but now I need an architect to design the building."

"If you like, I can reach out to some of my former classmates from Pitt," I say. "In fact, several recently moved to Philadelphia. I'm sure I could find someone to help you." I begin a mental list of who might be a good match for Juliette.

"No, silly," she giggles. "I want *you* to do it."

"Me?" I ask, dumbfounded. Why would Juliette be willing to work with someone on the other side of the country? There are plenty of talented architects in the Philadelphia area.

"There's no one else better for this project," she says. "Besides, when Marlee told me what you did with that woman's yoga studio, especially how you incorporated her birth chart into the ceiling and the floor, I was like, *damn, this girl has exactly what I need!*"

A blush comes over my face. I'm flattered Juliette would choose me to design her retreat center. "Thank you, Juliette. I'd love to take this project on. That is, if you're sure it will work with me in Bend."

"Of course it will. You don't have to physically be here. Besides, I've already taken tons of pictures of the property. I'll send those, as well as inspiration pics, along with the surveyor's report."

"What's the timeline?" I ask, conscious of my own. The last thing I want is to hold up Juliette's project.

"The contractor wants to break ground in the middle of August," she says. "So, as long as he has the final plans by the first of the month, he'll be able to submit them for permitting. He assured me it doesn't take long. I suppose that's one advantage of building in a small community, where everyone seems to know one another."

I scan my calendar. "That means we have about a month to get this done." My throat tightens. This is going to have to be a fast turnaround. Luckily, my schedule is winding down. Since I'll be out for maternity leave in four months, Sandy, Mark, and I agreed its best that I don't take on new clients. Of course, I'll do whatever I must for Juliette.

My mind begins to cycle through all of the things that have to happen between now and August 1st. "We'll want everything firm by the third week of July, just to be safe," I say, switching into my architect mode.

"No problem," Juliette answers. "I trust you, Maggie. You get me. This will be easy peasy."

I wish I possessed half the confidence that she has in me.

"So, tell me your vision for this retreat center." I'm ready with paper and pen in hand.

"I'd like this space to have an inviting, natural vibe that inspires everyone who visits. As soon as we hang up, I'll send you pictures of the property. It's amazing! There's a stream that feeds our small pond. Not far from our house, which is nestled in a grove of large oak trees, there's a classic red barn with a real hex sign on the side of it! I want you to capture the feeling of the beautiful surroundings in your blueprints. Oh, and let's incorporate all natural elements, kinda like you did with the yoga studio."

"Absolutely," I say, nodding into the phone. "I think I know what you're looking for." I pause then ask, "How big would you like the center to be? Think about use. What type of events or workshops do you see yourself holding? How many rooms? What size should these spaces be to adequately meet your needs?"

There is a significant pause before Juliette speaks. "Definitely plan for a large room, with flexible seating ... kind of an all-purpose space. But nothing sterile. I want it to feel warm."

"OK. How many people should it hold?"

"Hmmm ... I know this is aggressive, but one hundred and fifty? Maybe two hundred?"

I write the numbers down. "And the smaller areas?"

"I'll need several rooms for practitioners and private sessions. And an office for me. Oh, and a yoga studio, of course." Her voice lifts when she says this.

"What about locker rooms? Cooking facilities?"

"Nope ... not necessary. We'll just need bathrooms ... and maybe a small area with a fridge, cabinets, and a sink. I could always add another building in the future. There's certainly enough space on the property."

I jot down more notes, then ask Juliette about her budget. "I'll work on the numbers and email them to you this afternoon," she says.

"Great." I gaze over my notepad. "I think I have enough to get started. Let me play with some ideas. Maybe this weekend, we can carve out time to go over preliminary drawings?"

"Absolutely. And before I forget ... remember to add your special juju. You know how I love energy work, astrology, crystals ... all that stuff!"

Juliette, like Toph, is asking me to do what Francisco foresaw, to combine architecture with astrology. Yet, Juliette wants a touch more. I lean my elbows on my desk and rest my head in my palms. *How in the hell did that man know this would happen?* Then a more foreboding thought surfaces. *Will I be able to come up with blueprints to meet Juliette's expectations?*

***

After work, I head downtown for an appointment with my hair stylist. I'm twenty minutes early, so I decide to check out some of nearby stores. Maybe the girls will want to shop when they're here.

Along Bond Street, I notice that what used to be a women's lingerie store is now a children's clothing boutique. As I pass the window, I see the most adorable mobile. Hanging from what appears to be a wind-up music box are a yellow chick, a pink pig, a purple cow, and a blue lamb. Unable to resist, I go inside.

Gently, I wind the music box atop of the mobile. As "The Farmer in the Dell" begins to play, a saleswoman approaches me.

"It's adorable, isn't it?" she asks, eyeing my belly. "When are you due?" The sweetest smile appears on her face.

"Not for a while," I say, then add, "the middle of October."

She smiles. "Do you know if you're having a boy or a girl?"

"No, we've decided we want to be surprised."

"Then this would work perfectly," she says. She unhooks the mobile from the plastic fishing line attached to the ceiling. I can't help but stroke the soft farm animals. Would my baby like this? I place one hand one my stomach and feel a gentle nudge.

"I'll take it." This is the first baby item I've purchased. Suddenly, I have an urge to tell Bobby, but it will have to wait till after my hair appointment. I'll show him tonight.

***

Getting my hair cut was just what I needed. Or maybe it was the mobile. Then again, my lifted spirit could be due to my phone call with Juliette. Regardless, I'm unable to contain myself when Bobby walks through the door.

Harry greets me with a quick nuzzle, then trots to his dog bed.

"Nice hair," Bobby says as his fingers graze through my slightly shorter, blown-dry blonde strands. He pulls me toward him. Just feeling the warmth of his body against me causes my core to stir.

"Figured I was due," I say. "It's been a while." I stand on my tip toes for a delicious kiss.

"Ready for your friends to come?" he asks. He walks to the fridge and comes back with a seltzer for me, a cold beer for himself.

"I am. I've really missed everyone," I admit before changing the subject. "You'll never guess what I bought today," I say, then hand the large white bag to Bobby. His brow scrunches.

"Am I supposed to guess?"

"Just open it," I grin.

As he pulls the tissue paper from the bag, his eyes search to see what's inside.

"It's for the baby," I say when he pulls out the mobile. "I thought it would work for a boy or a girl." I stumble to get out my words, wondering if it's bad luck to buy something for our unborn child.

"It's amazing," he says. "Perfect. Just like you." He puts the mobile down then places his hands on my hips. "I love the farm idea."

"I thought it could be the theme for the nursery. Maybe we can paint the room yellow ... find a green rug."

"Anything you want," he says, then kisses my belly. "What do *you* think?" Bobby speaks to the baby, not me. "Are you cool with farm animals?"

I could not be happier than I am at this moment.

"Hey, I think I just saw movement," Bobby says. I place my hands on my tummy. Unsure whether it's a foot or an arm, something's definitely happening down there.

"I believe it's a 'yes' to a farm theme," I laugh.

***

Over dinner, I tell Bobby about my conversation with Juliette. "Have you ever thought about focusing on this type of architecture?" he asks. "I'm not sure exactly what 'type' you would call it, but you seem to have a talent in this area."

"I could talk with Sandy and Mark about it," I suggest.

"Maybe you might want to go out on your own someday," he says with a shrug of his shoulders. "I know the timing isn't perfect right now, but it might be after the baby's born and you're settled. You could even have your office here. Or, I could build a separate space for you on our property. Think about it." He doesn't push the topic. Instead, he stands and starts to clear the table.

Go out on my own? Could I do that? Would people be interested in what I'm offering? My eyes go to the mobile, which is sitting on top of the coffee table. Right now, my focus needs to be here, on our baby and us, plus my current work. Still, I can't help but wonder … *what if*?

Chapter 9

MARLEE

June 23rd

Maggie is in the kitchen of our Airbnb, wearing a flowered knit maternity dress that gently snugs her belly. She's putting together a charcuterie board, singing to a Dave Matthews song that pipes out of a small portable speaker.

"I figured you'd be hungry," she says, then opens the refrigerator and pulls out a bottle of Sauvignon Blanc. "And thirsty," she winks.

I take five wine glasses from the cabinet.

"Would you like some?"

"I *would*, but I'm sticking to seltzers," she smiles.

"I remember when I was pregnant with Patrick," I say. "Occasionally, I'd take a sip from Tom's glass. I figured a little would be fine."

"I do the same," she admits. "My doctor said it's OK, just not to overdo it."

"My mother smoked and drank when she was pregnant with my siblings and me," I laugh. "And we're all fine … sort of."

Maggie comes over for a hug. "It's good to be with friends," she says, wiping tears from beneath her eyes.

"It's been tough, hasn't it?" I ask.

She nods. "Bobby's been beyond amazing. In fact, he asked me to move in, so we can be a family." With the word *family*, her eyes stare off, as if searching for some meaning behind it. I suppose Tom, Patrick, and I live a traditional family life. Yet Maggie never knew her father.

"There's no perfect formula for a family," I say. "What's important is that the child feels loved. So … are you ready to move in with Bobby?" For weeks, she's insisted she doesn't want to get married, but living together is new information.

"I think I am," she says. "I just don't know what to expect. I've never lived with a guy before." She unwraps a pack of cocktail napkins then sets them on the table next to the cutting board. "Growing up, it was just my mom and me. And then, after she passed, I guess I got used to living alone."

She sits down on a nearby stool. "Bobby and I met several months after I moved to Bend. Our relationship became serious quickly. We could have spent every night together. It was me who insisted on having our own places." She pauses. "Then he asked me to move in *and* design the renovations to his house. It caught me off guard. What surprised me most was how much I *wanted* to do both."

"Isn't that a good thing?"

"Is it? Or am I just succumbing to a man, relying on somebody who could leave at any moment?"

"Let's go to the sofa," I say. By now, streams of tears trickle down her face. I can only imagine how difficult these months have been without talking in person with a close female friend. I know Sandy has been incredibly helpful with pregnancy questions, but Maggie hesitates to confide in her about other aspects of life.

"Do you really think Bobby would leave you?" I ask. "If so, why would he ask you to move in? Has he ever said or done anything that would suggest he didn't have your best interest at heart?"

"No," Maggie gulps.

"Exactly. I suspect there's more behind how you're feeling. You're someone who can pick up on other people's emotions, right?"

"Sure."

"Well, do you feel he's being sincere? If so, then where is your fear coming from? Do you think you're self-sabotaging?" Maggie knows Bobby loves her. But for some reason, she won't fully commit to this relationship. "When you first found out you were pregnant, you didn't want to tell Bobby, right?"

"Right," she says. I brush a stray blonde hair from across her face.

"I know you're afraid of being abandoned. I think some part in everyone fears that." Maggie looks at me, doe-eyed.

"You think I'm doing this subconsciously?" she asks.

"Honey, I think you're afraid. This is a big deal." I point to her stomach. "When you consider what your mom went through as a single parent, it's no wonder you're scared."

"Hey there," Juliette says. She settles into the sofa next to Maggie. "Why the long face? Aren't you happy we're here?" She's teasing at first, but then her eyes narrow. I stay silent. This is Maggie's to share.

"I'm sorry … of course I'm happy!" Maggie sniffs then wipes her tears away with the back of her hand. "You all being here is exactly what I've needed. There's just a lot happening, and quickly. I was telling Marlee that Bobby wants us to live together as a family, at his place."

"It's a beautiful spot," I add, hoping to give Maggie some time to collect herself. "Bobby inherited the farm from his grandparents. I believe he was the only grandchild, right?" Maggie nods. "When I was here in February, Bobby made us dinner at his place. The property's amazing. It has a main house, a barn, and a guest house."

"There's more," Maggie says. "Bobby wants to renovate the main farmhouse, so it's ready for us and the baby. He asked *me* to do the architectural plans." Maggie touches her belly.

"Seriously?" Juliette says. "He wants you to move in *and* design a renovation? I'd say Bobby's all in. Wouldn't you, Marlee?"

"That's what I've been trying to tell her," I agree.

"So, what's the problem?" Juliette asks. I'm not so sure she realizes how independent Maggie has become since we first met at the retreat.

"The problem," Maggie quietly says, "is that it's happening too fast. I feel … I don't know." She breaks out into deep sobs just as Annie and Sophia walk into the room. Annie pivots and excuses herself to make a quick phone call, while Sophia joins us, sitting down across from me in one of two club chairs. She reaches over the coffee table and softly touches Maggie's arm.

"This has been a lot to process," I remind Maggie. "You've had an unexpected twist in your path, forcing you to make serious choices. You've decided to become a mother, and you're starting to acknowledge Bobby's role with you and the baby. And now that Bobby wants you to move in with him, well … it's no wonder you feel overwhelmed."

Maggie nods. Annie comes back from her room with a box of tissues. She hands one to Maggie, then sits in the chair next to Sophia. Knowing conflict makes Annie nervous—which is kind of funny since she's a therapist—I wonder if she even made a call or used it as an excuse to leave.

"And you're not sure if Bobby is with you because of *you*, or because of the baby?" Juliette asks. Maggie nods again.

"Where is Bobby now?" Sophia asks, raising her beautifully arched eyebrows.

"He's at the farm," Maggie says between sniffs, "working on the house."

"Whose house?" Sophia bats her long eyelashes. In this light, she resembles a sophisticated lawyer who's trying to lead her distraught witness toward an inevitable truth.

"His," Maggie says.

"Maggie, this man is building a home for *his family*," Sophia continues. "And he wants *your* imprint on the house through *your* design. I do not believe he would do so if he did not see a future together."

"My goodness, Maggie. Can't you see what's going on?" Annie asks. She stands up and places both hands on her hips. "He wants you in his life. Not just for now … but forever."

"Annie is correct," Sophia says, her eyes soft with compassion. "Why is this so difficult to accept?" Her eyes narrow as if trying to comprehend Maggie's reluctance. Maggie bites her lower lip, then glances at the woven rug below.

"I think I understand," Juliette says with a soft, almost child-like voice. "After I told Michael what happened in Costa Rica, with René, I couldn't believe he still wanted to marry me. *I* never would have forgiven *him*. Then, when I got back from Peru, he shared that he'd been with someone else."

There's silence for a moment. I knew about the Michael situation, but it's news for everyone else.

"I had no right to blame him," Juliette continues. "We weren't engaged at the time. Plus, we never said we wouldn't see other people. But it hurt … a lot." She gulps. "And that's when I understood … it happened, and now it was behind us. It didn't matter. I finally realized why he didn't end things last year."

"Somehow, I'm having trouble seeing the parallels between these situations," Annie says, looking perplexed. Juliette rolls her eyes then tries a different approach.

"What I'm trying to say is that we make assumptions all the time, *especially* when it comes to men," she says. "Maybe it's because so many men keep their true feelings hidden. I don't think we give men enough credit, honestly, especially those guys who come off as super masculine … cowboy types." She looks at Maggie. "We stereotype them, imagine we can read their minds and anticipate their behaviors. However, we're often totally off base. The bottom line is, you're afraid Bobby will leave you, just as I was scared Michael would walk out on me. But Michael never has, and I can't imagine Bobby ever would."

Maggie's eyes widen as she digests what Juliette is saying. Sophia gently smiles. "Do not be so hard on yourself," she says. "Everything seems magnified when you are expecting. I have not met Bobby yet, but Marlee tells me how wonderful he is, and how much he loves you."

"Has he ever given you a reason not to trust him?" Annie asks, shifting a little into her counselor role.

"No," Maggie answers.

"You are not your mother," I say. "And your father didn't choose not to be part of your life. He never knew your mom was pregnant. Bobby's doing everything in his power to create a family."

"You're right," Maggie says. Her face softens. A slight grin begins to form.

"So," Juliette says, sitting up and slapping her knees. "Are we gonna meet Bobby, or will he be working on the house all weekend?"

Chapter 10

MAGGIE

June 24th – 27th

We make a right onto the dusty gravel road lined with juniper bushes. The faded red barn is visible in the distance. "We're here," I say. "Bobby shares this driveway with neighbors, an elderly couple. They were here before his grandparents. Sweet people." My pulse quickens. As much as I want my friends to meet Bobby, I can't wait to see the progress he's made on the house.

Marlee turns toward Sophia and Annie, who are seated in the backseat. "You are going to love Bobby's property. In February, everything was covered in snow. It was pretty then. I bet it's even more beautiful in the summer."

Maybe Marlee's building the place up a bit too much. "There's still a ton to do," I add. "Right now, Bobby's focusing on getting the main home ready for the baby. After that, we'll need to tackle the barn. We've talked about buying some horses and chickens. By the time we finish with *that* project, it will be time to update the guest house."

Marlee touches my arm. "It's nice to hear you say *we*."

I'd told Bobby we'd be here late morning. He said a buddy or two would be around helping out. Up ahead, there are seven pickup trucks, a small Caterpillar backhoe loader, and a large pile of lumber. A guy with a long straw-colored beard hauls two-by-fours over his shoulder. Empty Gatorade bottles lie on the ground nearby. An overturned cardboard box, with two large Dunkin' boxes on top, serves as a makeshift table. This is a full-on construction site.

Harry comes bounding over as soon as he catches my scent. I lean down to greet him when someone yells, "You look'n for Bobby?"

"Yes," I yell back.

"He's upstairs, working on the plumbing. You're Maggie, right?"

"That's me."

"Pleased to meet ya." He walks towards us then wipes his hand on the front of his shirt. "I'm Clyde. Bobby and me go way back. I worked with him on his first job, right after he moved to Bend."

"I know your name," I say, shaking his hand. "You two climb together, right?"

He nods. "Partners in riding and climbing. Bobby's a helluva good climber. He ain't too bad on a mountain bike, either." I wonder if Clyde's aware of how nervous that all makes me. I know … it's silly, but stuff happens.

"I'll let him know you're here," he says. He nods to all of us, then sneaks a second glance at Juliette, which is no surprise. "I think you'll be pretty impressed with what's going on 'round here. By the end of the weekend, you won't recognize the place." Clyde turns toward the house and heads through the front door.

"This place is freaking awesome," Juliette says. She spins to take in the panoramic view. "Look at those mountains!"

"What are their names?" Sophia asks. She takes off her designer sunglasses to get a better look at the snow-capped mountains to our west.

"Those are the Three Sisters … South, Middle, and North."

"How beautiful! Why are they named 'the Sisters'?" Sophia asks. "They look so different from one another."

Annie grins. "Maybe they are exactly like three real sisters … individuals with distinct personalities and appearances. I know, because my two sisters are nothing like me." She laughs at her own joke.

"Depending on where I'm at, the Sisters seem to shift," I say. "I can't tell which is which. It's like they change locations when I do."

Just then, Bobby walks out of the house. Dressed in faded jeans and a close-fitting navy t-shirt, I have to catch my breath when I see him. While we've only been apart one night, I crave his touch.

His blue eyes sparkle as he walks towards us. "Hey," he says, then kisses my cheek. Harry jumps up and gives Bobby a sloppy lick with his tongue.

"You know Marlee," I say. "This is Annie, Sophia, and Juliette." They each shower Bobby with compliments about his farm. He nods and thanks them, the muscles in his face softening.

"How many guys are here today?" I ask.

"Seven now, a few more coming later," he says.

"How can they do that? Don't they have other jobs?" Annie asks.

"Sure," Bobby grins. His eyes narrow, like he's keeping a trade secret. "Around here, contractors usually don't work Fridays, unless there's a hard deadline. They'd rather be outside fishing, biking, camping, stuff like that. These guys are buddies of mine … and a few owe me favors. Do you want a tour?"

Bobby and I lead everyone through into the house. I whisper to him, "Thank you. We won't stay long."

"Not a problem," he says.

"I just want you to meet my friends, and for them to see our new home." Slowly, I'm becoming more comfortable with this idea. As we approach the entryway, I feel a sharp sensation in my abdomen. Then another.

"What is wrong?" Sophia asks, moving next to me.

"I'm not sure. I feel fine now." Then it happens again. My eyes go wide, but I let out a laugh. "I think the baby is kicking. This has never happened before."

Bobby turns and looks at my stomach as a small bump moves across my belly. His eyes big in amazement, Bobby places his hand on top of my shirt. Neither of us speak, but I can read his body language. *This is our child.* As quickly as the movements began, they cease.

"Do you think something's wrong?" I ask, turning toward Sophia.

"All is fine," she says. "Your baby will be active, and then you will feel nothing for a period of time. It is perfectly normal."

"I think the baby likes this house," Juliette says. Marlee nods in agreement.

Walking into the partially gutted first floor, Bobby asks me to explain what we're doing with the interior.

"Sure," I say, clearing my throat to adopt my *professional* tone. "As you can see, several of the supporting walls are gone. Temporary beams are holding up the second floor. Over here is the family room," I continue, pointing to where the fireplace will be, describing how we'll configure the furniture and the type of rug we're looking for.

"Do you want to check out the upstairs?" Bobby asks.

"Hell yeah!" Juliette says.

We form a line like ducklings and follow Bobby up the temporary plank stairs. "Guest rooms," I say, "and my office over here." Before long, we're back to the main floor, over to where the master bedroom, bath, and nursery will be.

"The baby's room is going to be right off the kitchen," I say. "We're adding wooden beams overhead. And the closet will have a slider, to resemble a barn door."

"Have you chosen a theme?" Sophia asks.

"Farm animals, of course," I laugh. "Crib and changing table will go there. We're having them made from recycled barn wood, looking to use as many natural materials as possible."

"Oh, this will be perfect," Annie says, her eyes wide in wonder. "You've thought of everything."

I shrug. "I love thinking about these kinds of details. I do it all day long for work. Now I get to do it for my own baby."

***

In the morning, I'm the first one awake. A faint snore comes from Annie's room. Unlike our time together at the retreat, we're not spending this trip discussing Annie's clairvoyance, Juliette's energetic abilities, Sophia's holistic practice, or Marlee's newly discovered channeling—the very things that made me coin these women The Healers. I guess we no longer need each other to validate our gifts. Now, we can just *be* and have fun. I like it better this way.

I turn on the coffee pot and look for something to eat. I'm hungry, even though I stuffed myself at dinner last night. Opening the box from Sparrow Bakery, I pull off a piece of pastry. The morsel melts in my mouth. Three bites later, I make myself stop. If I don't, I'll eat the whole thing. Already, I'm conscious of the weight I'm gaining … and I'm not so sure it's *all* baby.

Juliette is the next person awake. Dressed in burgundy tie-dyed yoga pants and a black tank top, she carries her yoga mat with her and looks around the room. "Good morning," she says.

"What a fun night," I offer.

She nods. "Yeah, but now I need to ground myself after all of the red wine I drank." She heads out the back door to the patio.

Marlee comes downstairs next. She grabs a mug and pours a cup of coffee, then settles onto the sofa. "I haven't had that much fun in a long time," she laughs.

"I am glad I declined the limoncello that Juliette ordered for us," Sophia says as she walks out of her room, wearing a silk robe adorned with cherry blossoms. "Though I certainly drank my share of wine," she uncharacteristically winks.

"Did we really sing 'Sweet Caroline' at that karaoke bar?" Annie asks, her auburn hair a mess, as she joins us.

"Yes," I say.

"Oh shit," she sighs. "Where's the coffee?"

I grab a mug from the cabinet and pour her a cup.

"Ahh … much better," she says. Her voice brightens after a few sips.

"Here … let's watch," Marlee says. She takes her phone and pulls up a video from last night.

"Oh, dear Lord," Sophia starts to laugh. "We sound horrific."

"Speak for yourself," Juliette says as she comes in from outside. "My voice is really good. In fact, Juana always complemented me when I sang the *Icaros* during ceremonies."

"Bet you weren't drunk when you did that," Annie says.

"What happened to your grounding?" I ask.

"Kinda hard to focus," Juliette admits, "especially hearing everyone recap last night." She heads to the kitchen, turns on the kettle for tea, then settles into the couch near Sophia, who's consumed by her phone.

"Is everything OK, Sophia?" I ask her, wondering if she received a message from a patient.

"I am not sure," she says. Uncharacteristically hunched over her cell, her voice quivers.

"What's going on?" Marlee asks, moving closer to her.

"It is a text from Lizzy. Jared is in the hospital. She says he is OK, but he had a scare." Her face turns ashen. "I must call Lizzy." She quickly walks into her bedroom and shuts the door to call her daughter.

"Maybe I should reach out to Tom," Marlee says. "He might know something."

Just as the tea kettle whistles, Annie straightens her spine and tightly shuts her eyes. Marlee stares at Annie, biting down on her lower lip. Juliette ignores the boiling water. She's more curious about Annie's behavior.

"She's *seeing* something," Juliette whispers. I sit as still as I can on the sofa, waiting until Annie returns from wherever she is. "What did you see?" Juliette asks once Annie opens her eyes.

"Jared, on the floor of their living room," she says. "Lizzy walks in … she finds him … then she calls 911."

"But Lizzy lives in New York," Juliette says, finally turning off the kettle. "Why would she be home?"

"She is visiting for the weekend," Annie says. "Spending time with her dad while Sophia is out here with us." Then she adds, "Sophia told me this yesterday."

"Can you go back to Jared?" Marlee asks. "Can you see what happened?"

Annie returns to a trance-like state. "It's his heart … I see him clutching his chest … then falling."

"But Lizzy found him … and he's OK?" I ask, my awe of Annie's clairvoyance mixed with concern for Jared and Sophia.

"Yes … the paramedics arrive …" Annie pauses, watching the scene inside of her head. "When they do … he's breathing … and conscious. They check his vitals … give him oxygen … take him to the hospital." She stops before continuing. "He is still there … Lizzy is with him."

I let out a deep breath, thankful Lizzy was home to find her dad. "How scary this must be for Sophia, not being able to be with her husband," I say.

"Annie, do you want to tell Sophia what you saw?" Marlee asks. "It might be helpful."

"I should," she says, then heads toward Sophia's door. After a faint knock, Sophia lets her in.

"Thank goodness they found him," Juliette says. "Imagine the alternative."

"I know," Marlee agrees.

"There are bagels and cinnamon rolls in the boxes by the fridge," I say, feeling helpless about it all. "Does anyone want anything?"

"Yes … I'm starving," Juliette says. I grab a roll for her and a sesame bagel for myself. I guess I can add stress to the list of things that make me hungry.

***

"How is she?" I ask when Annie steps out of Sophia's room. She'd been in there for close to thirty minutes.

"Not great," Annie says. Her thin lips form a straight line. Her eyebrows furrow. "She's booking a flight to Philadelphia," she adds. "The doctor told Lizzy that Jared is fine, but Sophia insists on being there with him." Annie pauses then adds, "Sometimes being a physician is a curse … you know too much of what can go wrong."

"Of course," I say. My heart sinks. Annie clears her throat.

"I told Sophia I would go with her," she whispers as her eyes dart between the three of us. She stops on me. "I am truly sorry, Maggie," she says. "I've been looking forward to us all being together with you for *so* long." She doesn't need to explain. We all know how Sophia was by Annie's side during her entire pregnancy. Sophia was even there when little Ella was born.

Tears begin to fall down Annie's cheeks. "Oh, Annie," I say, walking over to hold her. "We understand." I wipe away her tears with my fingertips and pull her in for a deep hug. "You are putting Sophia ahead of your own needs. It's not easy, but you're listening to your heart." I step back and offer an encouraging smile.

"Thank you," she says, dabbing at her eyes.

"Why don't you stay? I'll fly home with Sophia," Marlee offers. "I was just here in February. I know how much you could use this time away."

"Thank you, but I want to do this." Annie stands a bit taller.

"Of course," Marlee says. "You should pack … I'll check on Sophia." She stands and heads toward Sophia's room.

Juliette glances at me, sensing my sadness.

"Don't worry, Maggie. We'll still have fun."

"I know … it' just … "

"Did you think this was our last time together?" Juliette says, then waves her hand. "I was going to bring this up later tonight. Maybe now is a better time." A smirk appears on her face.

"What?"

"Our next trip!" she says, delighted. Her turquoise eyes widen in a mischievous manner.

"Where were you thinking of going?"

"Well …" she begins, but before she can finish, Marlee and Sophia return.

"I am so sorry," Sophia says. "But I must leave." Sophia's eyes fall to the floor.

"I totally get it," I say, though I suspect my voice cannot mask my disappointment.

"Is there anything we can do?" Juliette asks.

"Not at the moment, but thank you," Sophia offers.

"Except getting you to the airport," Marlee reminds. "We'll all go."

***

In the afternoon, when Marlee goes for a long run, Juliette and I spend close to two hours reviewing the preliminary plans for her retreat center. Juliette seems to love every idea I share. Now, I'll have several weeks to fine-tune things before she gives them to her builder.

As much as I enjoy designing traditional buildings, this project intrigues me more than any other plans I've drawn ... even more than Viv's studio. Knowing Juliette, she's going to expect me to dive deep into the astrological and spiritual elements. I wonder about the timing of Viv's project. It's as if it was practice for what I'm doing with Juliette.

Once Marlee returns and showers, the three of us head to the river. Maybe a paddle along the Deschutes before tonight's concert is exactly what we need to take our minds off Sophia and Annie leaving. Three miles downstream from where we started, we lie on our backs, relaxing in the sun as the current carries us along.

"This is amazing," Juliette says, gazing into the pale blue sky. Above the shoreline, a hawk circles its nest, squawking to keep intruders away.

Marlee glances at her watch. "They probably landed in Salt Lake City by now," she says. "It's only a short layover until they board the flight to Philly."

I say a prayer that their next flight goes well. Marlee's phone buzzes. "Jared is at Lankenau Hospital," she says, staring at her cell. "Tom thinks he'll be released tomorrow. The doctor wants to keep him tonight for observation." She puts her phone back into the dry bag, then secures it under elastic roping.

"I was just thinking," Juliette begins, "it's crazy how much our lives have changed since last year." She pauses, dangling her hand in the cool water.

"What if that's how it's supposed to be?" I ponder. "I mean, life isn't meant to be stagnant, right?" I prop myself up on my elbows. "Just look at this river. It's always moving. Maybe we're just like the Deschutes ... built for change, completely capable of flowing from one point to another."

"You're right," Juliette says. She stretches her arms above her head. "I have no idea where this will all lead, but I'm pretty certain of two things."

"Which are?" Marlee asks.

"One, I'm going to be with Michael, and two, you will always be my best friends."

My board bumps into hers. I turn toward Marlee, who paddles next to us.

"Life *is* a journey," I say. "I mean, I never imagined I'd be living in Bend … or pregnant … or about to move in with Bobby. But it all feels *right*." There's an unusual lightness in my voice as I talk about the unknown.

"Exactly!" Juliette's eyes widen. She reaches out to grab our hands, then pulls us together. "We never know what the future will bring," she smirks. Marlee and I giggle. "But wherever I land, you are both only a phone call away."

"Bend, Boston, the Poconos …" Marlee laughs. "Who would have thought?"

"I know," I sigh. A tranquility settles over me. That's when I recall what Juliette started saying earlier. I look at her. "Hey, you were about to share an idea for a trip a few hours ago."

Her lips purse. "Oh that. I'll let you know before we leave."

Marlee quickly interjects, "This reminds me of when you planned our sessions at Nueva Vida, how you didn't want to reveal what you'd done." Clearly, Marlee was not amused.

"Did I steer you wrong?"

Marlee looks at me. She shrugs her shoulders, resigned to the fact that we'll most likely do whatever Juliette conjures up.

***

Sunday afternoon, the three of us walk a dusty river path. "I can't believe you leave tomorrow," I say. A wave of sadness falls over me.

"I wish we could stay longer," Marlee replies.

"We'll all be together this January … at my wedding," Juliette chimes in. Funny enough, she's not preoccupied with wedding plans, nor does she behave like someone who may soon become a shaman. I thought her time in Peru would have changed her. To me, she's the same Juliette I met in Costa Rica.

"Your wedding will be amazing," I say. "I hope I lose all the baby weight by then, so I can fit into my bridesmaid dress." I recall Annie uttering those exact words last year when Juliette and Michael were *supposed* to be married the following November. Now, it's me who's pregnant and anxious about my post-pregnancy body.

"Do not worry about that," Juliette says. She stops walking and turns toward me. A mystical glow lights her face. "It is taking you nine months to provide the perfect environment and nutrients for your child," she says. "Your body will require time to calibrate after the birth. There's nothing to fear. Instead, see it for what it is … a gift to create life." Her voice deepens, her skin appearing almost translucent. Maybe she has changed after all.

"I guess I've been so focused on gaining weight that I haven't stopped to consider what my body is actually doing," I agree.

"It's hard to grasp that a little person is inside, getting bigger and stronger each day," Marlee adds. "When I was pregnant with Patrick, I felt exactly like you do. I had no idea what it would be like to be a mom. It actually took some time for me to fall in love with my son. He was so little, and I was afraid."

"What were you afraid of?" Juliette asks.

"I suppose I was afraid of not knowing how to care for my baby … or of doing things wrong," Marlee says. She looks at Juliette, smiling when she admits this.

"But you're so caring," I say. "I always assumed motherhood came naturally to you." Never in a million years would I suspect Marlee had reservations about her nurturing abilities.

Marlee shakes her head. "I was the youngest of five, so I was never around small children. I was the little kid."

"Did you babysit?" I ask.

"A few times, but not infants," she says. "After I had Patrick, I had to learn to trust myself … to believe I was capable of being a good mother … and that I wasn't going to do anything that might harm him." She laughs. "Oh, and those Lamaze classes … let's just say that Tom and I were dropouts. I could never breathe the right way. I was so out of touch with my body, I didn't know how to relax when they told me to."

"But you're able to do so now, right?" Juliette asks. She tilts her head toward Marlee, as if encouraging her to realize her progress.

"Yes," Marlee agrees, "but it took time for me to tune into my body and trust what it tells me. Thinking was always so much easier than *feeling*." She pauses then looks at me. "Did I ever tell you about 'Margaret'?"

I shake my head no.

"Margaret," Marlee begins, "was the name I gave to the voice inside my head. For years, this voice criticized me. She always pointed out every little thing I did wrong, as well as when I failed to act."

"Do you still hear Margaret?" I ask, aware of my own internal judgy comments that for years have made me doubt myself.

"I haven't for a while. It took me time to realize Margaret was holding me back. For so long, she kept me from stepping out of my comfort zone to do what I really wanted to do."

"How did you get rid of her?" I ask. "Did you do this on your own?"

"Actually, it happened during the retreat." Marlee recounts how every time she went to take a step forward, Margaret would pop up and say something to cause her to second-guess herself. "Maybe it was working with Francisco, or perhaps it was during the private session with Daniel. He showed me how to channel the real voice inside. Eventually, Margaret went away." A grin comes across Marlee's face.

"But what will you do if she comes back?" I ask.

"I suppose if she returns, it will mean that I've taken a step backward, and that I should pause and listen for the real voice of my intuition." Marlee's eyes glisten as she talks.

"Was Margaret around when Patrick was born?" I ask.

"Constantly. In fact, I think that's when she first appeared. Tom was a natural with Patrick. But as much as he wanted to help, he wasn't home much. It was early in his career. He had a hellish schedule. Whenever he had time off, he usually needed to catch up on sleep."

"And the critical voice made you second-guess everything you did?" I ask.

"Exactly."

"Well, I think I've got a Margaret of my own," I say. I stop and stare at the trail.

"Tell her to leave, immediately," Juliette says. She places a hand on my shoulder. "There is no room for her. She's not good for the baby. Remember, the baby absorbs everything. What you eat, drink, say, and think."

"I never thought about that." I shudder at the idea of my unborn child taking in my toxic thoughts and words.

"That's why it's important to speak to your baby," Juliette says.

"What should I say?"

"Tell him how much you love him … how you can't wait to meet him."

Immediately I return to the moment I first discovered I was pregnant. Those were definitely not the thoughts I was having. In fact, I felt the opposite. My pulse quickens. What if my fears of being pregnant impacted the baby?

"Wait, Juliette … you said *him*. Is that an assumption? Or, do you know something?" My voice shakes when I ask. Marlee, too, looks a bit unnerved. Her eyes dart from Juliette to me.

"Oh, I've known you're having a boy ever since Marlee first told me you were pregnant," she says.

Since neither Bobby nor I wanted to know the sex, I'm unsure how to process this information.

"Juliette," Marlee begins, probably aware of my reaction. "Maybe Maggie wanted to be surprised about the 'boy or girl' thing." Marlee's brow furrows, as if scolding Juliette a little.

"Oops," Juliette bites her lower lip. "My bad. Sorry."

Once again, regardless of whether Juliette becomes a shaman or not, she's still Juliette. And a part of her will always enjoy being right.

"Are you sure?" I ask, slowly massaging my stomach. A boy would certainly make Bobby happy. Then again, he'd love a daughter too. He did say either would be perfect, but I know there's a side of him that wants to teach a son how to fish, ride a dirt bike, and build a fence. Not that he couldn't do that with a daughter, but Bobby's a pretty traditional guy.

"Yep," Juliette nods. "Definitely a boy. In fact, I've been talking with him."

"What? How can you do that?" Marlee asks, her mouth wide open in disbelief.

"While in Peru, I learned to communicate with unborn babies. I find out all sorts of stuff. Their gender, why they chose their parents, what they are here to learn. I know it sounds strange, but they speak to me … energetically, of course."

Marlee and I exchange questioning glances.

"Seriously. That's one of the things I focused on when I worked with people in villages. I helped pregnant women communicate with their babies."

"Can you help me talk with mine?" I ask. Part of me is still doubtful, but I'm curious too.

"Of course." Juliette walks to my side, places one hand on my stomach, the other on my back. Then she shuts her eyes and begins breathing deeply. I remain still, hoping whatever she's hearing from the baby is good. After a moment, she removes her hands, clears her throat, then looks at me.

"He wants you to know that he chose you as his mother because he has lessons to teach you, and you have much to share with him. He knows that his dad is exactly who you are meant to be with. His coming to earth was a way to ensure that you didn't allow your fears to sabotage this relationship."

I gasp. How can Juliette say this. This is ridiculous. She cannot *read* what an unborn child is thinking … that is, if unborn babies are even able to think.

"There's more … something *he* desires."

"What is it?" Marlee asks.

"Your baby wants a real family."

"A *real* family … what does that mean?" I gasp.

Juliette tilts her head to the side. "Maybe he wants you and Bobby to make a permeant commitment," she offers.

"You mean … get married?" I feel the blood pumping through my veins. Why does everyone, even my unborn child, want us to get married? Why can't we keep things as they are?

Chapter 11

MARLEE

July 18th – 21st

The house is quiet. Too quiet. Tom's in the OR all day. And Patrick's somewhere between New York and Maine, in a canoe, probably having the time of his life. I'm unable to suppress a smile at the thought of him making new friends and camping under the stars. Still, some part of me is apprehensive about all that might go wrong. I shake these negative images from my head. Once again, I'm projecting fear for no reason.

Catching myself in action is my homework. Maybe working with Juliette is paying off. I glance at my watch, noting it's already 2 o'clock. Where has the day gone? I should be packing. We move in five weeks. Of course this doesn't mean we'll be gone forever. Tom's only committed to one year in Boston. If we hate it, we agreed to reevaluate the situation. That's why we're not selling our home. Still, I have to decide what goes to Boston and what stays in Radnor.

Instead of filling freshly taped cardboard boxes with linens, towels, and everything else we'll need, I'm researching spiritual resorts in Sedona. Juliette finally shared her idea the night before we left Bend. She proposed the five of us spend a week at a healing center in Bali next March. One look from Maggie told me everything. I suppose it's no big deal for Juliette to travel halfway across the world for a girls' getaway, even when she'll be in the midst of building her retreat center. However, it's a huge ask for the rest of us. Maggie's baby will be five months old. And it would be difficult for Annie and Sophia to leave their practices, as a week turns into nine days when you include travel time to Bali. Plus, there's the cost.

I shared with Juliette why this might not be the best spot. After pouting for a moment, she came around. That's when she suggested I find the perfect place. I sighed when she said it, and I'm still sighing at the idea. Is there a spot that will satisfy Juliette's thirst for enlightenment *and* accommodate the rest of us?

I shut my laptop and trudge upstairs. Maybe packing is a better idea right now. I sit on the guestroom bed and survey the room, wondering what I want to bring to the Boston brownstone we found a couple of weeks ago. It's a two-story townhome just off Newberry Street, with gorgeous, exposed brick walls, two fireplaces—one in the main living area, the other in our bedroom—and modern light fixtures through the entire space. My favorite room is the newly remodeled kitchen, with Viking appliances, poured cement countertops, hidden drawers, and ingenious storage. I love my Radnor kitchen, but this one sparked something in me, as if beckoning me to test new recipes and see what I can create.

All enchantment with the brownstone fades as my mind returns to the present. Tom and I spent years procuring everything for our home. It seems impossible to separate our possessions. Can we really extract certain pieces from our past to take to Boston? Then neither place will feel complete. Our things belong together, not more than three hundred miles apart.

And there it is … I'm wondering if we made the right decision again. Maybe Tom should have just stayed at Jefferson. No. Yes. I don't know. It would mean less money, but then life could continue as it's been.

My throat constricts. I'm going down my *oh so familiar* rabbit hole. This time, I catch myself before a full tumble. I won't allow uncertainty to trigger a fearful state. Just being aware of my patterned responses helps shake off the uncomfortable sensations.

I take in a slow breath and focus on how amazing our new place will be. With each deliberate inhale and exhale, the noose around my neck loosens.

***

Calmer now, I start a list on my phone: *Items to buy for Boston.* "Patrick's room needs a queen bed, linens, blanket, pillows, and quilt," I speak into my app. "We'll need the same for the master bedroom." Next up is my office. I look at the drawings the realtor gave to us. My current desk is huge. It will never fit in the brownstone office. "Small desk and chair," I say, then add "bookshelf," then "printer." The packing list gets smaller while the shopping list grows. We may be buying most of what we'll need *if* we want to maintain both places.

My mood continues to lift. Clearly there's no need to dismantle our home. Sure, I'll bring important pieces and photos, but moving from a farmhouse into a restored brownstone has limitations. I gladly accept this realization.

I leave the packing boxes on the guestroom floor, go downstairs to make tea, and then head to my office. I'm ready to adopt a new approach to organizing our move. I pull a fresh notepad from the drawer and pick up my favorite felt-tip pen, then jot out a list of necessities for every room in the brownstone, including what I dictated a few moments ago.

With a process in place, the idea of moving almost excites me. I type "bedroom furniture" into the search bar of my laptop, then watch dozens of options appear on the screen. Now I can have the furniture delivered straight to Boston and avoid renting such a large U-Haul.

Tom startles me as he kisses the top of my head. When did he get home? I never heard the garage door open.

"Researching a new book?" he asks with a touch of curiosity. I guess he's oblivious to the contents of the realtor's packet strewn across my desk.

"I'm looking for furniture for Boston," I say. I turn away from my laptop and toward him. "I finally understand why I've been having so much trouble getting started with the move. Our furnishings belong here." I show him some of what I've found online. "Most of what we have is too big to fit in the brownstone. Plus, things will look awkward. Our rustic farmhouse style won't work up there."

"So, you want to furnish our new place from scratch?" he asks.

"I'll be mindful of costs," I say, though I don't think he's too concerned.

"Marlee, you're making a huge sacrifice by agreeing to this move," he says. "Just promise me one thing," he grins. "You won't ask me about each purchase. I trust you to make this a home for us. It might be fun to start from the beginning."

But then Tom's smile fades.

"You're sad about moving too?" I ask, placing my hand on Tom's arm.

"Of course," he says. He gently sweeps a stray hair from my cheek "I love our home. There's a story behind everything … too many memories to forget."

"Do you think we'll come back?" I ask. "Or, is that something we're just saying to make the move easier?"

"I think we'll be back," he says, pausing for a moment. "Actually, this morning, I began considering a long-term plan. I was going to bring it up later, on our drive to pick up Patrick." He pauses as his fingers comb through his graying hair. "There's just so much going on right now."

"Of course," I agree. "You're trying to tie things up at Jefferson, and you're beginning to step into your new role at Mass General."

He nods. "Yes, plus I started wondering how long I'll be in the game," he adds. "You know … when will it be time to retire? What will it look like? Those kinds of things have suddenly crept into mind." He gazes into my eyes. He's never mentioned life after being a doctor.

"Does this have to do with what happened to Jared?"

"A little, I suppose."

"Well, what do you see yourself doing?" I ask. It's strange we haven't discussed this before. Retirement has always seemed so far away. But then again, Tom is approaching fifty.

"Well, it's been a dream of mine to teach at a leading medical school," he says. His jaw relaxes when he admits this. "I figured it would be my way to give back to the profession, maybe even impact some folks on their way to becoming surgeons." He moves and sits in the empty swivel chair next to my desk, the spot where Patrick used to do his homework in elementary school. I wrote articles for the *Inquirer* while he completed math and spelling assignments.

"Boston has great teaching universities," he goes on. "Then again, so does Philadelphia. Maybe that's when we'll move back. Or, if we love Boston, we can use our home in Radnor as a getaway." He shrugs, resigned to the fact that plenty can happen between now and then. He takes both of my hands and brings my fingers to his lips. "As long as we're together, and we keep our close connection to Patrick, that's all that really matters."

***

This afternoon, Patrick returns from his canoe trip. He's bound to be exhausted after five days of paddling along more than seven-hundred miles from New York to Maine and back. The last thing he'll want to do is get in the car for a four-hour-plus drive. With that in mind, I reserved a room at the Colgate Inn. We could spend some time getting to know the town. Plus, we'll all appreciate a restful sleep before driving home in the morning. The last word resonates. How much longer will I be referring to Radnor as home?

Fifteen minutes into the drive, I reach for my laptop and open a blank document. I'm hoping for a spurt of inspiration, but I have no idea where to begin.

I journal every morning, always beginning with the question, "What am I to know?" But I haven't written anything I'd consider literary since my book came out … and I feel rusty. Not just rusty. I'm completely unmotivated. Is this what writer's block feels like?

Last Wednesday, I stopped by our local bookstore to see if they needed more copies of *The Best is Yet to Come*. The owner casually mentioned that she'd be interested in carrying my *next* book. Then she asked what I was working on. I forced a smile and replied, "I'm playing with a few ideas." I wasn't prepared for her response.

"If you'd like, I'd be happy to read your manuscript before it's published," she said. This conversation has been weighing on me ever since. Is it time to start my next book? I can't imagine doing so. The summer has been too busy, and it's only going to get busier. How could I dive into a new novel now?

Funny enough, once we settle in Boston, I suspect I might have *too much* free time. There's no reason I couldn't try to write then. Tom will be busy balancing administrative duties and a significant surgical load, all while getting to know an entirely new hospital system, plus doctors, nurses, technicians, and support staff. I'll need to find something to do.

My gameplan was to return to Radnor for a few days at the end of September. After all, how long will it take to unpack everything? And I don't know a soul in Boston. If I have a writing project, life in my new city might be a little easier. I could visit local coffee shops, or maybe even join a writers group.

With a stronger sense of conviction, I return to the empty document. The blank space doesn't intimidate me right now. I contemplate various scenarios and possible themes. When my fingers touch the keyboard, I start typing in what feels like an explosion.

First, I play with a strong-willed antagonist, a charming yet somewhat questionable man who tries to derail a vulnerable woman from her life's purpose. Next, I devise the supportive friend who stands by her side, committed to convincing her that she's too good for the antagonist's advances. Close to an hour later, I pause, shut my eyes, and let my mind play with possible plot lines. Maybe it will be a mystery. After all, the characters fit the part. What if the woman is moving to a new town, leaving this man behind? I can certainly relate to the moving part. It would be easy to write about opportunities and anxieties that come with such a transition.

Then another possibility appears. *The Best is Yet to Come* centers on shifting our perspective, letting go, and trusting what's ahead. Could I expand on that theme? If so, how? After all, isn't that exactly what I'm doing with Juliette?

With my first book, I received guidance from both Francisco and Daniel. Yet that was when I was with them in Costa Rica. Maybe I could ask someone else for help? But who?

Why not me?

Out of nowhere, the voice appears. While I've been consistently channeling this voice through my daily journaling, I usually don't *hear* it. Besides, how could the voice help me write a book?

As if meant to convince me otherwise, "Do You Believe in Magic" by the Lovin' Spoonful comes over the stereo. My mom used to sing that song to me when I was little.

Taking this as a sign, I close my eyelids. Counting my inhales and exhales, I consciously extend the length of each breath. Only after I reach a state of calm do I ask whoever this voice is for help.

"What should I write about?" I silently inquire, hoping this unknown being can hear me.

I wait. Moments become minutes without any response. Still, I don't give up. I go deeper within, trusting that if anything is meant to happen, it will.

Two, three, five minutes pass. I hear the blinker turn on and off, signaling Tom's passing a car ahead. Finally, just as I'm about to give up, the voice speaks.

Choose happiness.

Two simple words. I'm grateful for the clue. Now what do I do with it?

***

"Mom ... Dad!" Patrick hollers when he sees us. Quickly, I turn toward my favorite voice in the world. While my instinct is to rush to him and ask a million questions about his past five days, I don't. He's surrounded by new friends and guides. He'd be mortified.

Instead, I force my gait to slow. Faking a casual demeaner, I calmly approach my son. As I debate whether a hug is appropriate, Patrick envelops me before I make the call.

"Did you have fun?" I ask. For years, I've asked this question whenever I've picked him up from a playdate, a soccer game, or even a dance. Today, the question isn't necessary. The look on his face says it all.

"It was such a blast. Everyone is great. Super chill. These are *definitely* my people." He grins ear to ear. Tom joins us, and Patrick gives him a bear hug.

As we walk toward the car, he turns back to wave at some kids. "See you in a couple of weeks." His voice, which is normally upbeat for a teenage boy, now borders on peppy. But one response catches my attention.

"Tomorrow night … *Assassin's Creed*?"

My mouth falls open, but then I remember that's a video game. Seconds later, a soccer ball flies in our direction. With ease, Patrick catches it. "Thanks, Trevor. I almost forgot." He laughs, not a care in the world. After nearly a week on the river, he's totally at peace. These are *his people*. Our son will be fine.

***

Over a relaxing dinner on the patio of the Colgate Inn, Patrick gives us a blow-by-blow account of his paddling trip. He goes into great detail about meals, how they cooked them, even the trick to starting a fire when it's raining. Then he mimics his tentmate's snoring, which causes Tom to convulse with laughter.

After the server clears our plates, Patrick casually mentions a girl named Anna, an incoming freshman.

"Where's she from?" I ask, failing to disguise the enthusiasm in my voice. His only real *romance* began the summer after eighth grade. But that relationship ended before his sophomore year.

"Connecticut, near Stamford," he says. "She's really cool. She likes everything I do. She even played on her high school lacrosse and soccer teams."

An unexpected twinge of suspicion flows through me. "Oh, that's nice," I say, even as my mind begins to roam through a litany of questions. Who is this Anna? Is she nice? How important is she to Patrick? So soon?

Tom glances at me, picking up on the fact that my thoughts are elsewhere. Now I'm almost embarrassed by my reaction. If Patrick likes her, I'm sure she's wonderful … at least I hope.

***

"How is Jared?" I ask Sophia as we walk along a trail not far from her house. It's been a month since Jared's incident. He's just now getting back to work.

"He claims he feels fine," she says. "I think he looks too thin." She doesn't make eye contact. Instead, she stares at the path ahead.

"Thank God it happened when Lizzy was visiting," I say. I take a closer look at Sophia. The woman who normally mirrors an Italian Audrey Hepburn now appears older than her true age, fifty-seven. Creases surround her eyes, and wrinkles I've never noticed stretch across her forehead. She's dressed in baggy running shorts and a loose sleeveless shirt. She's not even wearing makeup.

"I'm concerned about you," I say, not able to hold it in.

"I am worried about Jared," she shakes her head. "He follows certain practices that help his well-being, but still …" She stops and turns toward me. "Jared is pushing himself too much at work," she confides. "Things have changed. His call schedule should be easier, but it has gotten worse. There have been so many shifts in health-care … but I know I do not need to tell you about that. I am sure Tom has shared the many changes occurring at the hospital."

She starts walking again, but at a slower pace than earlier. "I suppose I hold much of the blame," she hangs her head. "Whenever Jared wanted to talk about retiring and moving to Manhattan, I would change the subject." A slow sigh escapes her mouth. "Jared is ready … but I am not. I have been selfish, only thinking of my career."

"Sophia, please don't blame yourself," I say. I place my hand on her shoulder. "It's natural for you to want to grow your practice, especially after all the work you've done with Jack. I remember how impactful it was when you to returned to Costa Rica to study with him last fall."

A slight smile appears on Sophia's thin lips. "Jack and I consult on a weekly basis. We discuss my patients and how to enhance their well-being. In fact, he invited me to return this October, for additional training."

"That's wonderful. I'm sure you're excited to continue." I pause, then shift back to Jared. "Until the incident, Jared had been the picture of health. He had never shown any signs of needing to slow down. Out of all of Tom's friends, he takes the best care of himself."

"I suppose you are right," Sophia agrees. "It is all so complicated." Tears fill her eyes. She pulls a tissue from her waistband and blots at them. "There is more going on," she admits, then exhales. "Lizzy quit her job … in January! She hid it from us. We only found out last month … just before you told me about Boston."

My hand goes instinctively to my heart when I hear this. Sophia's eyes meet mine. "Her brother, Max, came to us out of concern. He felt she had fallen into a state of depression. That is why Lizzy was home. Jared wanted her to meet with our neighbor, the psychologist."

"Oh, Sophia, I am so sorry." Having no idea what to say, I choose to stay silent. The dots begin connecting. That's why she was so upset I didn't tell her we were moving. It triggered her recent pain about Lizzy hiding her job situation. It's all adding up.

"Why didn't she tell you work was getting too stressful for her?"

"I do not know," Sophia says, shrugging. "She resigned, then spent the past four months feeling inadequate. I feel as though I failed as a mother."

I look at my dear friend. A lone tear falls down her cheek. How difficult these months must have been for her. As close as I am to Sophia, our relationship is relatively new. She talks about Lizzy and Max often, but I don't really know their stories.

"Sweetie, you haven't failed as a mother," I offer. "Lizzy probably just needed some time alone, to process things."

Sophia hangs her head, then softly says, "Lizzy was always our high-achiever. She graduated *magna cum laude* from Columbia. We were so proud when McKenzie hired her."

"Sometimes, having the ability to perform at a high level doesn't mean it is what's best for you," I say. "I don't mean to overstep, but it doesn't sound like Lizzy wants that lifestyle."

Sophia nods, but says nothing. We're mostly quiet for the rest of the walk. Ten minutes later, we're back in the parking lot. My phone pings as I get back in my car. So does Sophia's. It's a text from Annie on both of our phones:

Mary's father just had a stroke. Tomorrow morning, she's returning to Ireland to care for him. I feel so badly for her, but we depend on her. There's no one else to watch Ella. Can you think of anyone who could fill in?

"Shit," I say, shaking my head as I reread her text. "I can cover Annie tomorrow," I add, then double check my phone's calendar. "But that's only temporary. She'll need a full-time nanny."

"This is horrible," Sophia says. "Annie cares deeply about her patients, but Ella is just a baby."

"What about Lizzy?" I ask. "She needs a job, and Annie needs a sitter. It *could* be perfect. Do you think Lizzy would be interested? Does she like children? Plus, would she consider being in Philadelphia for a bit, while Mary is away?" I fire one question after another at Sophia.

Sophia tilts her head toward the sky, considering this possibility. "There is nothing I would love more than having Lizzy here in Philadelphia, to help her heal," she says. "Maybe it *could* work." Sophia's face softens, and a peaceful smile appears, something I haven't seen for a while. "I will talk with Lizzy."

"Do you think you should ask Annie first?"

"You are right, that would be the correct first step. I will call her on my drive home." Sophia slips into the driver's seat of her Tesla. "You have such a beautiful way of connecting people," she says. "It really is a gift. Most people become lost in the details of life. But not you, Marlee. You see the big picture."

***

"And just when I was about to give up on ideas for the book, the voice said, '*choose happiness*,'" I share with Juliette on the patio. "I wonder what that means?"

"Well, do you choose happiness?" she asks. Her voice is somewhat curt. Maybe she's losing patience with me. I shut my eyes to consider her question, then realize how unsure I am about my answer.

"I try to be happy," I say, "but do I *choose happiness*? I don't know."

"You've shared that you can identify your fears," Juliette says, starting our session. "And you realize how you project past experiences into future situations. In fact, the email you sent about your homework assignment contained excellent examples of you doing this with Patrick, as well as your thoughts about Boston. This is metacognition. You're becoming more aware of your thoughts."

I remember that term from college psych classes. I haven't given the concept much thought since then.

"You're recognizing moments when you attach prior experiences to future events," Juliette goes on. "Too often, you remember the bad stuff. This causes you to fear that the past will repeat itself. Can you see how this leads to *not* choosing happiness?"

"How can I shift this ingrained behavior?" I ask. "And … what does this have to do with writing a book?"

"I kiss what I have never before experienced," she says. Her tone is lyrical, somewhat ethereal. But I'm confused by her statement. I open my eyes and prop myself up on my elbows. "I don't get it. What do you mean?"

"Think about it, Marlee. *I kiss what I have never before experienced.* What do the words imply?"

"Well … there's a warm, welcoming acceptance in a kiss."

"Exactly. Another way of saying this would be, 'I welcome with an open heart that which is new to me.' Is that something you do?"

My throat constricts as I think about her question, making it even more difficult to admit the truth.

"No," I finally murmur.

"That's the point," she says. "You focus on what could go wrong. That's why your next assignment is to listen to the voice that said *choose happiness.* Stop worrying about what's next. Instead, remain in the present … *choose happiness.* Then think about how this might translate into a book."

I can't do that … can I? I take a calming breath and remind myself that I agreed to work with Juliette. I wanted to reach the next stage of my spiritual development. Still, what she's asking of me won't be easy.

"Juliette, it sounds uncomplicated when *you* say it … but choosing happiness can be hard. The future is uncertain." My jaw clenches.

"Our thoughts dictate our reality," Juliette quickly responds.

"True, but you're assuming I can control my thoughts."

"You can, but it takes practice. You know, I can help with this." She motions for me to lie back. Once she begins her clearing ritual,

I start to fall into a state of calm. She sets the smoldering sage in a large, sand-filled oyster shell. I close my eyes as she gently places her hands on my face, then flutters her fingertips on my forehead.

A light, feathery sensation quiets my mind and activates my senses. My thoughts dissipate. I'm suddenly more in-tune with what's happening around me. The sun grows more intense on my skin. The scent of honeysuckle wafts from the side of the house and fills my nostrils. Even the melodic song of nearby finches magnifies. I'm somehow disconnected yet deeply aware.

Suddenly, I begin to *see* what appears to be tiny moths circling out of my head. Some are pastel-colored, but most are a mix of blood red, deep purple, gray, and dull charcoal. Do they represent various thoughts leaving my mind?

Juliette begins to chant. More moths appear, mostly the darker ones. Could they represent my trapped emotions? Do they depict my concerns, worries, and fears? They exit my body and spiral upward, flying off and out of view. This continues for several minutes. I'm amazed by everything that's leaving my body. Perhaps this explains why I've been viewing life as a half-empty glass lately. No wonder the concept of *choosing happiness* overwhelmed me. Now that Juliette's freeing my negative thoughts, I can be more optimistic. I *can* choose happiness. Maybe I can even write a book about it.

Juliette stops chanting. The last of the moths disappear into the brilliant blue sky. Slowly, I return to my body. I feel different, lighter somehow. Even my breathing seems effortless.

I open my eyes and notice an unusual crispness to my vision. Edges look sharper. The potted flowers sparkle. When I look at Juliette, her skin appears iridescent, like it did when we met for lunch this spring. Her turquoise eyes glimmer, resembling a crystal that catches the sun's ray.

"How do you feel now?" she asks. She moves to the base of the lounge chair, taking both of my feet into her hands to ground me.

"Amazing … carefree," I hum. Even my voice sounds softer. Perhaps it's due to how relaxed my neck and shoulder muscles are.

"We must be conscious where our attention goes," she says. "Otherwise, we get swept away by negative ideas, spiraling downward emotionally and energetically. If we choose to become curious about the unknown, to *kiss what we have never before experienced*, we can step into a higher version of ourselves."

"Higher version?"

"Where we vibrate at a higher frequency," she says, "and focus on the positive. Where we feel fewer and fewer negative emotions. When we're in this state, it's easier to be present. We trust that things happen for a reason. Instead of fighting uncertainty, we embrace our faith. This causes our fears to lose their power. *That* is choosing happiness. It's how we elevate."

Chapter 12

MAGGIE

August 19th

Thud! My heart sinks as the morose sound vibrates through my ears. A bird flew into the window … again.

I run to the large balcony slider. There, outside, lies a robin. I carefully open the door and watch as this sweet thing rocks back and forth. Its small beak gasps in fits. After several moments, the bird remains on its left side, unable to right itself. A lump in my throat forms as its tail feathers fall.

"Fly away!" My voice is loud, determined.

Its left wing lifts and momentarily flutters. The bird's erratic breath comes and goes as its small, tufted chest heaves up and down.

"You can do it," I say. My words are soft, more like a prayer than an encouraging statement.

Twitches follow. Its back tail lifts less than a centimeter. Moments later, the death dance ends. For me, it's not over. An unexpected pain, coming from deep inside, shrouds me. I've just witnessed the end of a beautiful bird's life. Tears fall, quickly and fiercely. In less than a minute, I'm curled in the fetal position near the entrance of the balcony. The toaster pops. I can't move.

How could a bird flying into a window unravel me? Somehow, this common occurrence has poked a hole in the armor that encases my heart. Unsure when I first shut it down, I begin to wonder if my heart space has ever been truly open. I can express emotions. I remember crying multiple times each day for months after my mom died. Then there was the breakup with Pete. I felt terrible ending things. And of course, my grandfather's passing caused a great deal of sorrow. Then, when I found out I was pregnant, well, that pretty much unhinged me. Even now, I seem to cry easily.

Still, did I ever let myself fully feel … anything? Instead of permitting sufficient time and space to allow sadness to settle in, even if I may have sobbed, I always stood strong and stoic. I wasn't one to tend to my own broken pieces. I chose to brush all pain under the rug so I could go on with life. I suppose with each loss, I added a protective layer to the metal around my heart, making it nearly impossible to penetrate. But this morning, a tiny bird found a way through my armor.

I push myself up from the floor, then retrieve the cooled toast from the toaster. I can't understand why this bird triggered such a reaction. Could there be something underneath?

I settle on the couch and sip a little coffee before pulling my knees toward my chest. This once simple motion is no longer easy for me. There *must* be something else bothering me. What is it? Why can't I understand what's making me so sad?

Nothing enlightening pops into my head. Maybe it's because I'm thirty-one weeks pregnant, and my hormones are raging. Before I know it, I'm going to be responsible for a helpless newborn who will depend on me for everything.

Bobby's image comes into my mind, along with a string of questions. Why don't I let myself fully feel my emotions? Why is it so hard for me to trust? If I love Bobby, then what is holding me back from making a commitment?

I place both hands on my stomach and remember what Juliette shared during our last day together in Bend. It's about what *the baby* wants. I never told Bobby. Perhaps I've intentionally for-gotten her message. Besides, there's a good chance Juliette misin-terpreted the information. Maybe she just wants me to be happy, married like she's about to be.

Deep down, I don't believe that's true. I sit silently for a moment, then ask the exact thing I've kept myself from seriously considering: What if I marry Bobby?

I nestle my head onto a throw pillow, shut my eyes, and envision married life. We're together most of the time, but what I feel now is different. There's a shift in our commitment to each other. Our wedding vows encompass a promise to remain together, regardless of what life throws at us.

My breathing steadies, and my body settles deeper into the couch. I think to when our child is older. I see the three of us playing in the backyard, making pancakes, going on bike rides. From there, my mind travels farther into the future. Bobby's showing him how to drive the tractor ... then the truck. Our son is handsome and strong. He has Bobby's eyes and my hair. He looks at his dad with the utmost awe.

As I'm picturing these scenes, there's a flurry of activity in my uterus. Instead of kicking, I feel a flutter, like sweet butterflies are swirling around ... happy, joyful, and grateful to be alive. This baby has never done this before. Could this be his way of saying *yes*?

Assuming this was a fluke, perhaps even an imagined sensation messing with my mind, I get up from the couch. But it wasn't a coincidence. I know what I felt.

I take my plate of uneaten toast to the kitchen, and the swirling returns. Now there's more. I start laughing uncontrollably, as though someone's tickling me. I can't remember ever giggling this much. While this unexpected wave of happiness takes hold of me, I'm also filled with a strong desire to go to Bobby ... to tell him the word he's waiting to hear.

I look at my watch. It's quarter after seven in the morning. Bobby woke up early so he could go to the farm before work to finish up the kitchen backsplash. Quickly, I put on a pair of maternity jeans and a blouse, then slip into a pair of flats. I grab my purse and hurry out toward my car. I'll come back later and get ready for work. Right now, I have to see Bobby … to tell him I'm ready.

Excited, I can't help but drive faster than normal. I pass Shevlin Park. The next stretch has several sharp turns, but I've driven this road so many times, I know it like the back of my hand.

What will I say to Bobby? Should I propose to him? Should I share Juliette's message? Should I tell him what our baby …

Right then a speeding tractor trailer clips the back left bumper of my Subaru. My car swerves right, toward several large ponderosa pines. Frantically, I jerk the steering wheel left, but overcompensate. I hear a deep honk. My car's spinning. I can't stop. It's then I see the white truck …

PART TWO

Chapter 13

MARLEE

August 19th – 20th

My phone rings. I almost allow it to go to voicemail. Right now, all I can think about is Patrick leaving. No one in my contact list matches the number on the screen. Yet, something tells me to answer it.

"Marlee, it's Bobby." There's an uncomfortable pause. "Maggie … she … she was in a bad accident." Bobby doesn't sound like Bobby, more like a terrified man on the other end of the phone.

"What happened? Is she OK?" Panic runs through my veins.

"The doctors think she will be," he gulps. "An eighteen-wheeler hit her … and then she lost control of her car and collided with a truck. She's unconscious." The shakiness in his voice terrifies me.

I want to ask more questions, but first take a deep breath. The love of Bobby's life was just in a tragic accident. The last thing he needs to deal with is Maggie's frantic friend.

"How are you?" I ask. "What can I do?"

"I'm scared, Marlee," he says, his voice still quivering. "They let me see her. She looks broken… all purple and swollen … and …" He can't finish his sentence. I know where his thoughts have gone … to their baby.

"She's going to be OK," I say, without knowing, mostly to be hopeful. I hear him exhale. "You've got me … and Juliette, Annie, and Sophia," I continue. "Just tell me what you need, and it's done."

"I need a miracle," he says.

"A miracle?"

"She's always called you guys The Healers," he says. "I never understood what she meant. Is there some way … anything … you can do to *heal* Maggie?"

***

"Did Bobby mention the baby?" Sophia asks. She and Annie came as soon as I texted. Juliette is on her way.

"I couldn't go there," I say. "Bobby was a mess." I stare into my cup of peppermint tea. "And Maggie's still only thirty-one weeks pregnant." I stop myself from saying anything more. We're all aware of the implications.

"Well, we've got to do something," Annie says. She paces back and forth between the kitchen and family room.

"Annie, can you pick up on *anything*?" I ask.

"I'm not sure." She stops moving and sits on a stool by the counter. "I'll try."

I've never asked Annie to try to *see* anything. Every time I've been with her when she's done it, it just sort of happened. I'm not sure whether she'll be able to intentionally tap in. I know she does with her clients, but this is different. It's personal. She may be scared about what she might see.

Annie begins to go into one of her states, attempting to access the part of her mind that permits her to know what is happening, or has happened, elsewhere. Her eyebrows scrunch, her breath deepens. I sit in an uncomfortable silence and watch as her face becomes ashen. She forcefully turns her head toward the floor, as if shielding herself from something. Her entire body shakes uncontrollably.

Sophia jumps off her stool to stand next to her, ready to intervene if Annie crumbles. But Annie doesn't. Instead, her body steadies, and her shoulders fall away from her ears. Her breathing regulates. Then she opens her eyes.

"What did you see?" Sophia is quick to ask.

"I saw the accident," Annie says wide-eyed. "Maggie was alone, driving on a winding road. It appeared to be the same route we took to Bobby's house. I remember this one hairpin turn that made me nauseous." She swallows several times before continuing. "There's a tractor trailer right behind Maggie. The driver takes the turn too close. He hits the back of Maggie's car, causing her to spin out." Annie's hands go to her jaw. She rubs the side of her face. "Maggie's unable to get her car under control." Annie begins to turn pale, looking ill. "A big white truck is coming toward her from the opposite direction. They collide. There's blood everywhere," she goes on, looking vomitous now.

"The driver gets out of the truck. He's shaken but OK. He goes to Maggie's car and … pulls her out. But she's not conscious. He reaches for his phone and calls for help." Annie places her hands over her eyes. "The ambulance arrives in less than ten minutes. But it's the look on his face …"

"What do you mean?" I ask. In moments like these, I wish I could see what Annie sees.

Annie uncovers her eyes and stares at us. "He sees that she's pregnant. The man begins to sob, shaking his head back and forth. But then, he gets down on his knees, next to Maggie, and begins to pray." Annie stops.

"That is what we can do!" Sophia says, a glimmer of hope in her eyes.

"What?" I ask, unsure of what she means.

"Prayer," Sophia continues in a clear and crisp manner, as though she's found the perfect answer to Bobby's request. "I do not mean we have to recite traditional prayers, though we may," she adds, standing tall, her shoulders thrown back. "Many hear the word 'pray' and think of someone kneeling, with hands folded at their chest. That is surely one form of prayer, but there are many others. Some pray through meditation. Others communicate with God through yoga. I believe that whenever we converse with God, we are praying."

"We pray?" I ask. "That's how we grant Bobby his miracle? Prayer?"

"It's worth a shot," Annie says. "There's little we can do from here in Pennsylvania, while Maggie's in a hospital in Bend. Sure, I can tap in to see what happened. And Sophia's medical knowledge can help us understand what options are available for Maggie's care … and for the baby. Otherwise, I'm not sure there's anything else we *can* do."

"Then let's try it," I say, even though a part of me still questions whether requesting any type of assistance like this might actually help. "Let's pray."

Sophia moves toward the sofa and kneels on the rug. Her head tilts low while her lips move in silence. Annie lies down, shuts her eyes, and inhales deeply.

My friends all seem to know what to do. However, I am at a complete loss. I've never felt comfortable praying, maybe because I wasn't so sure anyone was listening. When I was a child, my mother taught me to kneel by my bed, hands by my heart, and recite, "Now I lay me down to sleep." We also prayed before dinner, heads bowed, quickly muttering a short phrase of gratitude. These types of prayers don't seem appropriate now. Occasionally, I pray for Patrick, but mostly as a response to my fears that something might happen to him. Today is different. To grant Bobby's wish for a miracle, we must link directly to God … or Source … whoever. Biting my lip, I realize I have no idea how to do that.

Just ask.

It's the voice. Could it really be that simple? Isn't a certain formality required? Don't I need a particular invocation to connect?

Ask. You will be heard. It truly is that simple.

A strange calmness steadies me. Instead of allowing uncertainty to interfere with my request, I shut my eyes, center myself, and begin sharing what's deep in my heart. *Please God ... please keep Maggie and her baby safe.* My words, while silent, echo louder than anything I know. I repeat the same phrase again and again, just in case God is busy listening to the infinitesimal prayers of others.

The three of us remain in our individual states of prayer for close to twenty minutes. Slowly, one by one, we reconvene at the kitchen counter.

"Do you think it worked?" Annie asks, her voice almost childlike.

"That is what makes prayer so complicated," Sophia says. "When we pray to God, we often think we know the best outcome."

"I don't understand what you mean," Annie says. She tilts her head.

"Sometimes, we are so focused on the immediate situation, as well as the solution we desire, that we do not see the larger picture. While it would be difficult to imagine anything better than both Maggie and the baby recovering, there are many unknowns and elements we cannot predict."

"Like if her child has severe brain damage from the accident?" Annie asks.

"Exactly," Sophia says. "Would having the child survive, only to die later, be what is best for all?" She stares at the floor. "There is no perfect answer. We cannot possibly understand the unforeseen ramifications of our prayers. I suppose that is why at times it appears as if God is not listening." She pauses, looking at me. "Perhaps *He* heard you, but He has other plans."

The doorbell rings. It's Juliette.

"I got here as fast as I could!" She throws her purse on the bench by the front door before joining us in the kitchen.

"Juliette," I say, as an idea begins to form. "When we were in Bend, you said you could speak with Maggie's baby. Are you able to connect to see how the baby is doing?"

"That's what I was trying to do ever since I read your text. But when I reach out, it's fuzzy, not like before. I'm not able to get anything definite, probably because I'm so scared."

Sophia places her hand on Juliette's arm. "Give yourself time," she says. "Insights may come when you are more relaxed and not pressuring yourself for answers."

Juliette sits down on an empty stool and rests her head in her hands.

"How did your conversation with Bobby end?" Annie asks.

"I offered to fly to Bend as soon as possible. He thanked me but asked me to wait. Maggie's father, John, is on his way there now. And Bobby's parents are driving in from Bozeman." I pause and sigh. "I feel so helpless. There must be something we can do, besides pray."

"I'm sending energy to Maggie and the baby," Juliette says. "I started the flow as soon as you told us. Distance healing is still new to me, but I've had some success with it in the past. I'm hoping that with everything I learned in Peru, my juju is getting stronger." It's so strange to hear hesitancy in Juliette's voice. She's always so bold and confident.

"Maybe one of us should go," Sophia offers. "I understand that John is Maggie's father, but they have only recently met. He does not know her like we do. I believe she needs a woman by her side to ensure ..."

Juliette gasps, interrupting Sophia. "He's alive … and thriving … the baby … they took him early … a C-section." Her eyes widen.

In a matter of seconds, our mood skyrockets from despair to hope.

"What about Maggie?" I ask, petrified of what her answer might be.

"I can't tell," Juliette says. "I can only reach out to the baby."

"But the baby is all right?" Sophia asks.

"Yes," Juliette says, smiling and nodding, her voice measured. "He's fine."

Annie becomes quiet. Her eyes shut, and her body slightly sways.

"She's seeing something," Juliette says.

Annie's body stills, and her eyes remain shut. Slowly, the color returns to her face … and Annie *returns* to us.

"Maggie's OK," she says, her eyes widening. "She's breathing on her own, but she's still unconscious. Oh, and I know where she was going. She was headed to Bobby's place." The slightest smile breaks over Annie's face. "That *was* the road we'd been on. She was going there to tell Bobby she was ready to get married. She was about to say yes!"

***

An hour later, Patrick walks in and finds me sitting alone at the counter. My friends have gone, and the house seems uncomfortably empty. "What's for dinner, Mom?" he asks.

I look up at my grown child who leaves for college in two days. A tear falls down my cheek. "Today was kind of crazy," I say, then wrap my arms around him, inhaling his musky scent. I take a step back, exhale loudly, and explain what's going on. "Maggie was in a bad car accident." As the words exit my mouth, tears flow full force. I'd been holding them in all day, trying my best to stay strong. Now, the realization that I won't be able to make a special dinner for my son on one of his last nights home pushes me over the edge.

"I'm sorry," Patrick says. "Is she OK?" He gulps as he asks.

I offer the truth. "I'm not sure. We think her baby's going to make it. But we're still waiting for Maggie to regain consciousness. I'll be calling Bobby later tonight. Hopefully, he'll know more by then."

I trust Annie's clairvoyance, but I don't feel like delving into the entire afternoon's discussion with Patrick.

"Damn, that's rough, Mom."

"It sure is," I say, reaching for a tissue. "How was volunteering?" I offer my best attempt at a smile. Patrick has been helping out with summer camps through the local Boys and Girls Club.

"I can't believe today was my last day," he says in a melancholy tone.

"I know. How'd it go?" I give my full attention to Patrick. In less than forty hours, we'll be dropping him off at college.

"Good, but it was tough saying bye to some of the kids."

I rub his shoulders. He gives me a half smile, then walks off to the family room, flicks on the TV, and flops onto the couch.

When Tom arrives home from work, I bring him up to speed as well, adding a few more details than what I shared with Patrick. Tom used to question Annie's visions at first, but he's beginning to believe she has something special going on. I know he and Jonathon have discussed it on more than one occasion.

"I hope she's right," he says, "and that the baby's healthy." His eyes lock on mine. "How are you?" he asks, taking me into his arms.

"I'm better. At least now I have some hope."

***

After dinner, I call Bobby.

"Marlee," he says when he answers.

"Hey there. I've been thinking about you and Maggie non-stop … and praying. Please tell me you have some good news." I exhale. *Please God.*

"I'm a dad," he says. "Our son is healthy and beautiful. And the doctors are hopeful about Maggie." His voice, still strained, at least sounds better than when we spoke earlier.

"That *is* wonderful news, Bobby."

"They performed a C-section. I wanted to be there, but considering …" he stops, collects himself. "Anyway, Maggie's still unconscious. Her vitals are strong. The doctors think she'll wake up soon." Once he says it, he starts to break down. "God, Marlee … she's got to come through. I love her so much … and now we have a child."

"She will," I say with conviction, though I have no evidence to back this statement.

Yes, she will.

Loud and clear, the voice speaks, confirming what I'd just shared. I say the words again. "She will, Bobby. Yes, she will."

We chat for a bit longer. Prior to hanging up, I repeat my offer to fly to Bend. As before, he asks me to wait. A part of me is grateful. I don't want to miss taking Patrick to college. But I would, if Bobby and Maggie needed me.

"John is here now," he says, "and my parents will arrive in a couple of hours. Maybe you can come and stay with us for a bit, once Maggie's home." His voice sounds cautiously optimistic.

"Of course!" I blurt.

"It would be a big help with the baby." With each word, his tone lightens.

"I would love to."

Right then, my world becomes brighter. A light flickers at the end of this dark tunnel.

***

The kitchen is quiet. Tom left early for work, and Patrick is still sleeping. I pour a cup of coffee then head to the patio. The temperature is perfect, low seventies with little humidity. The sweet smell of summer's fading flowers reminds me that everything must come to an end. Soon it will be fall. Patrick leaves tomorrow, then we leave for Boston. Before I go too far into the future, I pause. I *know* what's ahead. I don't need to dwell on it.

I've worked so hard to cultivate this garden. Gazing at it now, I realize how different mornings will be once we're in Boston. Living downtown, I won't have a yard. Yes, there are parks nearby, but they won't compare to what we have here at home.

Instead of allowing my vibration to drop, I decide to appreciate what is right now … the vibrant golden black-eyed Susans, the rabbit nibbling on the blades of grass, and the hummingbird sucking sugar water from the glass feeder Patrick gave to me for Mother's Day. I can't predict what tomorrow will bring, but I can be grateful for what I have today.

I enjoy my coffee and the quiet, then return to the kitchen and mix up some yogurt and granola. Once at the table with my laptop open, I see there's a message from Juliette, reminding me we have a session this morning, our last before I move. "I'm ready," I type, then mention that the voice appeared last night when I spoke to Bobby.

Messaging Juliette makes me think about my homework from our last session. How often have I chosen happiness, or *kissed what I have never before experienced*, as she put it? Is that what I just did in the yard? Instead of fearing the future, I appreciated what is. I didn't worry about the unknown. This morning, I embraced an openness toward tomorrow. Doing so felt strange, but it also felt good.

Honestly, I'm amazed I'm not a mess. I feel invigorated, as if some of the fears that have held me back in the past have lifted. I'm confident Maggie and the baby will be fine, and I'm excited about Patrick's freshman year, even if tomorrow will be hard. Besides, Colgate's Family Weekend is only five weeks away. Plus, we'll see him during fall break, then for Thanksgiving. Before I know it, the semester will be over, and he'll be home for Christmas.

***

Patrick is heading out to say goodbye to an old friend as Juliette pulls up in her Jeep. He stops and lingers to chat with her, his face turning red. He's always had a crush on my young friend. I'm sure he's not the only guy who does.

"I can't believe he leaves tomorrow," Juliette says as she walks toward the door.

"I know," I agree. "But I'm becoming OK with it. Besides, it's time. He's ready."

Juliette grins at this. "I see you're acing your homework," she says. Then her tone becomes serious. "Have you heard anything from Bobby?"

"Nothing besides what I shared last night. It's still early in Bend. I don't want to wake him. Plus, John and his parents are with him now."

We make our way to the back patio. This time, Juliette begins our session with a prayer for Maggie and her baby. We hold silence for a moment, then discuss all that's happened recently, plus my latest assignment.

"You see the progress you've made, don't you?" she remarks. "You can now identify your fears. You're aware when you replay unpleasant experiences and become anxious about the future. But the most important step …" she pauses, closes her eyes, and holds up one finger, "…is that you know how to choose happiness and break this cycle."

"It won't always work, right? I mean, I'm going to slip up now and then."

"Of course you will," she agrees. "All of us are here to learn." With that, Juliette flips her hair and rolls her eyes, which makes me giggle. "I think you're ready for the next step."

"Which is what?" I ask, curious instead of fearful.

"Discovering your root fear. Once you identify *that*, it becomes easier to understand how your little and big fears relate to this underlying core fear."

"Everything's connected?"

"Yup. There are several major fears most humans possess. Figuring out which one is yours helps you put your puzzle pieces together."

"This sounds like shadow work," I say, "looking into the darkness, then shining a light on what's holding me back."

"Yes! When you shine light on what frightens you most, you take away its power. Slowly, other fears dissipate once the main fear no longer controls you. Does that make sense?"

I nod, waiting for her to say more. Instead of words, she points to the lounge chair. I guess it's time to begin.

Lying down with eyes shut, Juliette's fingers graze my temples in a circular motion. "Relax," she says. "You're safe. If things get too intense, we can stop at any time." She's mystical Juliette now, no longer my fun-loving friend. She seems older, at peace, all-knowing.

My entire muscular system softens as I begin to surrender. Within moments, I feel as though I'm floating. A warm breeze caresses my cheeks.

"Think back to when we first discussed working together," Juliette says. "When you could not trust, could not let go, could not believe the best is yet to come. That's the title of your book, yes?"

"Yes," I murmur.

"Well, why is that?"

I consider her question, not speaking right away. I know all about my fear of uncertainty by now, but what's underneath it? Why do I become uneasy when I don't know what's going to happen? Lack of trust? Yes, but I already know *that*. It must be something bigger ... deeper.

My mind travels backwards in time, revisiting the parts of my life when I was the most fearful. After my mother died ... when I received my diagnosis. Is it death I'm afraid of? I don't think it's that simple. No, it's beyond dying. Could my core fear be connected to the part of me that isn't sure whether God exists? I pause. What if my fear were true and there is no God?

Shivers start to run up and down my body. I dig deeper. If there is no God, then after we die, it's just ... lights out ... over and done? I'd cease to exist. Or would I be somewhere else, *all alone*? Those last two words stick in my mind. My arms begin to shake. Then my legs follow.

"What is it, Marlee?"

"I'm afraid of being all alone." As I admit this, tears well in the corners of my eyes, then spill down my cheeks. I let them fall freely, not bothering to stop them.

"And if you are alone, what does that say about everyone else in your life?"

"They've left. They're no longer with me."

"Aha ... so you have arrived at your core fear ... abandonment by those you most love. Now do you understand why Patrick going to college is impacting you so much? And why it's so hard for you to leave Philadelphia?"

Juliette's right. It's all connected. So is my fear that my relationship with Tom might change once Patrick's gone. Deep down, conscious or not, I'm scared of being left by those I love. Of course it makes sense. My parents have both passed, and I'm basically estranged from my siblings. Thank God for Sue and Pete.

Juliette's hands move above my body. I cannot feel her touch on my skin, but there's no denying the energetic pull. "I'm helping you release this core fear," she says. "This is huge, Marlee. Not many people can so easily identify theirs."

Sometimes I wonder how much simpler life would be if I were one of those people. At this moment, it's as though someone is stretching my arms and legs in opposite directions, yanking them to the point of almost, but not quite, breaking. Then suddenly, my limbs go limp on the lounge chair.

"Now that I know my core fear, what do I do about it?" I ask.

"Acknowledging your fear of abandonment releases it from the shadow," Juliette says. "Now you can start to see how it has dictated your behaviors and actions over time, maybe even dominated them. You'll be amazed by how much it's kept you in your comfort zone. But now you can choose differently. This is tough work. Abandonment is an issue for many of us … myself included."

"But how do I choose differently?" I ask.

"There are two main ways," she says. "Self-love is the first. When you accept yourself, you realize how much others love and care about you … that the people closest to you will never truly leave. But if you're constantly self-critical or judging others, it's natural to think they feel the same way about you. As for the second …" she pauses. "It's a bit more challenging." She tilts her head and gives me an "I dare you" look.

"To fully release your fear of abandonment, you must develop faith in something higher than yourself." She looks deep into my eyes, as if trying to imprint this thought in my mind. "When you truly believe that Source, God, Spirit—whatever term you are comfortable with—loves you unconditionally, you realize you will never be alone."

"You know I struggle with that," I say. "I *want* to believe in God, and I mostly do. It's just that there's this part of me that keeps wondering *what if* God doesn't exist. Why is this so hard for me?"

"That's the uncertainty aspect coming into play," Juliette says. "You like to be assured, have all your 'I's' dotted, your 'T's' crossed. But life isn't always that way. If it were, there'd be no adventure, surprise, growth … only predictable outcomes. Of course, it's your choice. You don't *have* to do anything. If you decide *not* to examine your lack of faith, you'll remain where you are, safely nestled in your comfort zone. Is that what you really want?" She scrunches her nose as she asks me this.

Of course, Juliette knows the answer. So do I. Yet, doing what she's asking may be the hardest thing I've ever attempted … much more difficult than Patrick leaving or us moving. This is the ultimate surrender … trusting that something I can't see, hear, or feel exists. I may as well take a huge leap off a cliff, accepting there's no net below.

Chapter 14

MAGGIE

August 21st

I try to open my eyelids, but just the thought of lifting them hurts. It's not only my eyes either. I feel a steady throb of excruciating pain across my entire body. *What happened? What's wrong with me?*

"I think she's coming to," someone says. The voice is muffled. Then I hear the same phrase again. I know this voice. It's John, my father. *Why is he here?*

"Maggie, can you hear me?" There's a slight pressure on my hand … it's Bobby. But then I hear crying. *Bobby's crying. Why?*

There are strange noises in the background … a steady cadence of beeps, drips, buzzes. Then a woman speaks. "She's responding," she says. "Maggie, if you can hear me, I want you to wiggle your toes."

I try to follow this voice's instructions. Am I actually wiggling my toes?

"Good job," the woman says. I keep at it. Not just my toes … I want to shake everything, any part of me that will move. I try to sit up, but the pulsating pain hits me again.

"Try to relax. You've been through a lot," the voice says. "I'm Dr. Jenner. You are in St. Charles Hospital." Her tone is kind yet direct. "Maggie, you were in a car accident. Do you remember anything?"

Slowly, images form in my mind. I'm spinning. There's a honk. Then a white truck comes toward me. The thoughts cause my pulse to quicken. I wiggle my toes again.

"I know this is scary," the doctor says. "But trust me … you are going to be fine."

I rack my brain trying to see glimpses of what happened before everything went blank. There's a curvy road. But where? Why was I on it?

Panic sets in. The quiet, steady beeps shift to a frenzied string of warning alarms. *My baby … I have a baby … where is my baby?*

I strain to move my arms to my stomach but can't. I press my lips together to try to make a word. "Ba … ba … baby…" Something warm presses against my cheek … a kiss … Bobby's lips. His breath brushes against my ear. "Our baby is fine," I hear him say.

A peace comes over me. I drift back to sleep.

***

"You're gonna be OK, babe," Bobby whispers. He squeezes my hand. There's a sharp sting when the doctor lifts the bandages. My eyelids tighten reflexively, adjusting to the fluorescent lights.

"Try to open your eyes," the doctor says. A hand touches my forehead. It takes a few moments, but I start to see four people around me—Bobby, my father, a woman I presume is Dr. Jenner, and a young technician. No one says anything. They're all waiting for me. I try to talk, but my lips are swollen. Slowly, I try to form a sentence. "What happened? Where's our baby?"

"We realized it was best for you and the baby to proceed with a C-section," Dr. Jenner says. "One of our top obstetricians performed the surgery. You were unconscious from the accident. That is why you can't remember any of this."

"Our son is healthy," Bobby says. "He's a fighter." I look at Bobby. His eyes are bloodshot, not the sparkling blue I'm used to. Standing next to him, my father appears older and more serious than I've ever seen him look.

"A tractor trailer," my father begins to explain. "It was speeding. It hit you from behind. You lost control of your car. Then a pickup truck struck you head-on." He pauses, reaches out and touches my face. "Maggie, you were lucky." Tears well in his eyes.

Slowly, the images appear in my mind. "I remember," I say. It hurts to talk, but I get the words out. "The truck that hit me … " I freeze. "The driver?" I ask.

"He's fine," Bobby says. "He's the one who called 911. When the EMTs got there, he was with you, holding your hand and praying."

"Praying?"

"Yeah," Bobby softly says. A stranger tending to me and asking God's help … is that what saved me? Saved us?

"Where's the baby?" I tentatively ask.

"He's in NICU," Dr. Jenner says. "He's doing beautifully."

"When did this happen?" My words come slowly. I'm not sure I want to know the answer.

"Friday morning, two days ago," Bobby says, biting his lower lip.

"I've been out this entire time?" I gasp.

"Yes. The doctors were giving you medication. They didn't want you to come to until your body was ready to handle everything." Bobby chokes up a bit when he shares this.

"When did my dad get here?"

"Friday night. My parents arrived yesterday. They're at the house, finishing up some things." A look of gratitude comes across Bobby's face.

"And our baby was born on Friday?" The timing of everything confuses me.

"Yes … not too long after they admitted you." Bobby's face softens. "He's amazing, Maggie. Just wait. He has your nose." My heart lifts.

"You're sure he's good?" Words come easier now.

"Better than good. All his vitals are strong. The docs want him to stay in the NICU, until his lungs are stronger. But you should have heard him holler when he was born. They didn't let me in the room. I was standing outside." Bobby grins. "You could hear his cries straight through the walls."

"I want to see him," I say, though want is the wrong word. I *need* to see our son.

"Let me see what I can do," Dr. Jenner says then leaves the room.

Ten minutes later, there's a knock on the door. A young, red-haired woman enters, introducing herself as Betsy, the second-shift nurse. "Maggie, would you like to meet your baby?"

Tears stream down my face as I nod my head yes. She makes a quick call from the room's phone. Within moments, another woman pushes a portable bed into my room. Together they transfer me onto it. With Bobby by my side, they roll me out of the room and toward the elevator.

***

"Oh, Bobby ..." There are no words to describe the sensations swirling through every cell of my body as I gaze at our newborn through the large glass window of the NICU.

"He's incredible," Bobby says. "*You're* incredible." His eyes lock on mine.

"He has your chin," I gulp as I take in our child from the short distance between us. "He's so tiny ... and wrinkly."

"He's nine weeks early," Bobby reminds. "He has no body fat. That's why he's in the incubator. Luckily, his lungs are strong. But the doctor told me to be prepared to see him on a ventilator, just in case they feel the need to support his breathing."

I gulp. The doctors say he is doing well, but things could shift. I say a quick prayer, asking God to keep my baby safe.

"It seems strange that we didn't pick a name before," Bobby says.

"I know." I sigh as I watch this sweet baby, searching for a name that fits. Suddenly, a thought comes to me. "What do you think of John?" I ask, wondering how Bobby would feel about naming the child after my father.

"I can't think of a better name," he says.

"Will your parents be OK with it?" I ask.

"Are you kidding? They'll love it." He smiles as he says this. "Mom's been texting every few minutes, asking how you are, how I am, how the baby is."

"Tell them to come here. They need to meet their grandchild." I mean every word. I can only imagine how much Midge, his mom, has been worrying. I assume Bobby's dad, Bill, acted stoically. That's where Bobby gets it from. But deep down, I suspect he's been as upset as Midge.

"I'll let them know to come and meet us outside of the NICU this afternoon."

"John Parker," I say. "I like the way it sounds. We can call him Johnny until he gets older." It hurts to smile, but I can't help myself. After a brief pause, I ask, "What about a middle name?"

Bobby tilts his head for a moment. "What about my grandad's?" he suggests.

"Samuel? Yes. John Samuel Parker. There you are," I say to our newborn, who seems to be sleeping. I softly tap on the glass, and John Samuel Parker opens his eyes ever so slightly. Crystal blue, just like his dad's. I hope they stay that way.

Chapter 15

MARLEE

August 21ˢᵗ

We're all quiet as Tom backs the Suburban out of the garage. The car is loaded to the brim with Patrick's things—duffle bags of clothing, more bags filled with sheets, towels, pillows, and a comforter, his X-box and games, and an equipment bag for two lacrosse sticks, lax balls, a helmet, soccer balls, and cleats. I added a couple of recyclable shopping bags filled with tins of cookies, pretzels, nuts, beef jerky, and other treats he can keep nearby and snack on when he misses home.

I glance in the rearview mirror and gaze at Patrick. His cheek pressed against the window, our son seems contemplative. I suppose he's taking in every moment as we head out. Last night, I cooked his favorite meal—grilled salmon, peas, mashed potatoes, and Caesar salad. We even opened a bottle of wine we'd been saving. I didn't mind him drinking a little. I'm sure it won't be the last time, now that he's off to college. Still, the thought of him attending parties triggers me. Before I go straight into a fear-based mode, worrying about what's ahead, I catch myself and visualize him making good decisions.

***

Four hours and ten minutes later, we pull onto campus and navigate our way toward Drake Hall. A young woman with a clipboard directs us to follow a line of packed cars filled with other incoming freshmen, their parents, and everything they'll need for the upcoming semester.

Once we park, a group of upperclassmen swarm the car. Each one wears a maroon t-shirt that reads "Welcome Freshman." A cute blonde girl asks Patrick what his room number is. In no time, five upperclassmen begin unloading the Suburban and carrying things up to the second floor.

"You're going to love it here," she says to Patrick. "It's *so* much fun." With that brief, friendly exchange, I realize he's going to be fine. More than fine. I know he's going to *love* this new life he's about to start. Gazing out toward the sea of students, it's evident our son has found his people.

It takes two hours to help get Patrick unpacked and settled in. He lets me make his bed, but my son insists on putting away his clothes. Sure, I tidy things up when he's not looking. And while he and his roommate, a kid from California, head across the hall to meet some other guys on the floor, I quickly reorganize his underwear drawer. Tom shakes his head.

"You really think his clothes will stay that way?" he jokes.

"No," I reply. "But it's the least I can do." Of course, I recognize my pattern. "I guess it just makes me feel better to do *mom* stuff one last time," I sigh.

Tom takes me into his arms. "You'll have plenty of *mom* moments to come. He'll be OK."

"I know," I sniff. "It's going to be hard to say goodbye."

"Absolutely, but he's ready."

"You're right," I nod.

"It's his time to figure out who he is."

I nod my head, agreeing with Tom wholeheartedly. Besides, getting emotional will only make this harder for Patrick.

"I'll keep it together," I laugh, wiping my nose with the back of my hand.

"Hey," Patrick says, bounding back into the room. "I just heard from our hall advisor that we have a meeting in, like, ten minutes. Then we're all getting ice cream. There are trucks on the lawns outside the dorms." His eyes sparkle. Without saying so, our son is asking us to leave.

"Well then, I guess this is goodbye," I say, choking back tears. But I don't need to walk toward Patrick. He rushes toward me.

"I'm gonna miss you, Mom," he says. "But you'll be up for Family Weekend, right?"

"Wouldn't miss it for the world," I say, embracing my only child. Yes, my voice cracks, but I refrain from shedding another tear. I pull away and look into my son's eyes. "Have fun, and be careful. And please stay in touch, all right?"

"You got it." He gives me another hug. I move away so Tom can say goodbye. Their parting is silent, a bear hug without words. Then Patrick rushes out the door and joins a few other kids in the hallway. When I look at Tom, it's clear that he's the emotional one. I'd prepared myself, committed to not getting upset. Maybe Tom thought it would just be another goodbye. I don't think he anticipated his reaction. I take his hand and kiss his cheek. "Let's go home."

He nods, choking back tears. He maintains his composure until we're safely inside the Suburban. Then he lets loose, crying for the first time in years … since his parents died.

I place my hand on his leg. As he turns toward me, his face softens. His fingers brush against my face. "I love you," he says. And just like that, I know we're good.

Chapter 16

MAGGIE

September 20th – 26th

Hibiscus mint tea steeps in a flowered ceramic mug. I place one of Midge's homemade blueberry muffins on a plate and slowly walk to the back patio. It's 7:30 in the morning, and the sun is already warming things up.

Yesterday, Bobby's parents headed back to Bozeman. Bobby is at work now, but he'll be home in a couple of hours to take me to the hospital. It's the first time I've been alone since the accident.

Being outside at our house feels so different from anything I've ever known. In Pittsburgh, my backyard was filled with peonies, a lilac bush, hostas, and black-eyed Susans. My mother had a birdbath, with lilies of the valley growing beneath it. Out here, our backyard is filled with rabbit brush, manzanita, and Oregon sage that covers the dry dusty volcanic soil. In the distance stand larches and ponderosa pines, with junipers interspersed between them. While Bill was here, he added a few plants around the patio to make it feel homey. I suppose we'll plant a few more things before winter. And Bobby promised he'd build a greenhouse next spring. I've always dreamed of growing my own vegetables.

I lean my head back and think about what's ahead. Marlee flies in tonight and stays for a week. Then Juliette arrives two days before Marlee leaves.

They didn't need to come. I told them I'd be fine, but they weren't having it. Besides, Marlee announced they'd already purchased their tickets. She was adamant about being here to help when Johnny comes home. Something tells me Bobby is somehow behind their coming. Still, knowing Marlee and Juliette, they're willing participants.

Every time I think about taking care of our newborn—and a preemie at that—a long string of emotions begins to stir within me. There's fear … inadequacy … excitement … joy … awe … all muddled together. Sometimes it's overwhelming, causing me to feel unbalanced. I talked to Midge about it. She assured me these feelings are perfectly normal and that all new moms go through their own versions of it. Annie confirmed the same thing during our most recent call. She says she still experiences these emotions, even though it's close to a year since Ella was born. Annie explained how hormones shift during and after a baby's birth, making everything feel topsy-turvy. "Well," I said in response, "I'm definitely one helluva wobbly mess!"

Whenever I feel that way, Sophia is right there on the other end of a text message. Within minutes, she responds with traditional and holistic suggestions, offering me plenty of options. I love this amazing network of women around me. What would I do without them?

Still, there's something bothering me … something I can't figure out. I don't remember where I was going the morning of the accident. I recall Bobby telling me he decided to work on the house before heading to another project. But that doesn't explain why *I* was on that road. Besides, my office is in the opposite direction.

A beautiful monarch hovers by the milkweed that's just to the right of me. A swirling sensation moves through my stomach. *Oh my God! I felt fluttering butterflies that morning*! But it was more than butterflies. It was an overwhelming joy … a tickling sensation that made me laugh uncontrollably. Now I remember. Our baby was responding to the idea of us all being a family. *I was about to say yes to Bobby!*

The morning of the accident, I was finally ready to commit to marrying Bobby. It takes less than a moment to know that I still am. How do I tell him?

***

"Hey there," Bobby says as he walks onto the back patio. "Are you ready to go? Today's the last day we need to visit Johnny. Tomorrow, we get to bring him home!" His voice inflects as he leans down to kiss my cheek.

I look up. Bobby's been under so much pressure lately, sleeping poorly, not exercising, and eating way too much hospital food. But still, he glows when he talks about our son. I turn toward him, noting how his thick dark hair glistens with the morning light. I could not be more in love with this man.

"I am ready," I softly say, my eyes gazing deep into his.

"Great … then we should get going."

"No, Bobby." I pause and carefully stand up out of the chair, instinctively holding my incision. Now directly in front of Bobby, I take his hands in mine and look deep into his eyes.

"I just remembered why I was driving on that road the day of the accident," I say. "I wanted to see you." I swallow several times, my eyes remaining locked on his. "To tell you that *I'm ready … to be married.*"

Bobby pulls me toward him, his lips searching for mine. Even though his embrace hurts a bit, I don't care. He still wants me … wants us. He whispers, "I've been waiting so long."

Wrapped in his arms, there's no doubt in my mind … I'm absolutely ready. When I finally take a step back, my eyes naturally go toward the horizon. The distant mountains glow in the morning light. The ponderosas appear majestic, and the tall grasses dance in the wind. I turn to my right, where at least two-dozen monarchs flit around the milkweed plant, swirling in circles, dancing in delight.

***

I insist on going with Bobby to pick up Marlee, even though he suggests I stay at home and rest. Twenty minutes later, we spot Marlee standing outside of Redmond Municipal Airport. Bobby helps her with her luggage. In no time, we're on our way home. After a barrage of questions about Johnny and me, she updates us on Patrick's first weeks at college as well as their move to Boston. When there's a pause in the conversation, I share our news.

"You're getting married!" Marlee gushes. "Congratulations!" From the backseat, she places her hands on my shoulders and gives me a warm squeeze. "I'm so happy for you both!"

"Maggie finally came to her senses," Bobby teases as he turns onto the parkway.

"When's the big day?" Marlee asks. "What will you do? Will your dad be there?" Her questions come flying out one after the other.

"We really haven't talked about it yet. We just decided today."

"We?" Bobby playfully asks. I laugh then place my hand on his leg.

"I'd like it to be simple," I say. "The courthouse, or something like that."

Bobby smiles. "Whatever you want," he says, even though something in his tone suggests he has other ideas.

"You know," Marlee starts, "Juliette *could* marry you. She's officiated other weddings, and we do have a day in our stays that overlap."

I take out my phone, pulling up the calendar.

"You mean we could get married on Tuesday the 27th?" My jaw drops open when I ask this.

"Why not? You could have a small gathering at your new home. It would be so lovely, and I know Juliette would be honored to perform the ceremony."

I look over at Bobby. "What do you think? Would your parents be able to come on such short notice?" I wonder if my dad would be available.

"Sounds good to me," Bobby says, grinning. "And you know my mom. She'll be here in a heartbeat, wearing a blue dress, or whatever you want the mother of the groom to wear." He starts to laugh. Midge has probably already discussed this with him.

However, I'm not sure about my dad making the trip again so soon. He was just here. Besides, he has his own family in Florida. Still, maybe he *could*. Even though it's late in Florida, I send him a quick text, letting him know we just decided to make everything official. I ask if there's any way he'd be able to join us. Three minutes later, my phone pings.

"Oh my God! My dad responded … he's coming!"

"Then we're set," Bobby says. He gently squeezes my hand. I bite my lower lip and nod, amazed at how quickly it's all happening.

"Not so fast," Marlee chimes in, breaking the spell some. "There are still many details to handle … like food, music, flowers. But don't worry, I'll take care of everything." Her tone is even, as though assured this is the easiest thing to do.

Why is everyone so calm? I'm now getting married five and a half weeks after giving birth while in a coma! I take in a deep breath and lean back into my seat, staring straight ahead. Am I crazy? Johnny is just coming home from the hospital tomorrow. As exhausting as it has been spending my days in the NICU, having a preemie at home will be even more tiring. *And now I'm getting married?*

As if she can read my mind, Marlee says, "Maggie, your only concerns should be Johnny and taking care of yourself. I'm here to help with those *and* manage your wedding plans. Trust me."

Without turning around to face her, I can sense Marlee's reassuring smile. I sink even deeper into the seat and let out a soft sigh before dozing off.

***

"Are you sure it's in correctly?" I ask Bobby as he triple checks the infant car seat. Instead of answering, he comes around to my side of the car and gives me a luscious kiss. "It won't just be the two of us anymore," he says, lightly touching my cheek.

Truthfully, since I've been home from the hospital, it has not been the two of us. Our house has been a revolving door … my father, Bobby's parents, and now Marlee. Still, I am beyond grateful for the company and unwavering support.

"I can't wait to meet Johnny," Marlee calls from the front step, waving goodbye as we pull out of the driveway. We invited her to come to the hospital, but she insisted on staying behind, claiming this was our time as a family.

"I think Marlee's pretty excited about planning our wedding," Bobby says as we make a right out of the long driveway.

"She's amazing, isn't she? There's no way I could do this without her." I pause, suddenly concerned that Bobby's mother may feel a little slighted. "Do you think your mom is bummed that Marlee is handling everything?"

Bobby smiles and shakes his head. "Mom's fine. I talked with her this morning. She's just happy we're getting married. She did offer to help, if there's anything we need."

"Are you kidding? She's done so much already. Getting the house in order while I was in the hospital … I don't know what we would have done without your parents and my dad. And Sandy too. She spent her free weekend packing up my apartment while my dad drove boxes to the house."

"Maybe we could find something for my mom to do that would make her feel special."

"What if we asked her to hold Johnny during the ceremony?"

Bobby gently places his arm around me. "She'll love that."

***

Bobby drops me off at the hospital entrance, then parks in the lot. Once upstairs in the NICU, we get busy signing paperwork.

In a few minutes, a nurse named Nelly reviews a number of baby basics with us, things we'd already learned in childbirth class. I'm grateful for the refresher course.

"Do you think you could stop by our house after work each day to make sure we're doing it correctly?" I joke, trying to be funny. Yet a part of me is dead serious.

"You will be a wonderful mother," she says then offers me a wink.

"Sometimes I really wonder," I gulp.

"Everyone has jitters. It's natural to be apprehensive, especially with your first child." Nelly reassures me with a warm smile.

"I just don't want to do anything wrong," I admit.

Nelly gently places her arm around me. "If you're ever doubting yourself, lead from your heart. Don't get too stuck in your head with worries. Allow your instincts to guide you." With that, she turns and heads toward the nursery.

In a few moments, Nelly returns with Johnny, who's swaddled in a cute yellow blanket covered in gray penguins. She hands him to me. When I first held him, I was nervous, afraid I was doing it wrong. But at this moment, the sensation of our baby in my arms could not feel more natural. Johnny opens his eyes. He appears to be searching into my soul, like the little bird in the children's book who kept asking various animals, "Are you my mother?" Just in case he's wondering, I softly say, "I am, Johnny, I am." I am his mama, and even though I might not know everything a mother's supposed to, I will do whatever necessary to protect my son.

"Are you ready?" Nelly's voice brings me back to the present. She then leads the three of us to the elevator. Once we arrive on the main floor, Nelly waits with me while Bobby heads to get the truck.

"Johnny … you've been through a lot," I whisper to my son. "We all have. And now we're going home … together."

***

I cannot imagine what life would be like without Marlee here. Moving through the days like a zombie, I feel and look like a total mess. Marlee insists that I take a shower each day while she keeps an eye on Johnny. And whenever I return to relieve her, she looks completely content holding and rocking our baby. She's a natural. I wish I were too.

Juliette arrives tomorrow. Our wedding's the following day. Things are moving so quickly. I wish I could savor these moments, but I'm so exhausted, I can barely lift my fork to eat.

Johnny lies in his bassinette next to the coffee table. Harry lies attentively beneath it, clearly the baby's newly appointed guard dog.

"I hope you like this," Marlee says. She places bowls of rice topped with sautéed vegetable with sliced chicken in front of us. She darts back to the kitchen and returns with dishes of mixed greens and a platter of avocado, fresh herbs, and sour cream. She fills her own bowl then joins us, sitting down next to me. A few bites into the meal, Johnny stirs and lets out a brief cry. Harry stands to alert us.

"He's fine," Marlee sweetly says.

"I can't help it," I say. "I jump whenever he makes a peep."

"You'll get the hang of it," she assures. She's been trying to convince me to give the baby time and space to settle himself. Self-soothing, as she calls it. Bobby agrees with Marlee's approach. I know I should trust my intuition, but it seems to be missing when it comes to mothering.

Johnny makes a few more gurgles, then falls into a peaceful slumber. Harry lies down and crosses his paws in front of him, like a statue that guards the Egyptian pyramids.

"How many hours of sleep did you get last night?" Marlee asks as she returns to the kitchen to take a pie out of the oven.

"I fed the baby before I went to bed. That was around 10 p.m. He woke up at 1:30 in the morning, then again a few hours later. So…" I start to yawn before I can even do the math.

"I know Johnny's still young and was born early, but it would be great for *both* of you if he gets on a schedule where you only need to wake up once during the night."

Hearing this, Bobby gives me an "I told you so" glance.

"He's just so tiny," I say. "And if he's hungry, shouldn't I feed him?"

"Yes," Marlee agrees, "but you need to get rest too. Otherwise, you'll become rundown." She joins us at the table. "What if Bobby gives him a bottle before he goes to bed?"

"That's a good idea," Bobby chimes in. "I'm up till 11 o'clock most nights."

While I still have the pump and plenty of bottles from when Johnny was in NICU, I haven't used them since he came home. "Isn't it *my job* to feed my baby?" I blurt. My shoulders slump. Tears start to form in my eyes.

"Oh, honey, there's nothing wrong with bottle feeding," Marlee says. She places a hand on my shoulder. "Remember, the nurses bottle-fed him in the hospital. What if you want … or need … to leave Johnny for more than an hour or two? Having him comfortable with the bottle is a good thing. Besides, it allows Bobby a chance to feed Johnny … and gives them time for some bonding of their own."

I take a moment to consider what she's proposing. I realize how *on call* I've been feeling. And I suppose I still am a bit guilt-ridden that I couldn't always be there in the hospital to feed him whenever he was hungry. Maybe I'm trying to make up for that.

"Imagine going to sleep by 9 p.m.," Marlee continues. "Bobby gives him a bottle around 11 o'clock. After that, Johnny should be able to hold off until 2:30 in the morning before he's hungry again. By that time, you'll have gotten close to five hours of sleep! Then, after that feeding, maybe he won't wake until 6 a.m."

"It's worth a try … right babe?" Bobby says. He wipes a few tears from my cheeks.

"OK … we can *try*," I agree.

***

It's clear that Marlee is a genius. I'm asleep by 9:15 tonight. Bobby takes the next shift. My feeding duty isn't until around 2:50 in the morning. I wake feeling surprisingly rested.

***

Marlee must have been a wedding planner in a past lifetime. When I accepted her offer to take care of things, she asked how much I wanted to be involved. The old me, before the accident, would have wanted to do everything. But now, with Johnny here, plus my recovery, I'm too damn exhausted. I gave Marlee carte blanche. And she's loving it.

All week she's been making phone calls, attending to every detail while taking care of us. Yesterday, she spoke to the florist and chose the flowers as she made a double batch of cookies. Friday morning, she casually listened to three playlists from prospective musicians while designing and emailing the wedding invites. She makes everything seem effortless, even if it's not. Before heading to the airport to pick up Juliette, she did three loads of laundry, prepped tonight's dinner, and made chicken soup. I told her I'd be fine with leftovers, but she insisted her homemade soup was the perfect lunch for a new mom. And she's been double-batching everything, leaving us with extras in the freezer. As much as I'm looking forward to spending time with Juliette, I'll miss Marlee's pampering. I don't think Juliette is anywhere near the cook Marlee is. Still, in all fairness, is anyone?

I hear my car pull into the driveway. Juliette's flight landed forty minutes ago. I offered to go with Marlee to pick her up, but she insisted I stay home and rest. One door closes, then another. Thankfully, the baby monitor stays silent.

I force myself up and walk as quickly as possible to the door. The accident and C-section were over a month ago, however I'm nowhere near to my normal self. I can't imagine running, even though my doctor said I'd be cleared to start exercising next month.

"The new mama," Juliette squeals when she sees me. "I've missed you!" She hugs me like she hasn't seen me in years, even though it's been less than three months. "How are you?"

"Good … exhausted … both," I laugh. "Each day gets easier. Marlee's been a saint. Just wait till you hear about everything she's done for tomorrow." I let go of Juliette, then wrap my arms around Marlee, who has been like a surrogate mother to me this whole week.

"It's me who wants to thank *you*," Marlee says. She clears her throat and motions for us all to sit down at the counter while she starts the kettle. "It's been wonderful being here and helping with your wedding plans. I doubt I'll ever have this opportunity again. Something tells me that whomever Patrick marries won't allow it." She laughs, but then becomes serious. "Honestly, this is a true gift, Maggie." She sniffs back tears as she offers me a sweet smile.

"Hey … no sad stuff," Juliette playfully scolds. "I just got here. It's time to have some fun!"

She hops off the stool, retrieves her suitcase, and pulls out a bejeweled tiara. "If you're getting married tomorrow, then tonight's your bachelorette party!"

Marlee grabs her phone and takes a picture as Juliette sets the crown on my head.

"Seriously, you're joking, right?"

"Nope," Marlee laughs. "We cleared it with Bobby. His parents will be here sometime this afternoon, and John's arriving a little later. Once everyone is settled, we're heading out!"

"Bobby's really OK being in charge of the baby?" I ask. Marlee just shoots me a glance. "OK, I get it," I grimace. "He's probably more comfortable with Johnny than I am."

Juliette wraps her arm around my shoulder. "Maggie," she says, "I'm sure you're an amazing mom. But you're getting married tomorrow. So, let's go out and have fun tonight."

"If I can keep my eyes open," I say, shaking my head.

"Be glad you've just had a baby," Marlee laughs. "Otherwise, Juliette may have dragged us all to Nashville."

"OK, OK … you win. But with nursing, I really can't drink."

"Haven't you heard of pump and dump?" Marlee asks.

"You can do that?"

"Well, I wouldn't make a practice of it. But I did it … on more than one occasion. We went to a wedding when Patrick was five weeks old. I was so excited to be around adults … and out of the house. Well, after three glasses of champagne, I was pretty tipsy. Luckily, I had extra breast milk ready in the fridge. When I got home, Tom fed Patrick. I pumped and …"

"What?"

"Watered the geraniums with it," Marlee giggles. I laugh, envisioning an engorged post-partum Marlee outside in her garden, in the dark, dumping alcohol-infused breast milk on her plants.

"Let's get serious for a moment," Juliette interrupts. "Marlee, clue me in on our plans for tomorrow?"

Marlee's vision of the wedding sounds absolutely perfect. I lose myself a little as she lays things out for Juliette … the small ceremony on the back patio, just eleven people … the caterer's country supper, everything local and organic … the floral arrangements full of dahlias, including my bouquet.

"But what should I wear?" I interrupt. "When I asked you earlier in the week, you told me not to worry. But I'm starting to." I bite my lower lip.

"Well, now seems to be as good of time as any," Marlee says. On cue, Juliette retrieves one of the roller bags sitting by the front door. Marlee takes it upstairs to her bedroom.

"What's going on?" I ask. Juliette ignores me and pivots to her own question.

"Did you want anything particular in your vows, or do you trust me?"

"Vows! Oh no! I totally forgot. My brain isn't functioning. Shit. I don't even have a ring for Bobby! What do I do about his ring? I totally spaced." A heaviness comes over me. This is all happening too fast.

"Oh Maggie, don't worry. I'll take care of the vows," Juliette says as she pulls me toward her for a hug. "Now the ring … hmmm … Bobby doesn't seem to be a jewelry kind of guy, right?" She takes a step back and laughs. But she's right. I nod. "OK, so why not do something totally original?"

"Does it need to be something he can wear?"

"Not necessarily," Juliette replies. "But it should be meaningful to both of you. Don't worry about it. We'll figure it out." She waves her hand as if this is no big deal, even though it is to me. *Think. What could I give to Bobby?*

Before I have an answer, Marlee comes down the stairs, carrying a large garment bag. She gently places it on the sofa. I move closer, speechless as she unzips the bag and holds up the most beautiful ivory lace wedding gown I've ever seen.

"This was mine," she says. "I knew there would be no time to find a wedding dress. So, I asked Juliette to pick this up at our house in Radnor and bring it with her. I'd be honored if you'll wear it tomorrow."

"Oh Marlee." I gently touch the bodice, admiring the intricate details. "Are you sure?"

"Nothing would make me happier." Marlee's eyes moisten with tears.

"Do you think it will fit? I haven't lost all my baby weight." My practical side takes over as I eye the waistline.

"Definitely," Marlee says. "I was never as thin as you naturally are." She smiles. "It should fit perfectly."

As she hands me the dress, I freeze for a moment. All I can do is stare at the gorgeous gown. "I never imagined having a wedding dress like this," I say. "I mean … my mother never married, so there was nothing of hers for me to wear. And since this is all so sudden, I knew there was no time to buy my own."

"Well, it's not like you can just pick one off a rack anyway," Juliette says. "Besides, you deserve something special."

"I'm dying to see you in this," Marlee cuts in. "Go. Try it on. Chop-chop!"

★★★

I hear a knock at the bedroom door.

"Would you like some help buttoning the back?" Marlee asks.

"Please," I say. When she steps in and sees me in her dress, a lone tear falls down her cheek.

"You look stunning." Marlee walks behind me and begins to fasten the buttons. When she's done, I walk into the master bath to look in the mirror. The gown is a little snug across my back, probably from my swollen boobs. But overall, it's a near-perfect fit.

About six seconds later, Juliette bops into the room. "Damn, you look awesome, Maggie! Now … let's talk about your hair."

"I don't know. Any ideas?"

"You *could* wear it up, but I kinda like it down," Juliette says. "Marlee, what do you think?" Juliette looks at Marlee as she lifts my hair from my shoulders, twirling it into a loose knot.

"I agree with keeping it down," Marlee says. "Maggie, your hair looks beautiful just as it is."

"Oh, I almost forgot," Juliette jumps back in. She hands me a black velvet box. When I open the lid, two exquisite sapphire earrings shine up at me.

"The dress is something borrowed, so I thought you could use something old and blue," Juliette says. "They were my grandmother's earrings, from my father's side."

"Oh my God, Juliette. They're gorgeous." I remove one from the box and gaze at the brilliant blue stone.

"We still need to find something new," Marlee says. As if on cue, there's a cry from the nursery. Johnny's awake.

"Does Johnny count?" I ask, giggling at my own joke.

"Why not?"

"He's going to be hungry," I say, snapping back to the moment. "Would you mind unbuttoning me?"

Marlee undoes the back of the dress, and I slip into my shorts and top. When I enter the nursery, I call out his name. "I'm here, Johnny." His face relaxes. He stops crying. Could he know my voice already?

"Let me see this precious baby," Juliette says. She walks in and beelines toward his crib. Johnny's eyes fixate on her. Is that even possible at his age? I swear he tracks her every movement. Sure, I know Juliette has many gifts, but I didn't expect that captivating babies would be one of them.

She leans over the railing and picks up Johnny. He snuggles against her, cooing as if they've met before.

"Ahh," I say.

"What?" Juliette asks in a whisper.

"You and he are old friends. Remember? From June? You talked to him. He told you he wanted us to be a family."

"That's right. And then it happened."

"I think he's thanking you."

Chapter 17

MARLEE

September 27th – 28th

The sun's rays warm the flagstone patio. I've learned that late afternoon is often the nicest time of day in Central Oregon. I'm grateful we planned the wedding for 5 p.m.

Late last night, after we returned from Maggie's impromptu bachelorette party, Bobby stayed up to build a wooden wedding arch, then tucked it away in his woodshed, out of sight. This morning, while Maggie was bathing Johnny, he walked Juliette and me out to see it. We both loved the craftmanship, but Bobby felt like it needed a feminine touch. "To make it more 'wedding-like,'" as he put it. She and I got busy adding branches, flowers, and greens.

Now Maggie and Bobby stand beneath it, in the presence of those dearest to them, and exchange vows. Cradling Maggie's bouquet, I watch as she places her carnelian pyramid, a gift from Francisco, into Bobby's hand. This is what she chose in lieu of a wedding band.

Her voice is shaky as she speaks. "Bobby, a wise man gave this to me. He told me its peak signified how we are limitless. We can be and achieve whatever we desire. And the pyramid's solid foundation reminds us we possess everything we need, to hold us up and keep us strong."

She pauses to wipe a tear from her cheek. "I give this to you as a symbol of my love. Together, we can do anything." She points to the top, smiles, then moves her fingers to the bottom of the pyramid. "But no matter what, our love, and our belief in us as a family … are all we require."

Bobby holds the pyramid in his left hand and reaches into his jacket pocket with his right. A second later, a beautiful silver ring, wide and sparkling, rests between his thumb and middle finger.

"Maggie," he begins, then clears his throat. "You are my sun, moon, and stars." He gazes into her eyes. "I've had this ring for several months. You've always been the one. And I was ready to wait."

A handful of sighs permeate through our small crowd. Mark kisses Sandy on the cheek. Midge, holding Johnny, blots her eyes with a tissue. Next to her, Bill records the ceremony, using the back of his hand to wipe his cheeks.

Bobby holds the ring high. "I know your connection to astrology, and that's why I had this ring designed for you. Amethyst is Aquarians' birthstone … peridot is the gemstone for your moon sign, Pisces … and aquamarine represents your rising sign … Leo."

Maggie beams back at Bobby. He grins then adds, "And you thought I wasn't listening when you told me about what you were learning in your astrology course." He laughs. "Maggie, you're different from anyone I've ever met. That's one of the many things I love about you. This may not be a *traditional* wedding, but I still wanted to include some diamonds … because I'm a traditional kind of guy." Gently, he slips the ring onto Maggie's finger. She stares at her hand, turning the ring as she examines its exquisite design.

Juliette waits a few seconds more, then adds the culminating words. "By the power vested in me … but more importantly … in conjunction with the energetic vibration of your love and commitment to one and other … I am honored to pronounce you husband and wife."

Bobby takes Maggie into his arms and kisses her fervently. Together, they step toward Midge, who hands Johnny to Maggie. The three nestle together. Harry barks twice in approval.

"Woo hoo," a beaming Juliette yells. As the three-piece blue-grass band starts to play, our small gathering moves toward Bobby and Maggie, embracing them with our love.

***

Back on the East Coast, Tom picks me up at Logan Airport, then navigates the perpetual Boston traffic to our brownstone. Walking into our new place still feels odd to me. It's home, yet it's not. Roxie is waiting, of course. She barks when she hears the door open. Still, nothing about the place seems familiar. I guess that shouldn't be too much of a surprise. We'd only been here for less than three weeks when I left to see Maggie. Coming back now, it's clearly time to make it feel like *home*.

I toss my dirty clothes into the hamper, carry my empty suitcase downstairs, and set it in the guestroom closet. Only then do I realize I'll be using it again in just eight days, for Colgate's Family Weekend.

Curious how I'll spend the time until then, I let my mind wander. Perhaps Roxie and I will go for some runs and get to know the neighborhood. Naturally, I can start working on my next book, the one about choosing happiness. At some point, I plan to check out Boston's historical sites, even if the idea of sightseeing alone feels a little sad to me. Maybe it's best to wait for a weekend, so Tom and I can do that together.

By the time I walk into our bedroom, my husband's already in bed, asleep. Of course he's exhausted. He's learning an entirely different system, meeting new co-workers, and navigating a city where he's never lived. I kinda feel guilty for having left, but Maggie needed me.

Yet, this past week was so much more than seeing Maggie and her new family ... or helping around the house. She trusted me to plan her entire wedding. I loved every second of the process. Maybe I needed to be needed.

Perhaps that's what I've been missing. When was the last time Patrick truly needed me? It's been years. Sure, I've had *mom* duties, but being truly needed … and appreciated … is something totally different.

As for Tom, does he *need* me? I handle all of the house things, our financials and so on, but he doesn't seem to need me the way I want to be needed.

Juliette and I discussed this topic a bit during our last session. She said that for me to fully release my core fear and step into my new phase of life, I must begin to let go of certain things. Part of letting go involves accepting that I'm not needed like I once was. Patrick is moving on. He's more than capable of handling life on his own. And my relationship with Tom should not be based on dependency. My job now is to trust and have faith in the process. Just thinking about it makes my throat tighten, which reminds me how challenging trust, letting go, and faith still are for me.

***

Tom is up and out before I awaken. By the time my feet hit the ground, it's after 8 a.m. Does time even matter right now? I have nothing on the calendar for today. Or tomorrow … or any day for the next week.

Roxie, nestled on her blanket atop our bed, stirs then curls into a ball. I'm in awe of how quickly she's taken to being an on-leash, city dog, but I bet she misses our fenced-in backyard as much as I do.

Dressed and armed with my morning coffee, I call for Roxie and we head out, perhaps creating a new morning ritual. After walking a few blocks, we turn right. Ahead of us is a sweet little park we discovered just before I left for Bend. Roxie loved the thick grass and scents of other dogs. When we arrive this morning, I sit down on an unoccupied bench. Roxie quickly saunters over to a miniature labradoodle. After an initial sniff test, the two begin to play.

I smile at the woman who's holding the labradoodle's leash. She smiles back. "Lovely park," I say. "Normal spot for you both?"

"Most mornings," she replies, smiling. "I'm Allison. That's Porter. He's a therapy dog."

"Handsome guy. How old?"

"He'll be four next month."

"I'm Marlee, and this is Roxie. We're new to the neighborhood. We just moved from Philadelphia."

"Ah, from one old city to another," Allison says.

"Yes," I agree. "There's something different about Boston … distinct. But I can't quite put my finger on it."

"It's the people," she says, "and the salt air. We're a hearty bunch. Maybe it's in our blood. Boston can be cold and dreary for long stretches, and spring takes forever some years. We don't seem to mind, or we try not to. That's why I have Porter. He helps keep me balanced when the days are short and dark." She bends down and gently pats her dog's head. No doubt, this dog makes a difference in Allison's life.

"I can't image not having Roxie," I say. Allison nods. "In Philadelphia … Radnor actually, a suburb … the moment our son started school, the house seemed so quiet and lonely. When I wasn't working or running errands, there was a heavy stillness. It was right about then that we got our first dog, Cricket. And now we have Roxie. She's pure joy." I gaze down at our border collie.

"Do you live alone?" Allison asks.

"My husband, Tom, and I just moved here for his new job. You?"

"I do now," her voice lowers. "For years I lived with my mother, but she recently passed."

"Oh, I am sorry."

"Thank you. It was a blessing. I was able to be with her." She looks toward the sky. "My mother was a beautiful human. And she aged gracefully. That made it easier on everyone."

"It doesn't always happen that way," I say.

"True. My mother became a widow at an early age. She invited me to live with her … after I'd left my husband." Her green eyes catch mine, sparkling a bit. I remain silent, choosing not to pry. After a moment of quiet, she continues. "He was a drinker," she says. "Not a very nice one."

"I'm glad you left," I say in a soft tone. She nods.

"Do you live nearby?" she asks.

"Three blocks that way," I point.

"I'm two blocks in the other direction," she says. "And how do you spend your days, Marlee?" she asks.

"Well, we just moved here the beginning of the month." I pause before adding, "Truthfully, I'm not sure what to do all day. Tom's new job is at Mass General. He's gone early and doesn't come home until evening. And our son just started his first year in college. He's at Colgate. So, for now, Roxie and I are still figuring it all out."

"Ah, a new phase," she says. "Empty nesters. When my girls, twins, left for school … there was a void without them around. I was caring for my mother, and they were always such bright spots. Luckily, I found Porter."

"I'm learning that with each passage of time, new gifts arrive … as well as new challenges," I say. "I think that's how we learn to master the lessons that come our way."

A slight grin breaks out across Allison's face, soon becoming a full smile. She starts to laugh. "Some of us seem to have more lessons than we bargained for, right?"

"Totally," I say, "but that's life, I suppose. It seems that you've certainly been dealt your fair share." I offer a compassionate smile.

Allison nods her head in a resounding *yes*. As she does, Porter trots over and leans into her legs.

"Here's something I've learned," she says. "Every time you jump a hurdle, your sense of self gets a little stronger. Eventually, you discover that you're capable of much more than you ever thought possible." She tilts her chin toward me. What a beautiful woman. Her cheeks brighten as she talks, and she seems younger than when I first said hello. "You know what else I've discovered?" she asks.

"What's that, Allison?"

"That if you ever doubt yourself, you only need to remember that you're not alone. There's always something much bigger right by your side." She glances upward for a moment, takes a deep breath, then looks at her watch. "Well, it's been lovely meeting you … and Roxie." Another grin etches across her face. "Porter and I are off to the women's shelter. We go there two days a week. Everyone loves Porter." She pets her pup. "I look forward to chatting again."

"Thank you," I say, wiping at a tear that starts to roll down my cheek.

"For what?" Allison asks, tilting her head.

"For helping me *see*."

Allison smiles, then starts to walk off.

I look down at Roxie and say, "What a special lady she is. And you seemed to like Porter, didn't you?"

As I lift my head to look at Allison, I'm surprised when she's no longer there. Instead, there's a shimmer of twinkling lights where she and Porter should be. I shake my head. What just happened? Where did they go?

Suddenly, a calmness comes over me. I glance around the park, quietly taking in its beauty. My eyes fix on the black-eyed Susans nestled in the shade of a tall oak. While this may not be my back-yard, this sanctuary of green space is certainly magical in its own right. Is Allison part of this magic, or am I merely imagining things?

Chapter 18

MAGGIE

September 30th – October 1st

Today's weather is perfect, sunny with intermittent clouds and a slight breeze. Lightly swaddled, Johnny sleeps peacefully in his stroller while Juliette and I walk along the river path. To my surprise, Juliette's proven to be extremely adept at changing diapers, burping Johnny, and reheating the meals Marlee left us in the freezer. And whenever she walks into the room, Johnny's eyes light up. There's definitely a connection between them. Bobby picked up on the way Johnny behaves around Juliette, even though he never heard the story of them *talking* before Johnny was born.

"You're really OK with the plans for your retreat center?" I ask, even though Juliette approved them two months ago. "Because there's still time to make minor revisions."

When Juliette asked me to design the center, I made it a priority to finish the blueprints ASAP. I knew how anxious she was to get started. I didn't want to hold things up. Thank God we finalized everything *before* the accident.

"Are you kidding me? They're awesome. You nailed it, Maggie. You totally got my vision. I wish everything with this project was as easy."

"What do you mean?"

Juliette releases a loud sigh. "We're already behind schedule."

"When is your projected end date?" I ask.

"The first of May. That was what Larry, my contractor, said when I signed the contract. But there's no way it will happen." Juliette loudly exhales.

I nod. I've heard similar concerns from a few clients over the past year. Plus, Bobby's shared his annoyance about unanticipated delays and lack of subs.

"Be patient," I say, even though I can feel Juliette's frustration. "Most of the guys do their best. Everything seems to go slower these days."

"Larry assured me his crew is lined up to pour cement next week … then framing will begin. The shell of the building should be finished around the time I leave for Peru, so the electricians, plumbers, and HVAC guys can do their thing." Juliette stops for a moment. "Once I'm back," her eyes widen, "windows go in … then drywall … all before Christmas. The *Farmer's Almanac* predicts a mild winter. Larry's confident he'll get the space enclosed before any major snowfalls. Plus, when I tapped in, that's what I *heard*."

Of course, Juliette wouldn't do anything that didn't seem energetically correct. "When do you get back?" I ask.

"Just before Thanksgiving. Michael and I thought we'd head to Boston to visit Tom and Marlee for a long weekend. It'll be great to see them. Plus, Michael's constantly raving about Marlee's Thanksgiving dinners. I don't eat turkey, but apparently her vegetarian sides are amazing." She shrugs her shoulders in a nonchalant manner, causing me to giggle.

"Your fall is super busy," I say, "and then you're getting married in January!" She nods and smiles.

"When do you return to work?" she asks.

"Mid-November. I'll be mostly remote for a while. We agreed I'll just go in for meetings." I let out a sigh before adding, "I'd hoped to finish all my projects before starting maternity leave, but then the accident messed things up. Luckily, Mark and Sandy stepped in with my bigger clients. I've managed to keep up with emails and do some minor problem-solving."

"Who's going to take care of Johnny when you're in the office?"

"We're not sure," I say. "Bobby said he'll do it, but I don't see how that will be possible with his schedule. We need a better option than that." I bite my lip, conscious there's no plan B.

***

I'm a little worried about Bobby. He looks exhausted. My husband—it still feels strange to say that—has been working non-stop. This isn't unusual, but he needs a break. The problem is he missed so many days when I was in the hospital, and now he has to play catchup. His guys covered for him as best they could, but there are certain things only Bobby can do.

After nursing Johnny, I place him in the bassinette and plop down on the couch. Juliette comes in from the patio, fresh from doing yoga. She leans her mat against the kitchen island, looks at me, and grins. "You should go shower," she says. "Then put on something nice. You and Bobby have a 7 o'clock reservation at Ariana's. I'm babysitting."

"What?" I ask? "How did you even get reservations there? It's almost impossible."

Juliette brushes my question aside. "When was the last time you and Bobby had time alone? Besides, I could use a relaxing evening with Johnny. No offense, but all the construction talk is getting boring." She winks. "And no more questions about whether you *captured my thoughts* in your designs." Then she puts her hands on her hips for emphasis. "Seriously, go shower. Your reservation is in less than an hour!"

***

Soon I'm cleaned up and dressed in a black cotton mini, wearing my grandmother's pearl stud earrings. Bobby and I walk to the corner table that's waiting for us in Bend's most elegant restaurant.

"Should I call Juliette?" I ask Bobby. "You know … just to make sure everything's OK?"

"I'm sure she's fine … and so is Johnny. If Juliette has questions, she promised to text." Bobby taps his phone. "Let's enjoy ourselves. This is our time. Considering all that's happened … I think we deserve it."

"You're right," I nod. "It's just weird for things to suddenly feel quiet … even relaxed. After all we've been through, I'm not used to sitting still." I shrug and sip some ice water. Bobby reaches across the table and squeezes my hand.

"Our entire world has shifted." He takes a deep breath. "I didn't think I could love you more than I did, but when I saw you in that hospital bed, bruised and unconscious, and knowing that our baby was in NICU …" He swallows a few times. "You're even more beautiful as a mother," he says.

"Bobby …" It's hard to find the words, but I try. "I haven't spoken much about what happened on the morning of the accident." I pause, trying to center myself. "That was when I felt … when *I knew* … I was ready to commit to us. It's not that I didn't want to before then. I was just afraid you were choosing me and the baby out of obligation. But that morning, I finally understood that those feelings were coming from old stories I'd inherited from my mother. I realized I was ready to say yes."

Bobby's eyes lock on mine. "You wanted to trust me," he says, "but you were afraid to. Did you think I'd leave?"

I nod, slightly embarrassed at the truth. "I think it's because of what my mother went through. Learning I was pregnant scared the hell out of me. And then, when you wanted to get married … well, I didn't believe I *deserved* happiness." I cast my eyes toward the floor.

Bobby lifts my hand to his lips, gently kissing my fingertips. "That's where you're wrong, Maggie. You're the kindest, most loving woman I've ever met. You always give without thinking about yourself." He shakes his head. "You're my world … you and Johnny. I can't imagine life without the two of you in it."

"You had everything ready when I came home from the hospital," I say, doing my best to hold back tears. "I didn't need to do a thing. I can't believe everyone who rallied around us … your parents, my dad, Sandy, Marlee, and Juliette. And you orchestrated everything." The tears are flowing now. I don't bother to stop them.

"*Everyone* wanted to help. Everyone." Bobby leans closer and kisses me ever so softly. When I open my eyes, I notice our server approaching. He hands us our menus, then places a sealed envelope on the table, smiles, and leaves. I look at the envelope, noting our names scripted in gold ink across the top.

"What's this?" I ask Bobby, thinking he's pulling a surprise.

"I have no idea," he says. I tilt my head, waiting for him to let on. But he just shrugs. "Seriously."

"Well, let's see what's in it." I tear it open to reveal a simple note:

Best wishes for years of joy and happiness.
Love, Marlee, Juliette, Annie, and Sophia.
P.S. Your gift will arrive next week.

"Does it say what the gift is?" Bobby asks. "The last thing they need to do is get us anything, considering all they've already done."

"I know," I say, completely perplexed. "I guess we'll find out next week."

***

In the morning, Juliette and I hug goodbye, then Bobby takes her to the airport to catch her early flight. I'd love to go back to bed. Instead I curl up on the couch and listen to the baby monitor, waiting for Johnny's first sounds.

Thanks to Marlee's nurturing and Juliette's company, I'm finally feeling stronger. The thought of exercising doesn't seem as daunting. However, my doctor wants me to wait until the end of October before I do anything too strenuous. In the meantime, I'm planning to up my walks … a little longer, a little faster when I can. Plus, Juliette guided me through several restorative yoga classes while she was here. I can continue doing yoga on my own.

Truthfully, now that Juliette's gone, I'm worried about being lonely during the day. I still don't know many people in Bend. Most of my relationships are professionally based. And since I'm not back working, it's up to me to start meeting new people. My plan is to get out of the house every day, just Johnny and me. Tomorrow, we're going to the office to see Sandy and Mark. The next day, we're meeting Viv for lunch at Lemon Tree downtown. It'll be a test run to see how well Johnny does at a restaurant. And Viv wants to talk with me about *reading people*. She's convinced I have a special talent. I wish I could read Johnny and know what he wants. Sometimes, I get his signals mixed up, thinking he's hungry when he's just tired.

It's funny how many books tell you what to expect when you're pregnant, or how to care for your baby after he or she is born. But I haven't found one that prepares you for the solitude that comes with motherhood. I suppose it's something we're meant to discover on our own.

Chapter 19

MARLEE

October 6th – 9th

What am I to know?

Whenever you become fearful, pause. Try to connect with your intuition, your guides, or God. Go beyond yourself to that which is higher. This is not meant to escape reality. Instead, it will help you see reality for what it truly is, not the matrix humans live in. Over time, this process will help strengthen your faith.

In today's session with Juliette, you will journey out of your human body and into your true self, so you can better see. This seeing will allow you to realize how beautiful your life truly is … and that what you have been fearing is only your small self's insecurity. When you recognize these habitual patterns, you can choose another way. This is how you step into your power and act from love (a high vibrational state) instead of fear (a low vibrational state).

Free of uncertainty, anxiety, frustration, and judgment, you become filled with love, acceptance, and compassion. This is how you shine.

My fingers fall still. Today's transmission is over. I set the timer on my watch for forty minutes. My last session with Juliette will be remote. I don't doubt her energetic capabilities, but I am a *bit* skeptical about how she can do it via phone. Even though I'm a little unsure, I'm ready to show up and trust the process. Juliette knows what she's doing.

Before our call starts, I scan my packing list and grab a small suitcase from the downstairs bedroom closet. Once upstairs, I eye some possible outfits for this weekend. There's the drive to Colgate, then Friday's dinner, Saturday's football game, Saturday's dinner, and our drive home. Plus, I'll need two sets of running clothes. I take a few things out and throw them on the bed. I'm trying to envision how different combos will look … pants and tops for different events, plus my shoes. I don't get too far before my timer goes off.

I pour a mug of coffee then grab a handful of cashews before heading to my office. Caffeine and nourishment are what I need right now. At nine on the dot, my phone rings. With a bit of trepidation, I answer.

"Good morning, sunshine," Juliette's voice travels crisply though my cell. "Are you ready to do some journeying?"

"I'm willing to try my best." My words come out in gulps, not exactly striking a confident tone. "Honestly, this whole thing is making me a bit uneasy," I admit.

"Well," Juliette says, "let me explain how it works." She tells me to get comfortable … to lie down on the floor. I set the phone on speaker, roll out my yoga mat, and stretch across its length. "Do you have a blanket?" she asks.

"Should I?"

"You might get cold. Also, grab a pillow for under your knees."

I get up to find a blanket and pillow, then let Juliette know when I'm back and comfortably situated on my mat.

"Good," she says. "Now, take some deep breaths."

"Is this yoga class?" I laugh.

"Not exactly," she says. "But you can pretend if it helps."

I giggle, but is it really funny?

"OK, Marlee, today we're going on a journey where you will begin to witness things from a *new* perspective. To start, I want you to imagine you are in a meadow. Look around you. Wildflowers, in every shade of the rainbow, are everywhere. Feel the sun's warm rays. Glance at the white clouds that lazily drift across the sky." Her descriptive words and soothing voice help me ground into the experience.

While I'm somewhat able to *see* the scene she describes, I can't help but wonder about the *journey* part of things. What will it look like? Shouldn't we be doing this in person for it to *really happen*?

"You're walking through a field of wildflowers now," Juliette says. "Up ahead, you see a large rock. Move toward the rock. As you approach, you realize it isn't an ordinary boulder. This huge rock sparkles. When you get closer, you start to see why. It's embedded with magnificent gemstones … like a *bedazzled* boulder."

I'm with the image, watching the colors sparkle and shine.

"Place your hands on the rock," Juliette says. "When you do, steps appear in its side. Climb up the steps, Marlee, to the top of rock."

I envision myself ascending the rock's steps, then sitting down on top of it. I gaze at miles and miles of open fields surrounding me. I'd like to stay here, but Juliette has other things in mind.

"Watch as the landscape changes," she says. "The wildflowers fade. Even the rock disappears. Now you're sitting on the roof of a building in Boston. Look below. You can see your new brownstone."

None of this makes any sense. I want to say something, but Juliette continues before I can object.

"Look around," she says. "Take in the start of the fall foliage … the early glimpses of gold, orange, and red breaking into faded green leaves. Feel the cool breeze on your skin. Observe people walking on the sidewalks. They're dressed for yoga … work … school. They carry bags. They walk dogs. Even though they are strangers, they acknowledge each other. They smile, nod, offer 'hello' to those they pass."

My body relaxes into the experience, witnessing the kindness of everyone below me.

"Now, turn your focus to the steps of your new home. There you are, Marlee. It's you and Roxie, leaving the building. You're glowing. You reach down and pat Roxie on the head. She's *ecstatic* to be outside. She starts to take off running down the sidewalk, but you gently tell her to heel. Roxie listens, calmly falling into time with your step. As the two of you walk, you greet the people you pass. The sun's bright rays make everything seem iridescent. There's a buzz about the city. You can feel the electricity in the air."

It's easy to imagine this scene. Roxie and I have already explored the neighborhood. I haven't always felt *present* during our recent ventures, but I'm able to follow Juliette's cues and envision the two of us heading up our street.

"OK Marlee, now for some fun. I want *you* to come along … to follow yourself and Roxie and observe what happens."

The *me* who is watching from the roof begins to float above the street, trailing the other *me* who's tethered to Roxie. I see the river … the route we take when we run. Roxie and I begin to jog. In no time, we're increasing our pace. The sun is bouncing off the Charles River. Crew teams are practicing on the water. Each coxswain stands up front, encouraging the rowers on. Other people run on the same path with Roxie and me. It's not disorienting at all to watch myself like this. I'm oddly comfortable with the whole thing, entranced to the point where Juliette's words begin to muffle. I feel as though I'm part of this mental movie.

"Now the scene starts to change again," Juliette says, directing me back to the roof across from our brownstone. I begin to envision what happens next, then start narrating the scene.

"I'm peering inside the window of my townhome," I murmur. "I see myself in the kitchen. I'm cooking, glancing at the time as I often do. Tom is coming home from work soon. I'm making his favorite meal. We're celebrating our two-month Boston anniversary. I'm opening a bottle of red wine, letting it breathe. Then I start to stir the sauce that simmers on the stove. The phone rings."

"Pick up the phone, Marlee," Juliette says.

"It's Patrick. He aced his calculus test. He's having such an amazing time. His roommate is great, and his classes are going well." I pause, waiting for what happens next. "Tom walks in, looking younger than ever. He's holding flowers … they're for me. He pulls me into his arms. We kiss. I can feel his warmth envelop me." I actually smell the flowers that only exist in my mind's eye. They're my favorite, peonies, which are practically impossible to find in the fall.

"And now the scene moves again," Juliette says.

I follow where she tells me to go, again looking inside my new home. "Now, Tom and I are sitting at the dining table," I go on. "We're not alone. There's a new group of friends with us. Three couples … people from the hospital and their spouses. We're telling stories … laughing … drinking wine." From this scene my mind flashes to another that's similar yet different. I'm back in Radnor. It's not a scene, but a memory. We're with Sophia, Jared, Annie, Jonathon, Juliette, and Michael. It's the first time they came for dinner. However, the memory doesn't make me sad. I don't miss what I've left behind. Instead, I'm filled with an open curiosity about the new people around our table. Who are they? Will we all become friends?

Wait … switching back to the vision now, I see that these new people *are* already friends. I feel the beautiful energy in the room … a deep and abiding connection, almost exactly how I felt in Radnor with Sophia, Annie, and Juliette.

"We have one more scene," Juliette says. "Look around you. You're not outside your home looking in. Rather, you are inside a coffee shop, sitting at a large table. It's your writing group."

Ahh, I see them now. "We meet on Tuesday afternoons at the Thinking Cup on Newberry Street," I say, "several blocks from where we live. I'm sipping a latté, nibling on a cranberry muffin. My fingers move across my laptop's keyboard, as if the words write themselves. A grin stretches across my face. I'm finishing the first draft of my next book!"

"Marlee," Juliette whispers. "It's time to return to the large, glimmering rock from the start. Take one last look around. Then, I want you to slowly transition to the meadow. Let me know when you're there."

In the vision, I stand up from my seat, turn, and walk out the café's door. For a moment, the street is still a street. When it dissolves, I'm surrounded by wildflowers.

"OK," I whisper, barely able to move my lips.

***

Juliette is quiet as I open my eyes, yawn, roll my wrists and ankles, then bend my knees and pull them to my chest. Finally, I turn to one side, sit up, and find lotus position.

"I'm sitting now," I say toward the phone.

"Welcome back," Juliette laughs. "How was your journey?"

"You helped me see what's ahead … what our life in Boston will look like."

"And how do you feel about what you saw?"

"It's lovely … wonderful." A lightness comes over me as I speak this truth.

"Yes … it is," Juliette whispers.

"Was this meant to show me that I'm not perceiving things as I should?"

"Yes," she softly agrees.

"Even though there will be challenges in the future, I have the foundation for an amazing life in Boston, away from all of you."

"Go on."

"I'm the one creating these fears, even though everything is really going quite well. Better than *well*. But I need to trust."

"And believe," she adds. "Marlee, it may seem as though you left us, but the reality is, we are all living separate lives. Annie's immersed with Ella and her job. Sophia and Jared are already making plans around his retirement. They'll be traveling more. And when they're home, Sophia has her practice. Plus, with Lizzy in town, they're spending a lot of time together as a family. We're all in flux. And it's beautiful."

A wave of guilt floods my mind. I've only texted Sophia a few times in the past month, mostly having to do with Maggie or sending her pictures of Johnny. We haven't had a real conversation in weeks.

"Then there's Maggie," Juliette continues. "I don't have to explain her life to you. You know how she and Bobby are creating their dream. As for me, I'm up to my eyeballs in construction. We're all in the thick of it."

"I've been so focused on my own leaving that I've neglected to see that *we're all* moving on." Everything begins to click. "Our lives are going in so many different directions. We're not intentionally separating. It's just a natural consequence to following our own paths."

"Trust that everything is happening as it should," Juliette says.

"Why didn't I realize this on my own?"

"Well, you'll have to sit with that question to really get to the answer," Juliette says. "From my perspective, a part of you is worried about what moving to Boston will mean in the long run. Will you lose everything that's important to you in Radnor? Plus, big things like Patrick going to college and Tom taking a new job have compounded this fear. No wonder you felt overwhelmed. You couldn't see the big picture … the exciting things ahead in the distance. You only focused on what you were leaving, worried that *you*, too, would be left behind."

"Abandonment," I say. Ripples course through my body.

"Your core wound," Juliette concurs. "Luckily, you're aware of it. Now you can focus on healing it, which will help you trust in the unknowns."

"But I want to know what's next," I say, my voice cracking. "I don't like being unsure about the future."

"Life rarely, if ever, allows us to know," Juliette replies.

"So, how do I handle not knowing what's coming next?"

Her voice deepens. "I think you already know the answer. You must stay in the present and continue to strengthen your faith. When you believe in something greater, you can surrender your fears and trust that there's a plan. And remember, none of us are ever alone."

***

The next morning, I force myself out of bed, dress, and take Roxie for an early walk. The weather is about as perfect as I could imagine … blue skies and no humidity. The air is crisp yet warm at the same time. Standing on our stoop, I gaze at the sun and offer an intention for today. "May I let go of control and flow with life, trusting joy is all around me."

In a few hours, we'll be on our way to see Patrick. It's been over a month since he left. That's the longest I've ever gone without seeing my son since he was born. I miss Patrick … his voice … the musky smell of his hair … even his lacrosse gear strewn about the mudroom. I miss walking past his room and hearing him playing video games with his friends … watching him play soccer … and making his favorite meals.

Roxie pulls me forward to the sidewalk. Yes, it's more than Patrick's physical presence I long for. It seems like forever since we had one of our special talks, when I try to pepper in my motherly advice in a light-hearted, non-preachy manner. Often, Patrick looks for ways to change the subject, not wanting to hear my ideas on whatever we're talking about. But when he's receptive, we have some truly deep conversations. I suppose that's my way of helping him deal with whatever life throws at him. Maybe I need these talks more than he does. They seem to fill an internal void that's been growing parallel to Patrick's independence. The less he needs me, the more I crave connection.

I wonder if he misses me.

Patrick wanted us to bring Roxie, but we couldn't find anywhere to stay that allows dogs. When I told Patrick she wasn't coming, I reminded him that he'll be home in a few weeks for fall break. It was odd using the word "home" while referring to Boston. Patrick hasn't even seen the brownstone yet, except for little videos. Will it feel like home to him? I sigh. Will it feel like home to me by then?

Walking a few blocks, I realize I'm talking to myself. Maybe I'm not exactly talking to myself. I suppose I could be talking to something ... or someone. I go from thinking the words to mouthing them. Finally, I say them out loud.

"God, I hope Patrick likes it here. I know his friends aren't in Boston, but it's where we are ... for now." I swallow. Am I praying? Am I losing my mind? I suppose faith involves surrendering in order to have these types of conversations without judgment.

Roxie and I make our way around the block, hit our usual stops where she likes to sniff and pee, then return to the brownstone. Once inside, I pack her travel bag and place it at the bottom of the stairs for later. A co-worker of Tom's offered to take care of her while we're at Colgate.

"You're having your own weekend away," I say as she wags her tail. "And you're going to be a good girl, aren't you?" She smacks her lips and wiggles her bottom.

How is it that dogs can feel immediate happiness from praise, the mention of a favorite toy, or the promise of a treat? I wish shifting my own mood could be so easy. It would be amazing to transition from worry to joy with a couple key words and phrases. Wait … what if it really is that simple?

It is.

***

Tom's home earlier than expected. We hit the road just before noon. I'm quiet as he drives, thinking of how badly I *need* to see Patrick … to set my eyes on him … to hug him. He sounds great every time we talk, and his texts are generally upbeat. But the first semester of college is a big deal for everyone. No matter what I work on with Juliette, I can't help but worry about all the things that *could* go wrong.

I choose not to dwell on the *oh so* familiar negative thought loops during the drive. Instead, I do a little writing, then fold my laptop away and watch the scenery. I focus on breathing, allowing my thoughts to ease and shift toward positive images … happiness … health … self-assuredness … bliss.

Upon entering campus, I look at Tom and say, "Maybe we should surprise Patrick and bring the bag of treats to his room."

"Let's wait here," Tom says. Outside Drake Hall, he puts the car in park.

"But I have things for him," I clamor, my hand already moving to undo my seatbelt. "I made his favorite cookies … and chocolate peanut butter brownies … and …" My voice practically whimpers.

Tom laughs. "Would you have wanted your mother to come upstairs unannounced to your dorm room?" Tom tilts his head, as if challenging me to remember what life was like my freshman year.

"Well … I guess … maybe not." I can't help but break into a smile, realizing how awkward it could be for Patrick.

Tom takes out his phone to text Patrick that we're here. Several minutes later, Patrick is climbing into the back seat. He leans forward to hug us both. "I missed you guys!" He smiles. My heart melts. Then he gives me a sweet kiss on the cheek before he fastens his seatbelt. "Where are we going? I'm starved!"

Just like that, we are a family of three again. It's as though we never missed a beat. Patrick talks non-stop the entire way to the restaurant. There's not a doubt in my mind that our son is where he belongs.

That's when everything becomes crystal clear. I've been so focused on fearing what could go wrong during his first weeks at college that I failed to imagine all that could go right. Maybe when we let go of control and flow with life, we *can* experience joy.

***

My mind runs while my body does the same. I know I'm *supposed* to be in the present, but this morning, I let my thoughts wander. Last night's dinner with Patrick provided total assurance that he's happy and thriving. I can't help replaying every moment of it.

A ton has happened since Patrick left. I suppose he's experienced the most life changes, but has he? After all, we've all left our homes and moved on to new places where we are strangers.

On the outside, Patrick still looks like *my* Patrick. But last night he sounded different … calmer, and a bit more self-assured. I also noticed a change in his wardrobe. Instead of the usual t-shirt and jeans, he was wearing khakis and a button-down shirt.

"Oh my goodness, your hair," I blurted at one point.

"Do you like it?" he asked.

"It's combed! You look great."

"Thanks, Mom."

We ate at a place called Pino Bianco, which proved to be a pretty popular destination. Packed with parents and students, we didn't even get to our table before Patrick flagged down and said hello to a few dorm friends. As great as it was to meet these kids and their parents, I craved family time. Sensing my unease, Tom shot me a fast wink. I smiled and felt myself come back to the present … just being happy to be with Patrick.

After the waiter took a drink order and gave us menus, I kept glancing around the bustling restaurant. What were other families doing? Were they enjoying themselves? Most looked like they were, but a few seemed a little disjointed, disengaged, maybe even overwhelmed.

Patrick's eyes grew wide as he scanned the menu.

"Have you eaten anywhere other than on campus this whole semester?" I asked.

"Mostly pizza joints," he said. "Definitely nowhere like here. Can I get a steak?"

"Anything you want," Tom said. I nodded.

"How's the cafeteria's food?" I asked.

"Good, but not like yours, Mom," Patrick answered. I must admit, this made my heart feel gooey and warm.

We spent the next ninety minutes ordering, laughing, sharing appetizers, trying each other's entrees, denying that we had room for dessert, then ordering it anyway. Patrick went for the chocolate lava cake. Tom and I looked at each other. He'd always been a good eater, but tonight he seemed famished. When a round of coffees came, Patrick excused himself and headed for the restroom.

"Does he seem taller, somehow?" I asked. "Is that even possible at his age?"

"He definitely seems more filled out," Tom noted.

"What happened to our lanky son, up in his room playing X-box?" I asked with a laugh.

"He sounds happy," Tom said with a shrug.

"I know," I nodded.

"Do you feel better?" Tom asked, arching his slightly graying eyebrows.

"I suppose," I said. "But it's still early in the year. He's barely into the semester. I mean…" But I stopped myself, realizing I was imagining all that could go wrong instead of focusing on what seemed to be going right.

"Marlee, do you remember … we were once his age?" A hint of mischief stretched across Tom's face.

"That's the problem," I grinned. "I do."

***

After my run, I hop in the shower, then put on what I've jokingly dubbed my "game outfit"—jeans, a white shirt, a beige sweater, and my favorite pair of black boots. Tom changes into jeans and pulls his old Colgate sweatshirt on over a navy polo. I look at him and can't help but giggle.

"What?" he grins. "It's a tradition. Plus, this sweatshirt is good luck."

In twenty minutes, we're walking through a large, crowded parking lot looking for a maroon and gold flag attached to a gray Sprinter van. When we arrive, I'm amazed by the number of kids and adults hanging out together. Everyone's chatting, and most hold red solo cups. A fold-out table is laden with a huge tray of sandwiches, baskets filled with potato chips, pretzels, and popcorn, and a large bowl of potato salad. A separate dessert table is filled with Twizzlers licorice, chocolate chip cookies, and a gigantic cake with the phrase "Let's go Raiders!" spelled out in maroon frosting. I add our box of cupcakes to the table and watch as a group of kids dive in, scooping up close to half of what's inside.

I don't see Patrick right away. I guess he's running a bit late. "Let's have something to eat before the game," I say to Tom.

"Good idea," he says. "Would you mind grabbing something for me? I'll go get us some beers." He heads toward the keg, while I carry two plates toward the food spread.

In a few minutes we're sipping Coors Lights and enjoying a tailgate lunch. A gentleman in his late forties approaches us. "Welcome," he says. "I'm Bob. This is my wife, Carol. Our sons, Tanner and Conner, are over there." He tilts his head toward the keg, where two boys, twins, are pouring refills.

"Thanks for having us," I say. "You and Carol are so kind to do this for the kids. The hoagies are delicious," I add. They're as good as the ones we get at the Reading Terminal Market.

Carol looks quizzically at me. "Oh, you mean the Italian sandwiches?" She giggles and glances at my plate.

"Sorry," I laugh. "I guess *hoagie* is more of a Philadelphia word."

"Well, whatever you call them, I'm happy you're enjoying them. We try to have tailgates before all the home games," she adds. "It's fun to hang out with our kids and their friends."

"Plus," Bob lowers his voice, "this way, I can keep an eye on them … if you know what I mean." He clears his throat, perhaps for emphasis.

Tom and I nod. "We're Patrick's parents," Tom says. "Tom and Marlee."

"Oh, Patrick's such a sweetheart," Carol replies. "He always comes early, helps us set up … and clean up. Most kids *disappear* at that point." She winks. "You've got a good son." I feel my heart swell. Nothing is better than when another parent acknowledges our son's character.

I enjoy mingling, but we still haven't seen Patrick. Finally, I spot him talking with a pretty blonde who's dressed in cut-off shorts and a Colgate tee. Could this be the same girl he mentioned back in July, after his canoe trip? I nudge Tom and nod in Patrick's direction.

"Should we go over?" I ask. "Do you think he'll introduce us?"

Tom shakes his head. Once again, message received. I keep an eye on Patrick as he says goodbye to the girl then heads toward us.

"Hey, glad you made it! Sorry … got held up." He smiles and glances at his watch. "It's almost time for the game," he says.

I peruse the dessert table for a bit, then talk with some of the other families. Eventually, the three of us make our way to the stadium. Patrick never mentions the girl he was talking to. Maybe they're just friends. However, something tells me there's more to it.

Once we find our seats, Tom becomes unusually quiet. Is he mentally returning to his days as an undergraduate? He's shared a few stories, but I suppose he was different back then. Weren't we all? I remember when I attended University of Vermont. A lump forms in my throat. Thankfully, *something* was watching over me back then. Maybe God has been by my side all along.

***

"What a game!" I yell as we make our way out of the stadium with the rest of the crowd. "I can't believe that ending."

"We're the only undefeated team in the Patriot League," Patrick says.

"Where to next?" I ask. "We have a few hours before dinner."

"Well," Patrick starts, "if you want to head back to your place and relax, that's fine with me."

"Or we could hang out in your dorm," I offer. This suggestion makes Patrick and Tom squirm.

"Actually, I wouldn't mind a short nap," Tom says. "Then we can pick up Patrick outside the dorm around 6:45." Father and son exchange grins.

"OK," I say, trying my best to seem casual about it. Is it wrong that I feel a little dismissed? I'd wanted to spend more time with Patrick, just the three of us.

"See you later," Patrick says. He gives me a quick kiss on the cheek, then runs ahead to catch up with friends. I watch him disappear into a sea of kids.

"He's happy," Tom says.

"His friends seem great," I offer. "Their parents too."

"But…" Tom says, waiting for me to continue.

"Well … I mean … what else could I want?" I ask.

"But…" Tom presses.

"Well, OK … we wouldn't have had to stay in his room," I say. "We could have walked around campus … or gone out for ice cream … or…"

You want him to miss you more than he does.

It's not Tom talking. It's the voice. I'm startled by this unexpected message and take a moment to consider. Is it true? I thought I wanted him to be happy, which he seems to be. Could some other side of me also want him to miss me as much as I miss him?

The past twenty-one hours have reinforced how well-adjusted Patrick appears to be. None of my fears have come to fruition. It's as though I imagined scenarios to make him need me … because I need him. Is that it? Or is this one more story I've told myself over the years … how much it will hurt when Patrick goes to college?

As these puzzle pieces connect, I take a breath. I feel the gentle weight of Tom's arm around me. He and I wander down a winding path through campus. For a moment, it's just the two of us, surrounded by old stone buildings, sloping lawns, and large oak trees.

"Let's go take that nap," Tom says with a grin.

***

When I wake up Sunday morning, a distinct heaviness weighs on me. The weekend's almost over. Then I glance over at Tom in bed next to me and can't help but smile. Everything is fine. No … better than fine. My life is wonderful.

Tom and I are quickly adapting to life in our new city. This coming Friday, we're going out to a new restaurant in the Back Bay with some people from the hospital. On Saturday, we're going to do *touristy* stuff—checkout the Freedom Trail, have dinner at Mamma Maria in the North End, and top off the evening with cannoli at Mike's Pastry. I can't imagine a better day.

Most importantly, now that I know Patrick is happy at school, I can fully exhale and stop worrying that something will go wrong.

After a short run and quick shower, Tom and I pack up and check out of the rental. We drive to meet Patrick at a funky little diner four blocks from campus. When we're done, he walks us outside to say goodbye. He takes both my hands.

"I think I made a really great choice coming here," he says. "At first, I was worried about fitting in. But everyone has been so cool."

"I'm glad to hear that," I say.

"I just don't want you to stress out about me. OK, Mom?"

"OK," I respond with a soft smile.

"Really … I'm serious. I'm good."

"I can see that now," I say, my shoulders sliding a bit further down my back.

"And trust me, if things *stop* being good, you'll be the first person I call."

I look deeply into his eyes. "And I will always be here for you," I say. "Count on that." I hold his stare for an extra heartbeat, hoping to cement the message.

Then Patrick flashes me the grin I so love.

"So … see you in three weeks," I remind him.

"I can't wait to come to our new home," he says. Hearing him refer to our place in Boston as *home* catches me off guard.

"It's different than Radnor," I warn. "I hope you like it."

"If you and Dad are there, it's home to me."

Chapter 20

MAGGIE

November 9th

"I don't get it," I say into the phone to Marlee. "If Juana decides Juliette's ready to become a shaman, how will her life change?"

"I'm not so sure it will," Marlee says, sighing. "From what Juliette's explained, she can already do most of what she wants to. But having that title makes her more credible to others, I suppose."

"It seems to mean a lot to her," I add. "She told me how much she wants to be like Francisco. But wouldn't she be what people call an *urban shaman?*"

"Yes. I believe the main difference is that urban shamans can live anywhere," Marlee points out, "whereas traditional shamans usually exist in tribal environments."

"It's all so confusing."

"I agree," Marlee says. "The only shaman I've even met is Francisco. I'm not sure if he qualifies as an urban shaman or a regular shaman … I have no idea."

We both start laughing.

"I can't thank you enough for the amazing wedding present!" I say, though I've repeatedly thanked Marlee, along with Annie, Sophia, and Juliette for their brilliant gift.

"It's going well?" Marlee asks.

"Tara's amazing. She and Johnny have already bonded. We're so grateful to have someone so trustworthy and competent to watch Johnny when I need to go into the office." Even I sense relief in my voice. Tara, Annie's niece, recently moved to Bend and was looking for a part-time job. Lucky for us, Annie put two and two together, and The Healers gave us fifty hours of babysitting with Tara as a wedding gift.

"Are you ready?" Marlee inquires. "You return next week, right?"

"Yes, and yes." I say. "Part of me can't wait to get back in the groove. Returning to work will be good for my mind too," I laugh. Still, there's another side of me that wonders how difficult it will be to balance both Johnny and my job. "So, how's Boston?" I ask, changing the subject.

"We're loving it," Marlee's voice beams through the phone. I'm a little surprised at first. When she visited after Johnny was born, I could tell she was conflicted, maybe even remorseful about the move. But now …

"Has it been difficult to meet people?" I ask. "Are you making friends? I remember how hard it was for me when I first moved to Bend."

"Actually, it's been easier than I thought it would be," Marlee says, then mentions several of Tom's colleagues and their spouses. "Plus, one of Patrick's Colgate friends is from Cambridge. His mom and I have had lunch a few times. Last week, she asked me to join her book club." Marlee's voice lights up when she says this.

"I'm glad. Moving someplace new can be tough," I say before again changing topics. "Any news on how things are working out with Lizzy filling in as Ella's nanny?" I ask, now knowing first-hand how important the relationship between caregiver, child, and parent is.

"It's going wonderfully for everyone. Lizzy seems to love her new job, and Annie is thrilled with how smoothly the transition has gone. The last time I spoke with Sophia, she kept saying how grateful she is to have Lizzy home. She told me Lizzy's regained her self-confidence and is beginning to connect with old high school friends who live in the area."

"It sounds like it's a win-win for everyone!" I say, then add, "I miss Sophia. She is so wise and caring. I was so bummed she and Annie had to leave when everyone was here." I pause. "How is Jared doing?"

"Great. He just announced he's retiring in June. However, Sophia's continuing to work ... but she's not taking any new patients. I suppose that's her way of cutting back," Marlee laughs. "Oh, she asked me to remind you to send more pics of Johnny."

"And how is Patrick?" I ask, hopeful it's been an easy transition.

"He's amazing," Marlee says, then shares a few tidbits about his first semester. "Two more weeks, and he'll be here for Thanksgiving. After that, only three weeks till finals. Patrick seems to like our place in Boston, but he's planning to spend some of winter break in Radnor, to see old friends."

"That makes sense," I say. "Maybe some of them will visit him in Boston."

Marlee pauses for a moment. "Maybe," she says, her voice lowering. "I'm learning to be OK with things when I'm not sure how they're going to pan out."

"But it's hard, right?"

"Frustratingly so!" Marlee replies then laughs.

"Oh," I say, remembering something I want to share with her. "I'm having lunch with Viv next week. We've been getting together twice a month. She's helping me become better with *reading* people. Viv thinks I have a definite talent." My voice cracks a bit when I admit this to Marlee.

"I think Viv's onto something." Marlee says. "You do have a beautiful way to access the essence of others ... not only with your architectural designs, but in general. Something tells me you and Viv will become good friends."

"I'd love that. She's really special. And speaking of making friends, I'm taking Johnny to *Mommy and Me* classes. They start next month."

"Ahh, we did those," Marlee says tenderly. "You'll have fun."

"I miss you." My voice becomes unsteady. "I love our calls, but …"

"I know … I miss you too," Marlee says. "Juliette's wedding isn't that far away," she adds, perhaps trying to sound optimistic. "And then we will all be together at her retreat center's opening in June." Marlee pauses. "You're coming to that, right?"

"I wouldn't miss it," I say. "And don't forget, you can always come to Bend. Maybe Tom could come too. We could ski … hang out … whatever."

"You know," Marlee cuts in, "I think we're looking at things the wrong way. What if we're too focused on finding *new* friends, attempting to recreate what the five of us have? Just because we don't live near each other doesn't mean *everything* has to change. If we're creative, we can make this work."

"You're right!" I say, practically jumping off the couch. "We can still make plans to get together for a few days each year. And there are other ways we can stay in touch."

"Zoom calls," Marlee says.

"Zoom cocktails," I suggest.

"I like that even better," she says, her tone shifting toward something playful.

"I really needed to hear that, Marlee," I say. "I've been so focused on wanting new friendships that I've almost forgotten what I already have." I get quiet for a moment. Marlee asks what's wrong. "It's just … you've been to Bend three times to see me," I tell her. "You planned my wedding. I don't know what I would have done without you when Johnny came home. You cooked … even made sure I showered!" I laugh, then get serious again. "Marlee, you lent me your wedding dress …" Tears stream down my cheeks. "It's like our friendship has always been about you helping me, even in Costa Rica. I'm not sure I've been the best friend to you."

"Oh, Maggie, that's not true at all," she says. "I hope you understand what you've given me. Helping to care for you and your family was a gift. With Patrick gone … it felt good to be needed."

"I suppose I needed a mother," I say, amazed as the words leave my mouth. "I loved my mom, but there wasn't a lot of extra time for nurturing."

"I get it," Marlee says. "Just know that your mother loved you so much … more than you could imagine."

"How could you know that?"

"That's what mothers do … it's how we are. It's how *you* are, and will always be, with Johnny. We don't always show it, but our love for our children reigns over all else."

Just then, Johnny lets out a voracious scream.

"Lunch time?" Marlee laughs into the phone.

"Something like that," I say.

"Go nurture your little guy," she says. "Give him all the love and warmth you wanted … but never received."

Chapter 21

MARLEE

January 2nd – 3th

"I don't want to go back to school," Patrick says. He stares into the red and green plastic storage container that's half-full of Christmas ornaments.

"What?" I practically drop the hand-blown glass ball I'm holding. "Why? What's wrong?"

Patrick hesitates, afraid that what he's about to say will upset me. I wait patiently. Finally, he lifts his head but avoids eye contact. "There's something I didn't tell you."

My throat tightens. I knew there would be some sort of problem while he was at college. Why didn't he say something earlier?

"Right after finals were over …" He pauses before he even gets going, and sits on the floor, his head in his hands. "Well, this girl I was seeing … Anna … the one I told you about last summer … from the canoe trip … " He clenches his jaw. "I found out she slept with another guy."

"Oh, honey," I say. There's a pit in my stomach. That must have been who he was talking to during Family Weekend. I knew it. I look at my son and see his pain. Suddenly, I remember the betrayal I felt after a college boyfriend cheated on me.

"I don't know why she did it," he says. "She said she really liked me." He stops to look up at me. "We were close … really close."

It's then I wonder why Patrick never mentioned that he and Anna were a thing. He's never had a serious girlfriend, so he lacks any real relationship experience. Why did this girl cheat on him?

Part of me wants to ask about her, but I don't. Maybe Patrick will say more.

"I had just finished my last final. All the guys on my floor ordered pizza, and we got some beer to celebrate making it though the first semester."

He looks at me. I shrug. "Go on," I say.

"We were having such a great time. Then someone started buzzing the front door of our dorm. I went downstairs to let them in. On my way down the stairwell …" he pauses, visibly gulping, "for some reason, I looked through the window of the door that leads to the second floor. That's when I saw them … kissing outside of his dorm room. Anna was wearing his shirt … nothing else."

Now I'm pissed. Who is this little bitch? And what about the guy? Didn't he know she was Patrick's girlfriend?

Instinctively, I sit down on the floor next to Patrick and wrap my arm around his shoulder, pulling him into me.

"I don't know what to do. Everyone knew Anna was my girl-friend. But after I saw them in the hallway, I avoided her. I didn't answer her texts. I couldn't even say goodbye before I left the next day." Tears stream down his face. "Mom, who else saw her outside his room? I can't go back to school. There's no way I can face her … or him."

All I do is nod. My son is mortified. This girl really hurt him. Sure, some part of me realizes this will pass, but that doesn't change the way Patrick feels right now. I don't know what to do, or if I should *do* anything.

I listen to my heart and hold my son. Gently, I rock him back and forth, attempting to soothe the myriads of emotions he's feeling. Nothing I say can ease his pain or diminish his embarrassment. All I can do is love him … and let him know I'll be forever by his side. And that is exactly what I do.

Once he calms down, we resume our work removing ornaments from the tree's dry branches. We wrap each one in tissue, then place it inside of a cardboard slot. I watch as Patrick repeats this process with robotic-like precision, using the stepladder to reach the highest ornaments.

From there, we unwind the lights. He gently eases the strands away from the branches while I wrap them around my elbow and hand, secure their ends, and place them in the storage container marked *Christmas Lights*. We don't say much as we pack the season away. No words are necessary right now. The brownstone holds this quiet for another thirty minutes, until Roxie barks. Tom's home. Patrick looks at me, a little startled. I suspect he hasn't told his father about the Anna situation yet.

"Hey you two!" Tom says after climbing the stairs. "You've been busy." Instead of greeting him with a hearty hello, Patrick remains silent. He looks at his father, then back at me, as if hoping I'll share the story with Tom.

"Patrick, would you mind taking the tree to the sidewalk?" I ask. "The pick-up tag is on the kitchen counter."

"Sure," he says, then dashes out of the room. Once he's out of earshot, Tom looks at me.

"What's going on?" he asks, confused by our actions.

"Come, sit down," I say. Once we settle onto the couch, I explain the situation Patrick is going through.

"This Anna seems … well … misguided, at best," Tom says. "And that guy is an ass. Who does he think he is?" Tom shakes his head.

"I agree. But think about things from Patrick's perspective," I say. "He's mortified. His girlfriend cheated on him." I pause for a moment. "Patrick doesn't want to go back to school," I say softly, worried about Tom's reaction.

"What? Not go back to Colgate? That's absurd." Tom's voice is unusually loud. "I'm sure it stings having your girlfriend cheat on you, but he's certainly not the first guy this has happened to."

"True, but that doesn't diminish his pain … or the embarrassment he feels."

"OK … I get it. But not go back to school?" Tom goes silent, his eyes on the floor, clenching his hands into tight fists. I hear the front door open. Patrick is back in the house.

"Go talk to your son," I say. "He needs to know you support him." I pull Tom closer and lean my head against his chest. His breathing slows.

"Thank you," he says, and kisses the top of my head. I retreat to my office and give them space to talk.

***

Tom carves the flank steak, and I add a healthy portion of meat and roasted sweet potatoes to Patrick's plate. For good measure I include a few florets of broccoli.

As we sit and eat, it's clear that Patrick isn't his usual bubbly self, but he's definitely closer to normal. I do my best to infuse small talk into the conversation—asking about last night's Boston Bruins game, sharing the latest about Johnny, and telling them about the book I'm reading for book club.

I try to keep things light, fun, even a little spirited … intentionally avoiding all conversation about school or this upcoming semester. The whole time, even with a smile on my face, I'm angry with this Anna girl. Why did she do it? If she was unhappy in their relationship, couldn't she have just ended it instead of cheating? Was there something underneath her actions?

Patrick's cell, over on the counter with Tom's and mine, vibrates. He moves to go pick it up.

"Remember … no phones during dinner," I say, reminding him of the rule we've enforced since he first got his own phone in seventh grade.

Looking slightly annoyed, he returns to his seat and cuts a piece of meat. Just as he's about to put the steak into his mouth, his phone vibrates again. I shake my head, despite his pleading eyes, remaining steadfast in our policy. But the vibrations continue at an alarming rate.

"You better check and see what's going on," Tom says, motioning with his eyes toward the counter.

Patrick jumps out of his chair and grabs his phone. I watch as my son's jaw drops, his mouth wide open in shock.

"What is it?" I stand to walk toward him.

Patrick turns, a stricken look on his face. "My friends … they're letting me know there's a video of Anna that's gone viral." He freezes, unable to completely comprehend what's happening.

I walk to his side. One glance at his phone says it all. He begins to shake. The phone falls to the floor. I pull him toward me. "Breathe," I say, then rub his back. His muscles feel rigid, as if they might break with the slightest provocation. Tears well in his eyes. In no time, he's sobbing.

Alarmed, Tom picks up Patrick's cell. When he looks at the screen, his eyes bulge. He doesn't say anything, but I can sense his rage.

Despite all the fears I had about Patrick's first semester at Colgate, this is one situation I never imagined … and there's nothing I can do to fix it. The only option is to stand by his side and weather the storm with him. That's where my power lies … to love and support, not to make his troubles go away. If I try to solve all of Patrick's problems, he will miss out on life's lessons. And one thing I've come to realize is that when we don't learn from the lesson at hand, the universe will send more challenging situations in the future to teach us.

Tom moves toward us. He looks like he might break. But he doesn't. Instead, he locks his eyes on mine, places his left arm around Patrick and his right around me. We can't erase his pain, or delete a suddenly viral sex video of his ex-girlfriend. But we can provide support, hold space, and ensure him of our love.

My heart not only aches for Patrick, but also for this girl. We've never met, and probably never will, yet I hold a space of compassion for her too. Did she know what was coming her way? Whether or not she did, I mourn the loss of her innocence. No doubt the impact of this experience will weigh heavily on her for a long time. I just hope Patrick can release his pain.

***

The ache in my stomach is still there when I wake up, but I can feel it softening.

Tom and I learned a lot last night. We found out that Patrick's relationship with Anna started on the canoe trip, and that they were together all semester. Patrick confided that she was the first person he ever slept with. He was her first too. Everything was going really well. He was even going to ask her to visit him in Boston during break. Why did she cheat? It made no sense. We talked our way around hypothetical circles, then finally accepted that sometimes we don't understand why people do things.

Once Patrick and Tom settled down a bit, I went into the kitchen and made brownies. We sat around the kitchen counter and devoured the gooey, rich dessert. Chocolate might not cure things, but it definitely makes you feel better. Tom poured me a glass of Cab … then another … then a third. He and Patrick split a six-pack of beer.

It was 2:30 in the morning before any of us went to bed. On his way to his room, Patrick admitted he still cared for Anna, but he couldn't trust her. He asked me whether he should reach out to her, to make sure she was OK.

"She has to be feeling like shit," he said, his eyes toward the floor. "I think I'll let her know she can still talk to me if she wants to."

Never before had I felt so proud of our son. "That would be a really nice thing to do," I said.

He nodded, kissed my forehead, and headed to his room.

"Wait," I called, following him to the stairs. "You know, everything's gonna be all right." I placed my hand on his cheek.

"Thanks, Mom. I know it will. It's just that Anna's parents aren't like you and Dad. If they ever find out about that video, they'll disown her. Maybe that's why I never told you about her. She didn't understand our relationship. That was the one thing that always kind of bothered me about her. She thought parents were the enemy. She never *got* how we could be so close." He gave me a crooked smile then shrugged his shoulders. "I guess it never would have worked in the end."

One more hug, then Patrick went to bed, Roxie at his heels. As for me, I wasn't ready for sleep. I grabbed a heavy blanket and walked out onto the balcony. Gazing at the plethora of stars on the cold, dark, moonless night, I felt a surge of connectivity.

You are not alone. You never will be. There is an underlying thread joining the past, present, and future. Human souls are here to play in the proverbial sandbox of life, learning, growing, evolving. This is how we elevate.

***

This afternoon, Patrick reaches out to Anna. As much as I feel the urge to eavesdrop, I avoid that part of the brownstone completely.

"Well?" I ask when he's off the phone.

"She couldn't believe I called," he replies. Then he looks to the floor. "She's not coming back to school."

"I don't blame her," I say. "She must be absolutely mortified."

"Mom, she told me why she cheated. She said she never felt like she deserved me. She literally self-sabotaged with the other guy. She was afraid I'd eventually move on from her … and decided to move on first."

"Oh, honey," I say. He walks toward me for a hug. "It's sad, but a lot of women have similar feelings."

"Really?"

"Yes," I say. "For some, it just makes sense to do the hurting, before a man hurts them … because they think it's bound to happen. Juliette did that with Michael. Maggie almost did it, too, with Bobby."

After a moment, Patrick offers the perfect reply. "That's pretty messed up," he says.

"You don't know how right you are."

Chapter 22

MAGGIE

January 11th – 12th

Viv's already seated when I arrive at Drake. We've been meeting downtown for lunch twice a month. At first it was because Viv wanted to help me with reading people. But now, we're committed to our lunches because we enjoy spending time together.

Dressed in a black sweater dress with matching boots, she stands as soon as she sees me. "Come here, you," she says as she envelops me in a warm embrace.

"You look great," I say, conscious of my *oh so* comfortable jeans and boxy wool sweater. At least these clothes aren't stained with spit-up or baby food.

"As do you!" Her smile broadens as she takes me in. "Let me see the latest pictures of Johnny," she says as she motions for us to sit.

"This is one of my favorites." I scroll to the picture of him with my dad on the beach when we visited over Thanksgiving. Then I show her several from Christmas morning. "I have no idea why I wrapped Johnny's presents," I laugh. "Bobby and I had to take turns unwrapping his gifts."

"I did the same thing for Ben's first Christmas. Truthfully, I think I'd do it again if we ever have a second."

"Do you want more kids?" I ask, then chastise myself for being too personal. Yes, Viv's a friend now, but first she was my client.

"Honestly … no." Viv blushes a bit. "I like my life … our life. I finally seem to have found balance. When Ben was little, I lost my center. I struggled meeting his needs and mine. And Toph and I had no time for just the two of us. That was when I knew having another baby would completely derail me."

"I totally understand," I say. "I imagine that having another child would complicate things for Bobby and me. Maybe someday … but I'm nowhere near ready right now."

After our server checks in on us, I continue. "I've definitely lost my balance," I say. "Work no longer excites me like it used to. Before Johnny, I loved the challenge of designing commercial and residential buildings. I'd spend hours researching the newest sustainability practices and highest performing materials. But now, I don't have the time … or the drive. I'm lucky to finish projects by their deadlines." I take a sip of water. "Truthfully, I feel guilty when I spend too much time away from Johnny."

"A baby changes everything," Viv says and nods, then sits up a bit straighter. "That's when I started my own business. I couldn't keep adapting my schedule to the everchanging assignments at the yoga studio. So, I became a private yoga instructor. After that, I completed my level-three reiki certification."

"Did you miss working at your old studio?"

"I missed the people," she says, "but there was such relief when I finally gained control over my life." She twists a strand of long black hair around her finger. "My priorities changed. Having a baby will do that." Her eyebrows arch.

I sit with Viv's message as we place our orders. Is going out on my own something I could do? Bobby proposed the idea a few times, but I never took him seriously. Besides, don't I need more experience?

As if Viv can read my mind, she says, "You know, you have everything you require to start your own business. I'm happy to help."

"You really think I could do it?"

"Absolutely. But if *you* don't believe in yourself and your gifts, you can't expect others to." Again, she arches her eyebrows for emphasis.

It's then I recall Francisco's confidence when he told me I would use astrology and architecture to help others. I've already done that with Viv and Juliette. Could I do the same for more people?

"How would I begin?" I stare at Viv, hoping she possesses the blueprint I need to go out on my own.

"Come up with a business plan," she says. "Map out what you want to do and how you're going to accomplish it. Then set up a timeline to implement your goals. It sounds complicated, but it's not."

"Do you think other people would want what I offer?" I ask. "Because I'm not so sure."

"Yes! Especially *if* they can see what you've already created. You'll need a website, of course. You can use photos of my studio, plus what you're doing for your friend in Pennsylvania. Once you find your audience, something tells me you'll take off."

"I guess there are a lot of healer-types in the Bend area," I say. "Plus, I'm not limited to Central Oregon. I designed Juliette's retreat center from across the country." Slowly, what I once considered unattainable seems doable.

"Exactly," Viv smiles. "And if you hone your ability to read people the way you read me ... I think the sky's the limit."

***

"So, you're going to do it?" Bobby asks as he takes the meatloaf out of the oven. I glance at Johnny in his infant seat, fixated on his rattle socks.

"I just might," I say with an unexpected air of confidence.

My husband steps toward me and pulls me into his arms. "Babe, you are so ready ... more than you realize." He leans down and kisses me on the lips. I melt.

Once seated at the table, Bobby asks, "Have you thought about what you'll say to Sandy and Mark?" Of course, he knew this would be the biggest hurdle. They gave me my first job. And it's because of their generous offer that I moved to Bend.

"I think that's one of the reasons I've been hesitant to do this," I admit. I take a forkful of salad then wash it down with a sip of red wine. "They've both been so good to me. Supported me through the pregnancy … the accident … and maternity leave." I put my fork down. "I just don't want to disappoint them."

Bobby stops eating and places his hand on top of mine. "Part of having people work for you is hoping they'll become so good at what they do that they develop the ability to do it without you. Besides, you want to specialize. It doesn't sound like you'd be competing for clients."

My shoulders slide down with his reassuring words. "I guess you're right. And when people come to me who aren't a good fit, I'll refer them to Sandy and Mark." I feel my mood lift again.

"Exactly," Bobby agrees. "The same is true on their end. They know what they're good at and what their strengths are. That's why she referred Toph to you in the first place."

As Bobby points out the obvious, Harry comes over and places his head on my lap. Is he begging for food? Or is he saying that he, too, believes in me?

***

"Of course we support your decision," Mark says. He becomes quiet. Maybe he's figuring out how they'll handle the extra workload. Then he smiles. That's when I see something in his eyes … the same look Bobby has when Johnny reaches another milestone. Mark is proud of me.

"Oh Maggie," Sandy says as she gives me a hug. "We figured this day would come. You're an excellent architect … and you seem to have a special gift in designing spiritual spaces. Sadly, we don't attract those clients very often."

"If it's OK with you, I'd like to make the transition over the summer. This way, none of our current clients will be impacted." I pause for a sip of coffee. "I reached out to the Career Counseling Department at Pitt, planting the seeds for some of their best candidates to consider coming to Bend."

"Good thinking," Mark says. I figured he would appreciate this gesture, especially since he and Sandy also have degrees from Pitt. I believe it's one of the reasons they hired me.

Setting a concrete date for my last day at the firm creates an unusual mixture of emotions. As the feelings flow through me, what bubbles to the top is an overwhelming sense of excitement. I'm taking a risk and stepping into the unknown. Could I be following my destiny?

Chapter 23

MARLEE

January 14th

Juliette's been secretive about the entire day. From what little she's shared, this wedding sounds quite different from the first one they planned. Instead of getting married at a park north of the city, she and Michael have chosen to have their ceremony at Strawberry Mansion, where he first proposed. It's a historic building with a classic, old-style vibe … a lot like Michael, but totally unlike Juliette. Could she be learning to compromise?

The only instructions she's shared so far have been sparse—wear the dusty mauve dress we picked out together …. and be there by 4:45 sharp.

***

Tom, Michael's best man, looks more handsome than ever in his tux. As he and I enter Strawberry Mansion, I spot a short, gray-haired gentleman, dressed in a long red ceremonial robe and striped, black pants. He looks at me, places his hands at his sternum, and nods.

"You must be Marlee," he says in the sweetest accent. "The one who will stand next to Juliette when she marries Michael?"

"That's me," I say. "And you are?" I do my best to suppress a chuckle.

"It is a pleasure to meet you, Marlee. I am Juana." He bows.

Juliette's shaman is marrying them! Why didn't she tell me? I wonder if he realizes I'm Juliette's case study. A part of me twinges.

As a shaman, I suppose he knows mostly everything … and hopefully keeps it to himself.

"It's wonderful to meet you," I say. "This is my husband, Tom."

"Ah … the one who stands next to Michael."

"Uh, yes," Tom awkwardly responds. He looks at me as if to say, *Who in the hell is this guy*?

In my most upbeat tone, I say, "Tom, this is Juana, the shaman with whom Juliette studied."

"Oh," Tom stutters. "Good to meet you." When he extends his hand, Juana bows in return.

"The pleasure is all mine, Tom," Juana says.

When Michael walks in, I notice two things right away. As always, he looks like he's ready for a *GQ* shoot. But today he appears to be on edge, which isn't his normal vibe. He breaks into a smile when he sees us.

"You made it," he says, wiping beads of sweat from his forehead.

"Of course," Tom says, then leans closer to Michael. "It's gonna be OK, buddy," he whispers. "Relax."

"Yeah … I know," Michael says. He clears his throat then moves closer to us. "Juliette and I decided we'd both be involved in planning this wedding. I picked the place. She was cool with that." He pauses, lowering his voice. "But I'm not so sure about how I feel about Juana."

Juana wanders around the room, intrigued with the architectural nuances.

"I bet he knows you feel that way," I say, playing around.

"You're probably right," Michael nervously laughs.

"He seems fine to me," Tom's says. "Besides, marriage is all about compromise. Get used to it." He winks then slaps Michael on the back.

I excuse myself and go searching for Juliette. Within moments I see her sitting, gazing at a mirror in the room designated for brides.

"There you are," I say.

"Here I am," she replies, standing up to embrace me.

"I just met Juana. He seems very special," I say as I hold Juliette tightly to me. She takes a step back.

"I can't believe he agreed to marry us," she says. "It means the world to me. After all, he believes in my abilities." She looks at me with doe eyes. Never has she appeared more beautiful.

"You earned your title," I say. "Look how you've helped me."

"Really? You know, we *can* keep working together … if you want."

"Of course," I say without an ounce of hesitation. "I'd love to." I pause to reflect. "Our sessions have challenged me in so many ways. But I can't deny how much they've helped me grow … and find greater peace." I flash back to a few weeks ago, when I was able to help Patrick without trying to *fix* things for him. "I feel great," I add, "as good as I've felt in years. Actually, stronger … more vibrant … less worried about what's next."

"I think you're glowing," Juliette teases. She looks at me intently, then grimaces. "OK, enough about you. Can you help me with these damn buttons?"

***

Once Annie, Sophia, and Maggie arrive, Juliette presents us with silver bracelets, each adorned with a unique gemstone. For Sophia, Juliette chose prehnite, the healer's stone. Annie's eyes brighten when she sees hers—amethyst, a crystal known for its calming properties. Carnelian is embedded in Maggie's bracelet. This second chakra stone enhances self-confidence, creativity, and courage. The pyramid she gave Bobby on their wedding day is made of the same gemstone. And mine is turquoise, a stone that aligns with developing faith, seeing the bigger picture, and feeling at peace.

I clasp the bracelet securely around my wrist. Juliette hands each of us a bouquet of white tulips intermixed with Queen Anne's lace. We form a line and enter the main room where our husbands are waiting. One by one, we pair up, arm-in-arm, and walk down the aisle together. Then, when the music begins, Juana escorts Juliette toward the altar to an instrumental version of Iron and Wine's "Call It Dreaming."

Chapter 24

MAGGIE

June 27th

Welcome to Serenity

1:30 p.m.	Introduction, Meditation, & Breathwork —Juliette Sutton	
1:45 p.m.	Accepting Your Gifts Without Fear —Annie Thompson	
2:15 p.m.	Opening Your Heart —Maggie Carr Parker	
2:45 p.m.	Break	
3:00 p.m.	Speaking Your Truth —Dr. Sophia Robbins	
3:30 p.m.	Mastering Your Intuition —Marlee Ryan	
4:00 p.m.	Opening to Source —Juliette Sutton	
4:30 p.m.	Reception	

***

Even though I know today's schedule by heart, I reread the pamphlet for the umpteenth time, just to be sure. I still can't believe how everything came together. I shut my eyes and allow a moment of gratitude to wash over me.

"Are you ready?" Juliette gently nudges my shoulder, stirring me from my thoughts.

"I think so," I say. Then I admit the truth. "Just so you know, I haven't done a lot of public speaking."

"Oh Maggie, you'll be great," Juliette says, waving off my concern. "Just tell your story of how you cracked that protective shell around your heart." She gives me her trademark smirk. "Then share what happened after you did. Everyone will love how this lone wolf finally allowed herself to love another."

"Maybe," I shrug. "But won't that be a bit too *personal*?"

"That's how we grow," she counters. "When we become vulnerable in front of others, we give them the strength they need to take their own leaps of faith."

"It sounds like you're challenging me."

She says nothing … just tilts her head and smiles. I exhale loudly.

"Thank God Bobby will be here," I add. I feel *somewhat* comforted knowing I can look at my husband for reassurance.

"Let's do one final walkthrough, OK?" Juliette suggests. Perhaps she's also nervous, even if she hides it. Of course, she has every right to be anxious. She's unveiling her dream and has invited nearly a hundred and fifty people to witness. "Let's start as if we were walking in for the first time," she says.

I follow her outside until we are deep in the parking lot. Then we begin walking back toward the retreat center along the stone path lined with lilacs, Jacob's ladders, pansies, and lily of the valley. Potted ferns adorn the entranceway. Juliette opens the mahogany double doors and nods. The foyer's flooring is field stone, and the walls are a vibrant pewter-tinted stucco. My hope was to mimic a cavern. The water feature against the right wall is home to koi fish that swim under lily pads and occasionally brush against the surface. On our left stands a gray granite reception desk. A gathering of large white orchids frame pamphlets for today's opening.

Stepping back, I scrutinize the collection of oil and acrylic paintings Juliette and I hung. Each one symbolizes a meaningful stage of Juliette's spiritual path. My eyes move back and forth between a painting of Buddha that Juliette purchased in Tibet and one of Ganesh she brought home from India. Then, I study the artwork behind the reception area, a mural of the seven chakras.

"I love the lighting features," she says. "They totally amplify the cavernous feel."

"That was the goal," I nod. Large and small cans blend into the ceiling, while hammered copper pendants hang to provide more direct lighting.

"Everything looks amazing," she says. Then she claps twice, as if she's blessing the space. "OK, let's move on."

I prop open the double doors that lead to the main room where Juliette can hold large workshops and speaking events.

"This area will fit two hundred people, yes?" she asks.

"Technically one hundred and eighty *comfortably*, but two hundred maximum for sure." For a moment, I slip into my *nerdy architect* voice. Juliette shoots me a side glance then rolls her eyes.

"I love how it tilts downward like a theatre in the round," she says.

"I slanted the floor so everyone would have a good view of the speaker. Plus, look at these seating options … and the dark gray chairs with cushioned leather."

"Yup," she agrees. "I can arrange them in rows, or small circles … or whatever fits the vibe. Oh, and these white walls totally make the space feel twice as big as it is."

"The carpet is critical too," I add.

"Remind me why."

"First, the close-knit multi-colored gray creates continuity with the lobby. Equally important is its acoustical element. This carpeting will help diffuse unwanted sound."

"Your genius is in the details," Juliette glows. "And these amazing sculptures!" We look up in unison. Each abstract ivory sculpture is an archetype of an astrological sign. Positioned in niches at the top of the walls, together they form a zodiac wheel. Billowed pieces of off-white linen intermixed with long steel pendant lights complete this enchanting effect.

We walk to the podium. Juliette gently strokes the yellow orchids I placed there earlier.

"Everything is so beautiful," she says in a reverent tone. "It's perfect, Maggie."

As we continue our walkabout, my perspective begins to shift. A few minutes ago, it was hard to pretend I'd never seen any of this before. Now, as we continue to move throughout the center, I'm actually sinking deeper into something that feels like a dream … like visiting a place that's familiar yet hazy all at once.

The smaller rooms, where people will conduct private sessions, evoke different emotions … peace, inspiration, bliss. Paintings showcase wildflowers and flowing streams, while a variety of specifically chosen gemstones fill nooks. One room feels as expansive as the sky, complete with constellations that light the ceiling. Another room supports grounding and embodies the sensation of stepping barefoot into a lush forest.

"Ahh, my favorite room of all," Juliette says as we enter her office. "Look at that work space!" My eyes fall on the stone and mahogany desk she brought back from Brazil. Then I step back and scan the whole room … Juliette's musical instruments in the matching credenza … the slab of amethyst under her massage table

… and her collection of sage, gemstones, palo santo sticks, and other items she uses during sessions.

"The skylight is one of my favorite touches," I remark. "So perfect with the high windows."

"It makes the space feel bright and cheery," she adds.

"Look how the light plays off of the crystals we embedded into the wall," I say. I walk over and run my fingers along the collection of shapes and colors.

"I still can't believe how you combined my birth chart with Michael's," she says, feeling the gems as well.

"Well, I mean … that's what you wanted, right?"

I walk behind her desk and look at the photo of the two of them from their wedding day.

"You looked so … what's the word?"

"Relieved?" she laughs.

"Exquisite … but even that fails to capture it."

"Honestly, I felt radiant that day."

"Yes! I think I can see your aura in this picture."

She waves me off. "Enough of that." She claps twice. "One more space to go."

We head toward the yoga room. My inspiration for this area came straight from Nueva Vida with its wide white beaches, howler monkeys, and treehouses.

"Tell me again why you decided to elevate the yoga studio by half a floor?" Juliette asks.

"The tree houses," I say. I walk over toward the far wall to my left and stare out the floor-to-ceiling windows. "Have you opened these yet?"

"Yes! I love how easy the sliders are."

"You can bring the outside indoors on warm days."

"Exactly," she agrees. Walking barefoot, she steps slowly across the cork floor, as if wanting to feel each and every pore with the soles of her feet. She stops midstride and looks at me. "This is so much like the floor of the studio in Costa Rica, I can't get over it." Juliette looks up at the plants that hang from the ceiling. Then she continues toward the spring water that drizzles from the back wall into a small trough, mimicking an infinity pool. She stares, mesmerized.

"Maybe *this* is my favorite room," she says. "I really can't tell."

"It's OK to have more than one favorite space, depending on your mood and what you require," I tease.

Juliette's grin indicates she likes this thought. Her eyes flash. "The first yoga class is tomorrow morning. You'll be there, right?"

"You know I will," I say. "I'm a little rusty."

"Well, that's about to change," she laughs. "You once told me you're a better person when you're regularly doing yoga. Think of tomorrow as a kickoff … your personal yoga rebirth."

I smile, but Juliette can tell I'm uneasy.

"Did I say something wrong?" she asks.

"Not at all. It's just tough to find time in my schedule. I never know what's going to come up. Some days, I feel like I have no control over my life. I can't wait for the first of July. I'll miss working with Sandy and Mark, but I'm ready to go out on my own."

"Of course you are," Juliette says and smiles.

"I mean, there are a million risks with starting my own business. But since going back to work, I'm in the office way more than I'd expected … more than I want to be. I hate being away from Johnny. So … that's why I've been putting off yoga. Something had to go."

Juliette tosses her flaxen hair back and tilts her head. "But soon you'll be in charge of your schedule and working from home. You'll be able to recommit."

"I hope so. It takes a lot of time to start your own business. And Johnny's just nine months old."

"What if I live-streamed my classes? You could take them then, right?"

"Well, I mean … the time difference and all …"

"Right, right. Hmm. OK, what if I recorded them and sent you links. Then you could pull up a class whenever you liked. Hell, I could offer the same thing to other people too … maybe even charge a small fee, like an online membership." Her eyes widen. That's one of the things I love most about Juliette. Every idea leads to five more that often point toward greater self-sufficiency.

"It would be easy to make that happen," I say, doing my part to add a little fuel to her newest brainstorm. "You'll need a good camera and the right software to livestream or record. Would you imagine a subscription of sorts?"

"Hmm, I'm not sure. But hey, it would be free for you."

"I suppose I have no excuses then," I laugh. Juliette claps twice. As we start to walk out of the room, she grabs my elbow.

"Do you think we're ready?" she asks, biting her lip. "I mean, I've tried to make Serenity a place where people can come to heal … grow … and discover themselves." She takes a step closer. "What I'm asking is, do you think it's … good enough? Will it meet expectations? Will people believe in me?"

"What's going on?" I ask, placing my hand on her shoulder.

"Am I good enough?" Juliette asks, her voice quivering.

"I've never seen you doubt yourself or your abilities." I wipe a stray hair from her face. "Humility and grace are always great, but today is *your* day. It's time to show the world who you are and everything you have to offer."

Juliette smiles. I wrap my arms around her, giving her the biggest hug. "Serenity *is* you," I say quietly. "It's filled with your amazing energy and great wisdom. Your love and light shine through every aspect of this space."

Juliette's body shakes for a moment then slowly settles. She steps out of my hug and looks at me. "I freakin' love you!"

***

Juliette, as the last speaker, ties the entire day together with her usual dose of humor and charm. Still, she's dead serious about the ways energetic and holistic healing can shift our lives.

I realize as she's talking that she arranged the whole day to correspond with the chakra system. We started with her breathwork session … the root chakra. When Annie spoke, she discussed creativity, fear, and willpower … topics that align with the second and third chakras. My little talk, which we titled "Opening Your Heart," was all about the fourth chakra. Sophia focused on the importance of communicating your truth … the fifth chakra. Then came Marlee, who discussed the third eye … our sixth chakra. As Juliette shares ways to connect with Source, she's talking about knowing ourselves, our transformation, and our awareness. This state of clarity exists in the crown chakra … the seventh.

"Brilliant," I say under my breath, shaking my head and smiling at her. She catches my glance and winks back.

"My dream is for Serenity to provide support, guidance, and inspiration to everyone … whether you're facing a major life decision … searching for your purpose …or merely need a few days away to reset." Just as I expect her to end her talk, Juliette's energy shifts. She looks at me.

"My dear friend, Maggie, who spoke earlier … is the gifted architect behind this project. Serenity would not exist without her."

People begin clapping and looking at me. I can't tell if I should wave or hide! I decide to smile and accept.

"She's an extremely talented architect with an innate ability to listen … and understand what people need. This is the *special sauce* she adds to the mix. Maggie combines function with beauty … and creates spaces that exceed your wildest imagination."

OK, Juliette, I think to myself, *let's move on.* But there's more.

"As you know from her story, she went on a retreat after losing her mother. She knew she needed to make some major life decisions. Luckily, we happened to meet her there. Before we knew it, Sophia, Annie, Marlee and I were no longer four women trying to have an enlightening experience together. We became five friends on track to helping each other grow."

Wow, I think. *That really is when this all started. In many ways, the beginning of the life I now know.*

"A lot happened on that trip," Juliette continues. She glances at Michael and smiles. He smiles back. "In the months that followed, the real work continued. We all learned to say yes to the challenges that came our way. Life wanted us to integrate our new knowledge and insights. So we got to work. It was Maggie who first called us The Healers on our last day at the retreat. Here's something I hope Maggie realizes. She is a healer too. Her gift involves reading people … and making their dreams come true."

***

"Maggie, I have a little surprise for you," Juliette says once most of the guests are gone. Her eyes narrow, and that *oh so* familiar smirk comes across her face. "Would you like to see?"

"I don't know if I can handle anything more," I say. "The end of your speech … I mean …"

"Oh, shush," she says. "Follow me outside."

She leads me along a stone path. Bobby trails, carrying Johnny in his arms. The rest of The Healers and their husbands follow.

"What are you up to, Juliette?" I ask.

"Look," she says.

"Wow, you landscaped this entire area." Why hadn't I notice this before?

"I wanted to keep it as a surprise for you … until now. Go ahead … explore."

I take a few steps among flowers and ornamental bushes, then stop in my tracks at a huge structure in the middle of the lawn … a much larger version of the carnelian pyramid Francisco gave me during our retreat … the one I gave Bobby during our wedding.

Tears begin to stream down my cheeks. "Oh my God," I say. I turn to Juliette. "How did you?" I run my hands along the rock's ripples and varying hues … reds, gingers, auburns, oranges, each shade sparkling in the sun.

"Well," she begins, "since you're such an integral part of Serenity, I wanted something I could look at every day and think of you, even though you're almost three thousand miles away. Bobby helped a little." She winks at my husband, then fixes her gaze on Johnny. Immediately, he responds with the biggest smile and sweetest laugh.

"I sent a picture," Bobby shrugs, oblivious to Johnny's reaction. Still, I notice. No doubt, Juliette and Johnny will always have a special connection. I suppose that's why I asked her to be Johnny's godmother.

"I toured some local quarries and eventually found this piece," she adds, staring at the pyramid.

"I love it," is about all I can say.

"And soon, I'm going to add a plaque below the stone, to share your story. Actually," she pauses and looks at all of us. "I'm hoping we can all gather here once a year … to be together. We can make it our annual retreat … and maybe even hold an event at the same time… to share our journey with others." Juliette pauses. Her eyes are glassy. "I want you all to be part of my life, no matter where we live. What do you think?"

"I cannot imagine a more beautiful invitation," Sophia says, the first of us to speak.

"Count me in!" Annie adds.

"Any reason to get together is great for me," Marlee says. She squeezes Juliette in an affirming hug.

"Wow," I say. "You really did it."

"*We* did it," Juliette says.

"Yes, of course … but you *really* did it. You followed your heart and your soul."

"And so did you," she winks.

Chapter 25

MARLEE

September 9th

What am I to know?

Think back to a year ago. How has your life changed? What have you released? How have you grown?

When you and Tom moved to Boston, you thought you left everything you've ever known. At the same time, Patrick began his freshman year of college. But that was merely what was happening on the outside. Your inner transformation proved most meaningful.

You confronted your biggest fears … letting go of the safety and comfort of your home, community, and friends to venture into a new space where you knew no one, all while saying goodbye to your only child, something you've dreaded for some time.

Instead of crumbling, these situations prompted you to face your fears head-on. In the process, you learned to put your faith in God, listen to your true inner voice, and trust the unknown. Of course, Juliette nudged you along the way, helping you prepare for these difficult times through your sessions.

Looking back, was it truly that hard? Yes, there were challenges. But you also encountered beautiful moments which functioned as sources of light to help you through the difficult days.

Assisting Maggie and Bobby acclimate to their new life as parents … planning their wedding … providing them with nourishing meals … these acts of service may have nurtured you more than they nurtured them. Perhaps you now see that mothering Patrick is not the only way to care for others. You can support Tom in his career, listen to your friends, and write your books so others may benefit from your experiences and intuitive knowings. You are finding the path to follow your soul's journey. This is how you step into your power.

Being in your power is not about controlling situations, mitigating risk, or keeping yourself and others safe. It is showing up as your authentic self and accepting others for who they are. It is about trusting that whatever happens is meant to be.

Remember, this is not a blind resignation to fate. Instead, being in your power means you live in the present moment and respond to life's circumstances. You choose to release negative thought patterns and limiting beliefs that hold you hostage to fear. Even when you do not understand, you trust, because you know there is a Divine purpose to it all.

You are now able to recognize when your mind leads you astray, as the voice you named Margaret did for years. Control, fear, worry, or doubt do not keep you safe. Quite the opposite. Only when you release your fears, negative thoughts, and limiting beliefs … those things that keep you small and hold you back … can you step into a higher state. Through faith you find freedom.

You may not see it, but others look up to you. You can make a difference. However, you first must believe in yourself. Nothing else is necessary. We do not try to shine. The light comes naturally from within.

Believe, trust, let go … the best is yet to come.

My fingers stop moving. Today's session is over. I let out a brief sigh, then reread my words, hoping to engrave the message into my mind.

The last eighteen months have brought about a new phase of life. Yes, pieces of the past remain, but so much is different. I'm trying to *choose happiness*, just as the voice encouraged me to do. I have no idea what's next, but I'm beginning to have faith that everything will work out as it's meant to. It's finally clear that I'm unable to control what life throws at me, but I can control how I respond. That is where my power lies. And when I feel totally lost, I talk to God. If I ever wonder whether He's listening, I quickly remind myself He is always with me.

It's been more than three months since Juliette, Maggie, Sophia, Annie and I were last together. To stay connected, we've committed to livestreaming Juliette's 4 o'clock yoga class on Thursdays. Out west, Maggie has permanently blocked out 1 p.m. Pacific so we can all do it together. Once Juliette's students leave the studio, we pour wine, or tea in Maggie's case—she's pregnant with their second child—and update each other on our lives. I wish we could all be together in person, but I'll take what I can get. I miss them. Then again, the livestreams and Zoom calls are helping.

Tom and I committed to Boston. As difficult as it was, we put the Radnor farmhouse on the market two weeks ago. Five days later, we had an offer from a lovely young family moving from Chicago. Ironically, the wife is an obstetrician at Jefferson, and the husband is taking a position at the *Inquirer*. Funny how things happen full circle. I'm sad to say goodbye to Philadelphia, but I'm excited about our future. We're staying in the brownstone for one more year. After that, who knows.

Last April, Sue and Pete decided to move to Florida for good. Tom and I saw this as a golden opportunity and bought their half of the home. When Patrick finished his second semester, he and I moved things from Radnor to Eagle's Landing. Our furniture from the farmhouse looks great in the Poconos!

Patrick and I spent most of the summer there. Tom came every weekend, escaping city life for mountain tranquility. During the week, while Tom was in Boston and Patrick was working as a lifeguard at the lodge, Juliette and I hiked, water-skied, and practiced yoga. We even had a few healing sessions.

My friend circle in Boston continues to grow, sometimes in the most unexpected ways. I have a new running buddy named Sheila, who recently moved here from Kentucky. I kept bumping into her on the river path. Finally, we started talking and realized we only live a few blocks from each other. Now we have standing running dates on Tuesday and Thursday mornings.

Sadly, I haven't seen Allison. Roxie and I have visited that exact park multiple times, intentionally arriving at various hours. Yet we've never come across her or Parker. Sometimes it makes me wonder. Was Allison *really* there, or was she a figment of my imagination? Perhaps she was angel, sent to help support my transition to Boston.

Last week, I finished the rough draft of my next novel, *Choose Happiness*, which I hope to publish next fall. I attribute a lot of my "stick-to-it-ness" to my writers group, which is just like the one I *saw* when I journeyed with Juliette.

Patrick continues to thrive at Colgate, and yesterday he hinted at meeting a girl he thinks I'll *love*. Of course, this could be nothing. Then again, maybe she's his special someone. Only time will tell.

As for Tom … I've never seen my husband happier. He's certainly consumed with work, but he's thriving. When he comes home, there's a peace about him, something I'm still getting used to. Our time together is better than ever. And I've also realized something … I don't *need* Tom … I *want* him. There's a huge difference. He's definitely found his groove in Boston. Maybe I have too.

It's strange, but I find myself worrying less and being OK with not knowing what's next. Working with Juliette taught me that before I could release my fears and limiting beliefs, I had to strengthen my faith in God and learn to trust my intuition. I've always had the order backwards. I thought I had to trust and let go in order to believe. But now I know faith drives the bus. Once I accepted that, everything became easier.

I'm not saying that life is without challenges. What I'm saying is … I no longer feel alone. I *know* something higher has my back. Accepting this truth makes it easier to deal with rocky times and see a light at the end of the tunnel.

Roxie ambles over and sets her head in my lap. "OK, Roxie," I say. "One minute and we'll go."

I shut my laptop, swivel in my chair, and look out the window. The leaves are beginning to turn. I love how nature mirrors life. With each goodbye comes an unexpected hello. When we're rooted in faith, we can be assured that endless possibilities await us.

And so, *I kiss what I have never before experienced* … knowing the best is yet to come.

ACKNOWLEDGEMENTS

We are all healers in our own right. Each one of us possesses a unique gift to share with the world. Sometimes these talents are obvious. However, we often must patiently wait to discover our abilities. But when we *see*, we begin to know, shining our light so others may find theirs. Instead of fixing or attempting to control, we realize there's a Divine plan. And as we contribute our piece to this Universal puzzle, we discover love, joy, happiness, and peace. This is how we step into our power. This is how we heal.

Understanding this truth transcends to publishing *The Healers*. Just as each character plays a critical role in her personal evolution as well as the growth of others, this book would not be possible without the guidance and support of Dave Jarecki and Lieve Maas. *The Healers* is the first (and hopefully not last) project I worked on with Dave. As my editor, he pushed me to dig deeper and fine-tune my writing skills, showing me less is more. And the talented Lieve once again created a stunning cover and interior layout, as she walked me though the publishing process with patience and grace. I am beyond grateful for these partnerships.

Perhaps the biggest healer in my life is my husband, Scott. As we've traveled our individual and collective journeys, not only has he held my hand, but he has also encouraged me to use my voice and step into my true self. His belief in me as an author fosters an internal strength to write about things that matter, things that change us, things that help us elevate.

QUOTES

"The plain fact is the planet does not need more successful people. The planet desperately needs more peacemakers, healers, restorers, storytellers, and lovers of all kinds."

—David W. Orr

"Awakening is not changing who you are, but discarding who you are not."

—Deepak Chopra

"As women, we have super powers. We are sisters. We are healers. We are mothers. We are goddess warriors."

—Merle Dandridge

"A healer's power stems not from any special ability, but from maintaining the courage and awareness to embody and express the universal healing power that every human being naturally possesses."

—Eric Michael Leventhal

"The soul always knows what to do to heal itself. The challenge is to silence the mind."

—Caroline Myss

"A healer is someone who seeks to be the light that they wished they'd had in their darkest moments."

—Alan Watts

ALSO BY MICHELLE DAVIS

The Invitation—Book one of *The Awakening Series*

The Retreat—Book two of *The Awakening Series*

The Dog Walkers

Learning to Bend

All publications are available on Amazon.